PULS

The Complete Series

Part One, Part Two, Part Three & Part Four

From NY Times Bestelling Author
Deborah Bladon

Copyright

First Original Print Edition, July 2014
Copyright © 2014 by Deborah Bladon
ISBN-13: 978-1500677411
ISBN-10: 1500677418

Also by Deborah Bladon

The Complete Obsessed Series
The Exposed Saga
The VAIN Series

Coming Soon

Impulse

PULSE
The Complete Series

Part One

Chapter 1

"You can come up to my suite right now." The casual way he reaches out his hand is almost too tempting to resist.

"You think it's that easy?" I raise a brow. The inner rush of the martini is pulling my defenses away. I want a one night stand. That's why I'm here. He's beautiful. Maybe the most attractive man I've ever seen. All I have to do is tell him what I want and he can make it a reality. I know that he can. His body not only suggests it, it screams it.

"I know it is." He leans in close to me, his breath tracing a warm path across my neck.

"Do you do this a lot?" It's a loaded question.

"Do what?" His tongue playfully runs over my chin before he brushes his lips effortlessly across mine.

"Pick up women here for one night stands?" I move forward a touch, hoping to catch his lips with mine again but he pulls back. A small smile forces his full lips slightly apart.

"Is that what I'm doing?" His beautiful blue eyes slowly rake over my body.

"You are, aren't you?" My breath hitches as he slides his arm around my waist and I feel his arousal instantly.

"You want to fuck me," he whispers the words slowly into my ear. I shudder as his breath slides across my neck. "You want me to lick you until you scream, over and over again."

I pull back hoping that with the slight bit of distance I'll find my breath. "That's…" I stop talking the moment his hand moves down my back.

"The minute you walked in and saw me by the bar, you imagined being under me." His hand moves lower, skirting the edge of the hem of my dress. "You knew that before the night was over you'd be on your knees sliding my cock into your mouth."

"I want that," I confess softly. One night with a man like this was all I wanted when I arrived in Manhattan two weeks ago. One night of pleasure unlike anything I'd ever experienced. This was the man who was going to give me that. I knew it as soon as he turned and looked at me.

"We're going up to my suite now," he pauses and I realize he's waiting for my name.

"Jessica," I offer. I want to be Jessica to him. I'm Jess or Jessie to everyone else. I want to hear my real name on his lips as he's lost in pleasure.

"I'm Nathan," he counters.

"How old are you?" I don't know why the question escapes from my lips. I don't care how old he is.

"Older than you." His hand brushes the back of my thigh.

I smile at his response. "How do you know I'm old enough?"

"Old enough?" He cocks a brow and his face shifts slightly. He's even more devastatingly handsome than I first realized.

"Old enough," I repeat.

"I watched them card you at the door when you walked in." He motions behind me to the entrance of the club. "They wouldn't have let you in if you weren't at least twenty-one."

I'm twenty-three but he doesn't need to know that. He doesn't want to know. I can tell. Only one thing matters to him.

"Do you live here? You said you have a suite." I realize I'm stalling. I want this to last. I want to savor every moment this man is pressed against me. I want to drink in every part of him. I may never get another night with a man like this.

I moan as I feel his finger run lazily over the silk of my panties.

"Are you done with the questions, Jessica?" He stares directly into my eyes.

"Yes. Why?" I cringe internally, hoping that my incessant rambling hasn't turned him off.

"Because I really need to fuck you."

My eyes dart past his shoulder to where my roommate, Rebecca, is standing, her mouth agape, the cosmopolitan in her hand precariously close to spilling out all over the floor and the very expensive heels she bought last week. I give a weak thumbs-up behind Nathan's head. It's the signal we agreed to an hour ago when we arrived at the club. She didn't think I was serious when I told her that tonight I was determined to find a gorgeous stranger who would sweep me off my feet and into his bed.

"What are we waiting for then?" I hear the words and I swear it's my voice saying them. What the hell did they put in that martini? It's stolen all of my inhibitions away.

He only nods in response. The way his black hair tumbles onto his forehead at the slightest movement of his head gives him a boyish charm that's completely misplaced. There's nothing about him that speaks of anything other than tall, gorgeous and very much a man through and through. He silently takes my hand and I follow him as he weaves his way through the throngs of people moving breathlessly to the pulsing beat of the music.

"This is *the* club to go to when you want to get laid." Rebecca's words from hours earlier are haunting my body as I follow this stranger into an experience I know that I'm not going to soon forget.

"This way." He drops my hand and gestures towards the lobby of Aeon. The hotel, situated in Times Square, is known for being a tourist hot spot. Even though I'm now a resident of the city, I still feel like a sightseer in disguise. I try not to react while I'm soaking in all the beautiful ambiance the lobby has to offer. I turn back for one last fleeting look at the entrance to the attached club. This is my chance to abandon my plan and race back into the crowd.

"Good evening, sir." The soft voice of a woman calls through my thoughts and I watch Nathan turn towards the desk in the lobby. The way the petite blond with the blue eyes stares at him suggests there's more to their exchange than first meets the eye. The contemptuous look she throws me cements my assumption. He's fucked her. I can see the envy in her face.

The fact that he doesn't openly acknowledge her isn't lost on me. When I feel his hand on the small of my back I can't help but feel an inner rush. He's focused and determined. For this brief moment of his life, that's all for me. I'm the one he wants.

As we round the corner to the bank of elevators, someone else calls his name. This time it's a man. I stand silently as Nathan pulls him out of my earshot. They have a very animated conversation. I stare at the man I'm about to share a bed with, or maybe a table or a floor. I can't believe I'm doing this. In a span of two weeks I've gone from being completely unfulfilled while in bed with my ex-boyfriend back in Connecticut, to being on the precipice of what I expect to be an incredible night of raw passion. That is, if he can tear himself away from this man long enough to fuck me.

"Jessica." He turns, the smile spreading over his face. "Shall we?"

"I thought you'd forgotten about me," I tease. At least I hope I'm teasing.

"You?" He pulls my hand into his and deftly to his lips. "I have a feeling you're going to be unforgettable."

My mind is telling me it's just words. He's an expert at this. He likely fucks a different woman every night and this is just part of his regular repertoire.

"Like the desk clerk was unforgettable?" I mutter. I didn't say that loud enough for him to hear it, did I?
"The desk clerk?" His hand is on my back again as he guides me into the waiting elevator.

I offer a sheepish smile as I raise a brow in response. "I saw the way she looked at you. She's been up to your suite."

"Perhaps." He laughs. "She's not relevant. You are."

"Are we your type?" I briefly glance at the mirror adorning the wall of the elevator.

"What type might that be?" He leans down and frowns at me.

"Blonde, blue eyes, curvy." The words come out much louder than I anticipate. What the hell is wrong with me? You don't ask a one night stand this many questions.

"I don't have a type," he says smoothly.

"Everyone has a type." I take a deep breath. "We all do."

"What's your type, Jessica?" The elevator dings its arrival on the eighteenth floor and the doors fly open. He doesn't move.

"Tonight, it's you." I take a step towards him, pulling my finger down his silk tie as I walk out into the dimly lit corridor all the while hoping he's following me.

Chapter 2

You can do this. You want to do this. You've wanted this for so long. I replay the words over and over in my mind as I let him lead me by the hand down the corridor to a door tucked away at the end, just past the corner.

He smiles down at me before he pulls a key card from the inner pocket of his suit jacket, swiping it quickly he leads the way into the darkened room.

"Jessica," he whispers my name softly as the door clicks closed behind me. I love the way it sounds on his lips. I love his lips. I've been craving another taste of them since he brushed them briefly over mine back at the club.

I move to take a step forward but he turns sharply. His arm jumps to the door above me, the other resting on my waist. He presses against me and I can feel how aroused he is. He wants me just as much as I want him.

I drop my clutch to the floor, needing to touch him. I sensed, from the first moment he turned to look at me in the club, that he was all muscle. As my hands glide over his chest, I'm amazed by the definition. Even through the soft fabric of his dress shirt, I can easily make out the toned muscles of his chest and abdomen.

He licks his lips before he lowers his face to mine. I perch myself onto my tiptoes. Even in the nude heels I'm wearing, he's much taller than me. He growls as his lips cover mine in a lush and deep kiss. I open my mouth slightly wanting to feel his tongue exploring me. He pushes his along my bottom lip before sliding it over mine.

I pull my hands up, grabbing his hair in between my fingers, needing to pull him even closer into the kiss. I'm rewarded with a deep and guttural groan. His hand falls to my thigh. I have to lower myself back down to my heels. Just the mere touch of his hand on my bare skin is making me feel faint.

"I can't wait. I need to hear you come now," he says hoarsely.

I moan as his fingers push the fabric of my panties to the side. He pulls his index finger slowly along my slick cleft.

"So smooth. So ready." His lips claim mine again as he traces a circle around my clitoris. His touch is gentle, yet skilled.

My hands grip the front of his suit jacket as he pushes a finger slowly into me. I can't stifle a cry of pleasure at the sensation. I feel him smile through our kiss before he pulls his face away from mine.

"You're so eager. Your body wants me so much." His words only help to incite the desire that is already coursing through me. How can I already be this close to an orgasm?

"I do," I whimper. I don't want to hold back. I want this desperately. I want to finally know what it is like to be with a man who truly understands a woman's body. A man who can listen to my breathing and instinctively knows what my body needs. This man can do that. He's already proving it.

"You want to come hard, don't you?" His voice is unbearably sensual. It's dripping with desire. I can feel his erection pressed against me. He's ready too. Part of me just wishes he'd fuck me right now. The other part wants to soak in the luxury of his need to get me to rush to the edge right here, right inside the door of his suite.

"So hard." I'm so desperate to come. I feel my hips involuntarily circle under his touch. I push them back against the door, before pulling them closer to him. My legs spread to give him more access.

He growls. "I can't wait to taste this. I can't wait to watch you squirm under my tongue before I fuck you."

The shamelessness of his words pushes me closer to the edge. I can't think straight. All I can focus on is his hand. His fingers slowly slide into me while his thumb circles my clit.

"You're so close. I can feel it." His breathing is faster. He's so aroused too. He wants me to come. It's part of what he needs.

I nod and pull my tongue across his lips. He cradles my face with his other hand as he glides his lips once again over mine. "Come for me, Jessica. Show me how good it feels."

I race to the edge and my climax is hard and intense. I fall forward and he grabs my waist, pulling me into his body. The rush of pleasure that pulses through me is accentuated by the feeling of his chest against me, his remarkable scent and his lips pressed against my forehead.

"I," I can't say anything. I can't breathe. It was never like that before. I've never come that powerfully.

"We're just getting started." He leans back and runs his lips over my cheek. "I'm going to make us a drink and then I'll tell you exactly what I'm going to do to you."

I stand in stunned silence as he pulls his body away from me. I watch him slide the suit jacket from his shoulders and throw it over the back of a couch. He doesn't look back at me as he moves seamlessly to a counter. He pours an amber liquid in two glasses before turning to hold one up to me.

"The washroom?" I ask breathlessly. I have to compose myself before I get in bed with him.

He cocks a perfect brow. "Down the hallway. First door on the left."

I nod in response before reaching down to pick up my clutch from the floor.

"Jessica?" His voice calls to me as I enter the hallway.

I turn and instantly pull my hand to my chest. He's undoing the buttons on his shirt. As the fabric gives way, the muscular tanned skin beneath beckons to me.

"Don't be long. I'm not a patient man."

Chapter 3

I sit on the edge of the bathtub, my heel tapping a rhythmic beat onto the tile floor. I stare down at my phone. I've already been in here for five minutes. Why isn't Rebecca texting me back? I need her words of reassurance that I can do this without making a total, not-very-experienced-in-bed, fool of myself.

I almost slam my phone onto the side of the tub in utter frustration. I wanted this. I was the one who decided that my life in Bloomfield, Connecticut wasn't for me anymore. Being Jessie Roth, the girlfriend of Josh Redmond was utterly unfulfilling. When I met Josh during my training to become a paramedic, he seemed like the all American guy I wanted. Now, that I'd left him and moved to Manhattan, all I desperately craved was to experience life. Nathan was my first step towards that. Once, I jumped into that very large king bed I saw in the bedroom when I walked down the hallway, I'd finally get to have an experience I'd always craved. One night with a man who could make me feel things I'd only imagined. He'd already proven he knew how to make me come as soon as we walked into his suite.

I dial Rebecca's number and there's no answer. I curse before I end the call without leaving a voice mail. I have to do this on my own. I have to find the courage to just jump in head first and, at the very least, pretend I know what I'm doing. There isn't going to be any pep talk from my best friend.

I take a deep breath before I pull the black dress I'm wearing from my body. I adjust my black lace bra and panties before I smooth my long hair behind my back. If I'm going to do this, I'm going to do it with a bang. I tuck my phone back into my clutch, fold my dress and place them both on the counter. It's now or never. With one last deep breath, I open the washroom door.

The faint sound of low music greets me as I step back into the hallway. I can feel my heart pounding in my chest. I try my best to saunter down the hallway with some semblance of sexiness. I realize fairly quickly that I look more awkward than alluring so I pick up my pace and move swiftly back towards the room where I left Nathan.

My eyes shoot around the room when I don't see him standing next to the counter where he had poured our drinks. The one meant for me is still there, untouched, the ice almost melted. I move further into the room. He's not by the massive window that offers an uncompromising view of Times Square. As I turn to walk back towards the bedroom I see him. The man I imagined bringing me a depth of pleasure that I'd only fantasized about, the man who had made me come with just a few smooth glides of his hand is sprawled out flat on his back on the couch, fast asleep.

***

"Do you want to meet for lunch today?" There's a slight pause. "My treat."

I smile at my roommate's continuing insistence on paying for absolutely everything. "No. I'll make something and bring it down to your office. Maybe that curried quinoa salad you raved about?"

"Really?" Her green eyes brighten at the suggestion. "I told my boss all about that. She was almost drooling."

I laugh at the thought. "You're exaggerating."

"I'm not." She scoops up her keys from the kitchen counter. "Cassandra is actually looking for a private chef right now. You'd be perfect for that."

"If I had gone to culinary school I'd be perfect for that," I groan. "No one wants to hire someone who doesn't have formal training." I recite the phrase I've heard countless times at dozens of restaurants since I'd arrived in the city. I was down to my last few saved dollars and if I didn't land something soon, I'd be up to my elbows in dishwater just as a way to get my foot in the door. Cooking was my passion and I wanted it to be my career.

"I'll mention you to her this morning." Rebecca pulls a banana from a basket on the counter. "I can't wait for lunch."

I smile at her enthusiasm. "I'll be there right at noon."

"Hey, Jess." She tilts her head to the side and I know what that means. She's about to talk about sex. It's a telling gesture and one that she's always unconsciously done since we were in middle school together.

"He fell asleep," I murmur.

"What?" The shrill tone of the question forces me to take a step back.

"I went to the washroom and he was out cold when I got back." I shake my head. "It was beyond humiliating."

"So nothing happened?" She settles onto one of the wooden stools next to the counter.

"Something happened." I might as well just get the conversation over with. "When we got to his room he helped me come."

"So you had sex?"

"I had sex with his finger." I shrug my shoulders and bite back a laugh. "It was great finger sex."

She giggles causing her tall frame to shake. "At least you'll always have the memory of Mr. Fingers."

I roll my eyes at the nickname. "His name is Nathan. Not that it matters. I blew my chance. Or rather, I didn't get a chance to blow him."

"We'll just try again tonight." Her grin is genuine. "I was so jealous of how hot the guy was you left with that I didn't hang around long. Maybe tonight we'll both get lucky."

"Not me." I shake my head. "I'm bowing out. The universe is telling me that I'm not a one night stand kind of girl."

Her brows shoot up. "You're wrong. It's like swimming in the ocean, Jess. When you first jump in the water it's freezing and your body has to get used to it. Sleeping with men in Manhattan is like that. At first, you wonder how you'll ever warm up to the idea and then once you're in bed with a man who can make you come over and over again in one night, you'll never want to stop."

"I was almost in bed with a man like that." I hold her gaze. "It was a disaster. He couldn't stay awake long enough to fuck me."

"That's why we're getting back in the saddle tonight."

"I'm going to keep my feet on the ground and my ass in my own bed. Thank you very much." I tip my head to her as she chuckles and turns to leave.

Chapter 4

"I gave my lunch away," Rebecca screams above the loud buzz of the music.

I pull my eyes up over the edge of the glass that I have pursed to my lips. "I'll try not to take that personally."

"To my boss, Cassandra." She shoots her eyes around the crowded club not once settling them on me. "She loved it. She wants to meet you."

"You're kidding?" I'm teetering on the verge of jumping up and down at the news but I'm not sure the strapless black dress I'm wearing will cooperate.

"Tomorrow at eleven." She motions behind my head. "Bring something for her to eat and she'll hire you. The way to that woman's check book is definitely through her stomach."

I turn around and I realize she's gesturing to two men staring directly at us. I give out a loud groan at the thought of diving back into the one night stand pool after only wading in the shallow end last night.

"I'll take the blonde and you can have the other one." She slinks past me and grabs hold of my hand before I have a chance to protest. I don't want the other one. I don't want the blonde either. I want my bed and my pillow and a good night's sleep. Being back at this club after my humiliating experience in a hotel room, just a few floors above us less than twenty-four hours ago, is not the optimal way I'd like to be spending my Wednesday night.

"I'm Rebecca, this is Jess." She slurs both of our names before letting out an animated giggle. What the hell happened to her during the ten feet it took us to walk over here? Is she actually pretending to be drunk?

"What's wrong with you?" I see no reason to not call her out on her obvious bullshit.

"Jess, don't curse." She plants her index finger over my lips and throws me a wink.

I shake my head in utter disbelief. I stare blankly at her while she launches into a convoluted story about how she works as a lingerie model. Who in their right mind would believe that? From the wide grin on the blonde's face, I'd guess she just baited him hook, line and sinker.

"What do you do?"

It takes an endless moment before I realize that the male voice asking the question is actually coming from the man standing next to me. I turn my head and I'm a little surprised by how attractive he really is. His brown eyes almost match the hue of his hair. He's young, perhaps even my age.

"Hopefully by the end of the day tomorrow I'll be a personal chef."

"Cool." He nods his head up and down as if he's searching for the next words that should be coming out of his mouth.

"What about you?" I offer, all the while my eyes are glued to Rebecca. Judging by the way she's got her arms draped over the blonde guy's shoulders, I'd venture a guess that she won't be going home with me.

"What about me?" He leans in closer and I pull back yet again.

"What do you do for a living?" I enunciate every syllable. I don't want him to think that anything beyond a brief conversation is going to happen between the two of us tonight.

He holds his hand up to his ear and gestures. The pounding of the music is making it harder and harder for me to think straight, let alone hear him.

Despite the fact that I feel incredibly uncomfortable, I lean closer to repeat the question. The scent of him, a mix of cigarettes and cheap cologne assaults my senses right away. I need to get away from him, and from this place. Coming back here was a mistake and now that Rebecca has a bedfellow for the night, I can finally make a run for the door.

His breath is thick and hot on my neck as he whispers in my ear that he works as a maintenance worker at a building in lower Manhattan.

I smile and nod my head not caring an ounce about how he spends his days, or how he'll spend tonight. I look at my hands, studying the fine lines on my palms while he goes on and on about what his plans for next weekend are. There's finally a break in the muted tone of his voice. I look up and he's staring right behind me. His radar must be locked on another woman. Small miracles do happen. I move to take a step back and I'm instantly aware of a presence behind me.

A large hand presses against my stomach as the feeling of a man's hard body pushes into my back. "Jessica." His voice has a frustrated note to it. "There you are."

I turn slowly. I don't need to. I already know who it is just be the scent of his skin. It's him. He looks even more devastatingly handsome than he did last night.

Chapter 5

"Hey, sleepyhead."

A slight frown pulls at the skin on his forehead. "Are you going to introduce me to your friend?"

"No," I say impassively. I have no intention of talking to either of these men for longer than ten seconds, if at all possible. "He's not my friend."

His intense blue eyes scan my face before jumping back to the man standing behind me. "I need a moment."

"Dude, now?" I hear the pleading voice of the man I was just talking to. I'm feeling a rush of relief at the idea of being pulled from the clutches of the conversation I was having with him.

"A minute, dude." Nathan stares at my face as he throws the words back at him.

I smile at the sound of such a misplaced word on his lips. He's the definition of culture and refinement. The suit he's wearing tonight is grey pinstriped, the white shirt underneath open at the collar to reveal just a hint of that toned chest I got to see last night.

I don't turn to look as he pulls me by my waist into the crowd. I scan the masses trying to find Rebecca but the effort is useless. I can barely walk through the throngs of people. There's no way I'd be able to pick her out in this place.

I freeze once I realize he's pulling me towards the entrance of the hotel. "Wait."

His eyes lower to mine. "It's quieter there."

"No." I stand my ground on the edge of the dance floor. "I'm not going back up there with you."

"Why?" He leans down, his breath forging a path on my bare shoulder. My nipples instantly harden at the sensation.

"It wasn't meant to be." I try to add a lighthearted lilt to my tone but it comes across much more jubilant than I intend.

"I didn't get a chance to finish what I started." He reaches to pull me closer and I take a step back. I can't want him again. Last night was so humiliating.

"There are dozens of women here who would love to go upstairs with you." I turn and his hand stays steady at my waist. "Look at that one right there. She'd be all over you in a flash." I nod my head towards a striking brunette who has her eyes locked on Nathan. Who could blame her? He's the definition of beautiful.

"I want to go upstairs with you." His hand is on my stomach again, pulling me into him. "I don't give up easily."

I sigh at the sensation of his body against mine. I should just swallow my pride and go upstairs. I wanted him last night. Nothing has changed. As soon as I heard his voice tonight I was instantly aroused.

"I'm going to have you." He pushes the hair from my shoulder as his lips trace a path across my skin. "Come upstairs with me. One night, Jessica."

I turn, my hand snaking up his shirt before it settles on his chin. "One night."

A smile pulls on the corner of his lips as he takes me by the hand. I follow him silently as we walk through the hotel lobby again. When the young woman behind the reception counter calls a greeting to him, this time he doesn't react. His gaze is focused forward, his hand gently tugging on mine.

The moment we step into the elevator, his lips are on my mouth. I melt into his embrace. He's so tall, so strong, and so incredibly masculine. I moan slightly as he traces a path along my lower lip with his tongue.

I feel deprived when he pulls away from the kiss as the elevator stops on the eighteenth floor. He takes my hand in his again. There's silence as he dashes to the door of his suite, key card in hand.

I take one last, full breath before he opens the door, pulling me inside.

Chapter 6

I don't have time to react before he pushes me against the door again. I whimper at the reminder of the night before. I want more. I need more than just his hands on me. I push him back and he growls.

He spins me around until I'm leaning against the back of the couch. With one hand he pulls my dress down and my breasts pop free. I didn't wear a bra tonight. I didn't invest any time in what I wore or what I looked like. Getting a man into bed last night was my goal, tonight it was just to be Rebecca's wing woman.

"Beautiful," he whispers as he dips his head to take one of my nipples into his mouth.

I moan at the sensation. His tongue circles the swollen bud before he rakes his teeth lightly across it.

I claw at his suit jacket, wanting to feel his skin on mine. He acquiesces. He effortlessly pushes it from his shoulders and it falls to the floor. Before I have a chance to start work on the buttons of his shirt, he's pulled my dress to the floor.

He drops my breast from his grasp and stands upright. I stare at him. I see the desire I feel in his eyes. He's on fire. He scoops me up in his arms and walks quickly down the hallway to that expansive king size bed I only got to glimpse at from the doorway last night.

"I can't wait to fuck you. Look at you." He moves quickly to rid himself of his shirt before he starts unbuckling his pants. I can't help but stare at his hands. I want to see him. I want to see how aroused he is by my body.

He stops before he pulls the zipper of his pants down. I feel a deep, heavy sigh race through me. Please don't stop. Please.

He crawls onto the bed beside me, his lips coursing hot over mine. I grab his head with my hands, guiding his kiss. I reach for his tongue with my own, playfully pulling it into my mouth. I want this. I want to grab everything I can from this.

His lips leave mine and trace a scorching path down my chest. He briefly pulls my right nipple into his mouth, then the left. I moan at the feeling of his tongue on my flesh.

"I have to make you come," he purrs.

I brace myself as he pulls my panties off. "Please," I whimper. I need to come soon. Just thinking about him fucking me has almost pushed me to the edge.

He pulls his tongue slowly and deliberately along my slick, smooth slit.

I almost cry out from the pressure of his tongue when it touches my clit. "You're exquisite," he whispers into me before glides his tongue across my folds.

"Like that," I cry out. This feels so good. I grab his head with both my hands and I'm rewarded with a loud moan.

"Tell me," he says as he pulls his breath across me. "Tell me how."

"My clit," I murmur. "Lick it."

He flicks his tongue over it and I push my back from the mattress. I have to get closer to him. I have to come like this.

"That's it, baby." His breath on my sensitive folds almost pushes me over the edge. "You're so sweet. So good."

His words push me nearer the edge. "Lick it," I spur him on. "Make me come."

He dives into me and licks me hard as my hips buck off the bed. I've never been eaten like this. I've never come from a man pleasing me this way.

I press my head into the pillow as I fall into the pleasure. I let my body go. I can't control it. I almost scream as I feel the climax course through me. The orgasm is intense. I writhe beneath him, unable to control my own body.

He rests his head on my thigh as I float back from the trance. I run my hand along his forehead, coaxing him to move. I want so much to feel him inside of me.

"That was incredible," he whispers into my thigh as his lips graze my skin. "I could get addicted to that taste."

I float on the words. I don't care who he said them to last week or who will be sprawled beneath him tomorrow. I want this. I need it. I have to hear him tell me he wants me.

"Fuck me," I manage to say.

He raises his head and a sly grin pulls at the corner of his mouth. "Say it again."

"Fuck me." I almost close my eyes at the thought of him over me, his cock inside of my body, taking me back to the edge.

He moves to his feet and deftly pushes his pants and boxer briefs to the floor. I stare at him. He's more impressive than I imagined. His body almost sculptured. The lines are all so defined, his muscles well-toned. His cock is hard, ready and eager. I pull my tongue across my lip. I want it. I want to feel it between my lips. I want to pull my tongue across its wide head. It's so thick, so large.

He reaches to pull a condom from the top drawer of the nightstand next to the bed. I watch in silence as he rolls it over his cock before he's beside me on the bed again.

"I've thought about fucking you all day." He rests between my thighs, his cock in his hand. "When I woke up I could smell your scent on my hand. It was intoxicating. I wanted to find you. I had to find you. I needed to fuck you."

My body aches at the words and the heated glare in his face. I want him too. I know it's one night but I want to know. I want to know what it's like to be taken by him, to have my pleasure be dictated by him.

I push my legs wider apart as my hands fist in the bed linens. I ready my body for him. "Now," I whisper.

He groans as he leans forward, rubbing his cock over my clit.

I shudder at the contact. My hips lunge upward seeking him. "Please," I almost beg.

He leans forward until he's towering over me. I feel the tip of him at my entrance. "Tell me to stop if it's too much."

"No," I shake my head from side-to-side. "No."

"Fuck," he moans loudly as he pushes into me.

I gasp as he sinks himself into me completely. It's so much.

His hips grind into me and I'm breathless with every heavy thrust. I whimper at the sensations. It's all so good.

I clench my body around his and I'm given a deep guttural moan in return. "Christ, Jessica."

"Hard. Harder," I mutter through clenched teeth. I'm close to coming again already. Just feeling him inside of me is pushing me into a place I've never felt before.

He starts fucking me. His strokes are long and hard. His lips find mine and he bites my bottom lip before pulling his tongue tenderly across it.

I grab his ass, pushing him even harder, needing to consume him the same way he's consuming me.

He pushes harder, deeper, faster. I cry out from the pleasure. I can't speak. It's all so much. This is what it's like to really be taken by a man.

I feel a deep, guttural sound escape my lips as my body slides into the edge of an orgasm. He kisses me deeply and I breathe in his breath. I pull him into me in every way as I feel all the pleasure he's giving me take over my body. I come hard.

He reaches to cup my ass in his hand as I feel my body relax again. He kisses my forehead. "I'm not done. I could fuck your sweet body for hours."

He shifts back onto his heels and pulls my hips with him. He's still so hard, so rigid inside of me. I gasp as I realize that he's going to help me come again.

Electricity courses through me when his thumb touches my clit. My hips involuntarily respond and it's all the invitation he needs. He pulls my body closer with one hand as he pounds himself harder into me.

"Fuck, you're so tight," he growls. "Such a sweet little body."

I can't control myself. The heat of his words and the feeling of him thrusting into me are causing another orgasm to race towards me.

"I can't. This is so good," I gasp. "Fuck. Please."

"Take it. It's yours." He pumps himself into me as he circles my clit lightly with his thumb.

"I'm…" my voice trails as I'm hit head-on with an intense orgasm. I can barely contain a scream.

"Fuck, Jessica." He grabs both my hips pulling me into him. "Baby," his voice comes from a deep and distant place as he throws his head back, his own pleasure surging through him.

Chapter 7

"When can I fuck you again?" His index finger runs a lazy path across my hip bone as we lay on our sides staring at each other.

I reach to push a strand of hair back from his face. "It's called a one night stand for a reason."

The playful tone I tried to convey doesn't register in his expression. "It doesn't have to be a one night stand."

"It does." I pull back from his touch.

"Are you involved with someone?" His brows lift with the question.

"No." I answer quickly. "Are you?"

"If you're not tied down why can't we fuck sometimes?"

The genuine tone of his voice almost makes me break out a chuckle. It's so easy for him. It's obvious by the inflection in his voice that having random sex is a very normal part of his life.

"You have plenty of women to fuck." The words come out much harsher than I intend. "I mean, I'm assuming based on the fact that you live above the club that you fuck women on a very regular basis."

"I don't live here. I fuck here."

"Exactly my point." I manage. "You have a place designated just for fucking. You don't need to have repeats."

He shifts his body away from me. I can tell I've offended him.

"You don't need to explain anything to me." I pull myself into a sitting position on the side of the bed. "We had a lot of fun. I'm not looking for anything else. Let's just shake hands and say goodbye."

"Do you want to fuck me again?" The question is bold, direct and immediately I feel myself getting aroused by its brashness.

"Who wouldn't?" I toss back. "That was amazing."

"So, you come back and we have more fun."

"That's treading on dangerous ground." I stand and start the search for my panties.

"Why?" He reaches over the side of the bed and pulls them from the floor.

"It's not just random sex then, it's something else." I cringe. I wish I had just said a weak *yes* when he asked if we could sleep together again.

"Not if we both understand the other's expectations."

"What are your expectations?" I ask even though I'm not certain that I want to know the answer.

"I'm fickle," he admits. "I like variety."

I smile at the confession. It was obvious when he first approached me at the club that any interest he might be showing in me would be fleeting.

"I don't want or need complications. I just want to have sex." His tone is calm and direct.

"You make it sound so easy." I laugh. "You have to run into complications. There must be women who become emotionally attached if you fuck them more than once."

"Sometimes." His gaze falls to the bed. "If that happens I end things."

"You use women." My voice doesn't sound like my own. I sound too righteous. Why I am defending any other woman he's slept with in the past?

He recoils slightly at the words. "Did I use you?"

"No," I mutter. "I was very willing."

"If you come back next week, you'll be willing again, right?" He swings his long legs over the bed and stands up. My eyes fall to his groin. Even in a still semi-hard state he's very imposing.

"If I decided to sleep with you again, yes, it would be because I wanted it."

"Then stop worrying about what anyone else feels or thinks." He pulls his boxer briefs on. "I'm very honest with any woman I fuck. They know it's just for that. No strings."

"We won't get attached to each other?" I tilt my head to the side.

"It's a physical relationship." His hands pull on his belt as he does up his pants. "If either of us feels anything emotional, we end it."

"What about others?" I ask. I'm not expecting him to offer me anything exclusive. I just want to understand the boundaries of what he's proposing. Sex with a man like this is all I really need as I build my life in Manhattan. I could get my needs fulfilled without having to date.

"I don't ask and you don't ask." He winks. "It's not either of our business."

"You make it sound so simple." I reach to pull my heels back on.

"It is." He glances at his watch. "Today is Wednesday. You come back here next Wednesday at ten o'clock. I'll be here waiting for you."

I purse my lips considering the proposition.

"No strings?" I ask softly.

"No strings." He nods towards the bed. "Just more of that."

Chapter 8

"So essentially, you two are fuck buddies?" Rebecca whispers from behind her desk in the cubicle where she spends her days working for one of the biggest investment firms in the city.

"I guess." I shrug my shoulders. "I hadn't really labeled it."

"And you're good with him fucking a different woman every night of the week?" She pulls her lips across her teeth in a grimace.

"I'm not going to think about that," I lie. It's all I've thought about since I left Nathan's hotel room last night. Was I really okay with having sex one night a week with a man who was fucking most of Manhattan the other six nights?

"The sex must have been phenomenal for you to agree to that." She rolls her eyes. "I would have just taken what I got and ended it."

"I haven't even decided if I'm going back." Lie number two. I was already craving his touch again and the thought of waiting almost a week to feel his body inside of mine was causing withdrawal. I had to make myself come in the shower this morning just to find the focus I needed for this meeting with Cassandra, Rebecca's boss.

"You can go in now." Rebecca glances at the clock on the wall above her desk. "It's eleven. She should be ready for you."

I scoop up the plate of coconut macaroons I brought with me and knock tentatively on the door to Cassandra's office.

"Come in," she calls from behind the door and I take a steely breath before I turn the knob. Grabbing this job would make my entire life better at this point.

"Hi," I say meekly as I step into her office. I realize that I don't know if I should call her by her first name or Ms. Saunders. We've only met once, very briefly, a few months ago when I was in New York with Josh visiting Rebecca.

"Jess. It's great to see you again." She motions for me to sit in one of the luxurious leather chairs in front of her desk. "You brought me treats?" The wicked smile that crosses her lips makes my heart leap. Maybe Rebecca was right when she said the way to her heart was through her stomach. It was hard to picture given the fact that Cassandra was tall, graceful and could easily have passed for a model.

"Coconut macaroons." I place the small plate down in front of her on the desk.

She picks one up and admires it before popping it into her mouth. "You're hired," she sighs.

I pull my hand to my mouth. "You're kidding, right?"

"With food I never kid." She playfully points her index finger at me. "You're an amazing cook. Rebecca can't shut up about how great your food is."

I laugh at the backhanded compliment. "Cooking is my passion."

"You didn't study it?" The question was expected but I still feel my stomach lurch. This is the point in the interview where I always lose the job. I can't lose this one. Being a private chef was just the right foot in the door I needed. With a good wage I could start saving for culinary school.

"I took a different path and then realized that I couldn't stay out of the kitchen." I want desperately to skirt over the issue. I know I'm a great cook. I know I can do the job. I just need a chance.

"What did you do back in Connecticut?" she asks before devouring another macaroon.

"I was a paramedic."

Her brow shoots up. "So you have medical training and you can cook?"

"I know," I chuckle. "It's perfect for those rare occasions when someone chokes on my cooking."

She laughs. "It's actually perfect for my situation."

"How so?" I feel I'm making headway. This is the first time I've been in an interview about a position in the industry when anyone has thought my EMT training was a plus.

"I need a cook mainly for my two kids." She motions to a framed picture on her desk of two small children. "They have a nanny, but she burns water."

I smile. "Boiling water isn't as easy as it looks."

"Apparently not." She finishes the last of the macaroons before she continues, "I want someone who can come in a few times a day, five days a week and prepare meals for the kids."

Being a private chef for pre-schoolers may not have been my optimum choice but it was going to pay my bills and allow me to save for my culinary dreams.

"I love cooking for kids." I'm not sure where those words come from. I've never cooked for a child in my life.

"Occasionally I may need you to work an evening to prepare a dinner for me and any guests I might have, but as a rule, it's just going to be you, the nanny and the kids eating. You'll be on your way home by seven every night."

I just nod in response. I'm so close to grabbing this I can almost taste it.

"Here's the detail sheet I've been handing out to the other applicants." She reaches into her desk drawer and removes one single sheet of white paper. "Salary, benefits, hours and all that jazz is on there."

I glance down briefly and I have to hold back a gasp at the number staring back at me. The weekly stipend is more than I made in a month being an EMT.

"When can you start?" She holds the empty china plate I brought with me in her hand.

"This afternoon." I push myself to my feet.

Chapter 9

"Jesus, Jessica." He pulls a heavy breath through clenched teeth as his hands pull gently on my hair. "Where the fuck did you learn how to suck cock?"

I moan at the words. I haven't been in Nathan's hotel room more than ten minutes and already I'm naked, on my knees with his heavy, beautiful cock in my mouth.

"Like that. Fuck, just like that." He leans back against the couch, his dress shirt still buttoned, his pants hanging open.

I pull him from my mouth before I race my tongue over the crown. My hands circle the root, gliding up and down it as I suck on just the tip.

"Christ," he pants as he grows thicker and wider beneath my touch.

I groan as I'm forced to open my mouth even more. I adjust my knees on the carpet of the floor not caring what I look like. Not minding that my body is on full display. All I want is the reward his body is going to offer to me when he reaches his climax.

"Suck it, baby." He grabs my hair harder, controlling the rhythm.

One of my hands bolt to the couch behind him for stability. He's fucking my mouth so hard. His hips moving in a steady beat. I suck him harder, pulling more and more of him into my mouth.

"You're so good." The words are deep and heavy with desire.

I look up. His long lashes flutter closed, his eyes roll back in his head. I'm giving him exactly what he gave me last week. I want that. I want him to feel that.

I pull my grasp away from the couch and cup his heavy, full balls in my hand. I'm compensated with a pull on my hair.

"You're going to make me come." He thrusts harder into my mouth as I pump the thick vein with my hand.

"Yes," I whisper around his flesh. Yes, please, come. Come for me.

"Stop," he moans. His body trying to pull away from mine. "I'm going to come."

I push harder into him, forcing his cock deeper down my throat. I shake my head slightly. I won't pull back. I need this.

"Fuck," he growls as the first shot of heat hits the back of my throat. I moan at the sensation. I brace myself for more.

He pumps harder as he fills my throat with his desire. I struggle to handle it all. It's so much. I've never done this before. I almost gasp at the sensation but I can't stop. My body won't let me. I'm so aroused and wanting.

He pulls back as he softens slightly in my mouth. I feel his legs trembling. His hand is grabbing the edge of the couch tightly.

I look up and he's staring down at me, a wide grin enveloping his handsome face. I smile back, my tongue slowly gliding over my lips.

"That was…" his voice trails as he pulls his hand to his chest. "That was so intense."

I stand and press my lips to his. "I loved every second of that," I whisper into his kiss. I did. I want him to know that it was just as intense for me. I need to tell him that I can't come back here. That even though I've spent the last week engrossed in my new job, that almost every second I've jumped back to thoughts of him in this hotel room.

"I need to taste you." He pulls me closer. "I have to lick your clit until you come too."

"No." I run my finger over his jaw, marvelling at how much more handsome he looks with just the hint of stubble on his face. I wonder what he looks like in the morning, after he's slept and he's ready for coffee. I wonder what it's like to fall asleep in his arms. No. I can't wonder.

"I need to go." I reach for the red dress he pulled off of me the moment I walked through the door.

He grabs my wrist in his hand. "You just got here. We have hours."

"I don't." I lie. I do have hours. I could stay here all night if he wanted me to.

"Why are you rushing off?" He glances down and it's as if he suddenly realizes that his semi-hard cock is still hanging outside of his pants. He tucks it in, does up his pants and faces me again.

"I have an early morning meeting." I do. With Allie and Aaron, the kids I make scrambled eggs for every day.

"What's going on?" He pushes a piece of hair back behind my ear before he tilts my chin up to his gaze.

"Nothing," I sigh. I can't tell him that we just shared the most intense and intimate experience I've ever had and the thought of another woman on her knees in this room, doing the very same thing to him, is just too much for me. I know what I agreed to, but my heart hasn't caught up yet.

"I'd like to see you Friday." His lips feather over mine lightly.

"This Friday?" My mind can't connect the dots. He wants to see me again in two days?

"Can you come by Friday night at the same time?" He bends down to retrieve my bra and panties from the floor.

"I'll be here," I say it without thought.

"Perfect." He taps the tip of my nose with his finger before he walks over to the bar to pour himself a drink.

As I pull my clothes back on I try to chase away that nagging voice in the back of my brain that is telling me that he's quickly becoming someone I need.

Chapter 10

"Rebecca said you left your boyfriend when you moved here." Cassandra pours herself a cup of coffee before turning to face me.

"I did." I manage a weak smile as I load the kids' breakfast dishes into the dishwasher. "It wasn't working."

"How long were you together?" She reaches to grab a piece of pineapple from the fruit salad I prepared earlier.

"A few years." I nod towards a bowl. "Do you want me to make you some breakfast?"

She shakes her head. "Was it hard? Leaving him like that?"

"I guess." I shrug my shoulders. "I still care about him. We just weren't a good fit."

"It was like that with my husband too." She reaches for a piece of peach from the salad. "Ex husband," she corrects herself.

"When did you get divorced?" I ask because I've wondered since I started why no one talks about her ex.

"Two years ago." She pulls in a heavy breath. "We fell in love in college and planned this whole elaborate life together. We had the kids quickly. Everything seemed idyllic and then it all fell apart."

"I'm sorry," I offer. I don't know what else to say. I can sympathize with Allie and Aaron. My own parents had divorced when I was a toddler. Their dysfunctional relationship had set the stage for many awkward years of being juggled back and forth between their two houses and their two lives.

"Don't be," she mutters. "It just fell apart. We settled down too young."

"I'm sure it's been hard." I manage a weak grin.

"It has been." She reaches across the breakfast bar to touch my arm. "Don't rush into anything serious, Jess. I wish I had explored more when I was your age instead of wanting something too serious."

Her words shift through me. Maybe she's right. Maybe I had to stop wanting what I had with Nathan to go anywhere. Maybe I just needed to have fun.

"I'm having more fun now, at thirty-two, than I had when I was twenty," she says, her chin lifting.

"I'm glad." I like this slightly exposed and vulnerable side of Cassandra. Rebecca has only told me stories of what a bitch she can be at work.

"We should hang out sometime."

Her words catch me off guard. "We could," I offer weakly.

"Becky never told you we met at a club?"

I'm not sure if I'm more shocked by the admission or by the fact she called Rebecca by her much hated nickname.

I stifle a chuckle by biting my lower lip. "She didn't."

"I'll get her to a plan a girl's night out for the three of us. It'll be a hoot."

***

"She actually used the word *hoot*?"

"Not only that, she called you Becky." I laugh as I pull a towel from the laundry basket and fold it.

"It's like you're talking about another Cassandra, not the one I work for."

"One in the same. Why didn't you tell me you met her at a club?" I reach for another towel, inwardly scowling at the fact that Rebecca is sitting right next to me and can't seem to reach over to help fold our laundry.

"It's not a great story." She gazes down at her hands. "I was so drunk. She helped me in the bathroom."

"How does that translate into a job for you?" I push the basket closer to her, hoping she'll take the hint. I don't want to spend the next thirty minutes folding clean clothes.

`"She was drunk too." She finally reaches for a washcloth. "I told her I needed a job and she told me she'd hire me."

"So bizarre." I laugh loudly. "You score your dream job while you're falling over drunk and I have to fight tooth and nail to get the privilege of cooking macaroni and cheese for two spoiled four-year-olds."

"Such is life in the big city." She flashes me a grin. "So when are we going to go out and paint the town red? Tomorrow night works for me."

"I can't." I don't offer anything more.

"It's Friday night. Do you have a date?" She leans in closer, resting her chin on the edge of the basket.

"Not a date." I shake my head hoping she's not going to press for more.

"A fuck? Are you seeing him tomorrow?"

I nod silently. "This is going to be the last time."

"Where have I heard that before?" She giggles as she throws the washcloth in my face.

Chapter 11

"There's no way you've ever had a boyfriend." Nathan's breath rushes across my skin.

"That sounds like an insult." I wrap my fingers through his hair wanting him to claim my wetness with his mouth. He's already helped me orgasm just by touching me tonight, now I want to feel his lips slide over me.

"I crave every part of you." His lips glide across my thigh. "The way I feel when I'm with you is too good. It's too much."

I feel my breath hitch at his words. I want to ask him if he means that. I need to know if he really feels that good when he's with me. The thoughts drift into the vapor as he pushes my thighs to the bed, spreading me wider so he can lick me harder.

I moan heavily at the sensations as I pull on his hair. His tongue glides over my sensitive folds, parting them before he buries his mouth deep into my wetness. I arch my back at the intensity of his tongue, of his lips pulling me in.

"Nathan," I cry out and he stills.

"Fuck. Say it again." He tempts me with a soft lick over my clit. "Say my name."

"Nathan," I purr as I pull on his hair. "Nathan, eat me."

"You're too sweet." He tempts me yet again with just a soft stroke of his tongue. "I'm going to fuck you and you're going to scream my name."

I buck at the promise of his cock inside of me. "Do it now," I challenge.

"Say it. Tell me what you want," he growls as he pushes himself from the bed to retrieve a condom from the drawer.

"Fuck me, Nathan." I pull my hand over my mound, relishing in how wet I am.

"Touch yourself," he orders as he pulls the condom over his hardness. "Stroke that clit for me."

I hesitate. I've never touched myself in front of anyone. I lock eyes with him and I see the command there. He wants it. He needs to see me bringing myself pleasure.

"Nathan," I repeat his name as I let my thighs fall to the bed, completely exposing myself.

"Jesus," he moans as he kneels between my legs, his hand stroking his sheathed cock.

"I love when you fuck me," I whisper. "I love how you fuck me."

I pull my eyelids open and he's staring at me. His lips slightly parted, his eyes glazed over.

"Slide it in." I hold myself open. "I want you so much."

He groans loudly as he enters me in one swift movement. My body stiffens at the sensation and I open my mouth to cry out but no sound escapes. It's so much.

"Say it." A trembling moan covers the words.

"Nathan," I spit back. "Nathan."

"So good." He pounds himself into me, his arms on either side of my head. With every thrust he lets out a small groan. He's lost in the sensation. I'm lost in the feeling of him.

"Make me come, Nathan." I pull his name slowly across my lips. "Please."

He pulls out of me so swiftly I moan at the loss. "No," I pout. "No."

His body glides down mine and he scoops my ass into his palms. Before I can react his mouth is on my cleft, parting my folds, probing within me. I grab his head with my hands, pushing my body into his face.

It's raw and intense as he licks me hungrily. "Say my name," he pants before pulling my swollen clit between his teeth.

I scream it loudly, unable to temper my emotions. I can't believe it can feel this good. I can't believe any man can make me want so much.

I rotate my hips as I grind myself into his face. He groans with each movement, eagerly lapping up my wetness, coaxing my orgasm from deep within me. I feel it build and I let out a guttural groan as I feel the pleasure rip through me, blinding me to everything else in the room.

Suddenly, his head isn't there. I'm clawing for his contact and then he's flipping me over. I'm on my knees. His hot, heavy cock resting against my ass cheek.

"I have to fuck you, baby." He pushes himself into me with one swift movement and I stifle a scream in the pillow.

He yanks my body up as if it's a rag doll pulling my back into his chest, all the while pressing on my mound to angle his cock into me. I reach back, unable to feel him.

"You're the sweetest. You're so good," he purrs into my ear as he fucks me with long, hard strokes.

"Please," I whimper. "Please."

He grunts in response as he pounds his body into mine. "Jessica," he whispers. "Jessica."

I close my eyes, breathing in his words, his body and the intense orgasm that has gripped every part of me.

Chapter 12

"What kinds of books did you read when you were a child?"

The words feel so misplaced. I pull my eyes open to see his smiling face looking down at me. He's already dressed. The expensive suit he dropped on the floor in the doorway of the bedroom, now covering his body once again.

"What?" I shake my head as if to rid myself of the sentimental nature of the words.

"When you were a little girl, what books did you read?"

"Fairytales," I whisper. "Why?"

"I was just wondering." He stands again and pulls his grey tie around his neck. I watch as he deftly ties it, his eyes never leaving my face.

"Are you going home?" I pull my hair back as I sit up in the bed.

"I am." He leans forward again to tap me on the tip of my nose. "You are too."

"Yes." I feel deflated for some reason. Maybe it was because everything felt so utterly intense tonight and now just a few minutes short of one o'clock in the morning, he's forcing me out of the bed.

`"I can get you a cab," he offers.

I bite my lip to avoid a huge sigh. I don't want to get in a cab. I don't want to go home. I want to rip that navy blue suit off his body and crawl back on top of him.

"Are you a lawyer?" I toss out.

"Am I a what?" The way his hand freezes in mid-air as he's putting on a cuff link is confirmation enough for me.

"You're a lawyer," I say it with a wide smile.

"What makes you think I'm a lawyer?" He pulls his eyes back down to his shirt, threading the gold circular link through the fabric.

"You know that saying about walking and acting like a duck?" I stand and suddenly feel incredibly exposed.

He doesn't respond. His eyes slide slowly over my naked body.

"Quack." I reach down to retrieve my panties from the floor.

"Quack?"

I twist my hips as I pull my legs through the white lace fabric. "Quack as in you're a lawyer."

"Maybe you're the lawyer." He moves around the bed, my bra dangling from his fingers.

"You're deflecting which proves beyond any reasonable doubt that you're a lawyer."

"Put this on or I'm going to need to fuck you again." He rubs the front of his pants. The obvious outline of his erection straining against the material.

"Lawyers." I wink at him as I grab the bra from him.

"You'll be here on Wednesday night, right?" His lips graze a path across my forehead.

"I'll be here," I whisper knowing that there's very little that could keep me out of his bed.

***

"We're going to interview today for another roommate." Rebecca picks at the salad on her dinner plate. "I was going to do it alone because I thought you'd be working. You always work on Tuesdays."

"Cassandra took the kids to a friend's for dinner tonight." I heave back in my chair. "It's nice to see her spending time with them."

She nods. "There's Bryce, He's the first and only interviewee."

I twist my neck to the entrance of the restaurant. An attractive man is standing in the doorway. "He's going to be our new roommate?"

"My new bedmate with any luck," she says as she waves her hand in the air in his direction.

"Since when are we getting a new roommate and why a guy?" I know the questions aren't going to be answered but I have to ask them anyway.

"You must be Bryce." She stands and offers him a weak hug. "This is Jess. She's my roommate."

He nods and sits down between us. "I just moved here. I was hoping to score a place to live this week. Your ad didn't say when the room would be available."

Ad? Room? I'm guessing that the room he's talking about is the barely there extra room that Rebecca currently uses to house all of her designer shoes and clothes. I briefly wonder whether my room is going to become her secondary closet if this guy moves in with us. I barely have enough space for my own things.

"It's available right now." She smiles brightly.

I toss her a look and immediately realize that I don't have a leg to stand on. I just gave her some money for rent last week. It's her apartment. She's the one calling the shots.

"Rent includes everything?" he asks.

"Everything." She slides her hand in the air. "We're both really easy to live with."

He nods and I finally turn to really look at him. His blond hair is neatly styled. His brown eyes look skeptical but I can tell that he's really considering the offer. Moving to Manhattan is terrifying and it's even more intimidating if you don't have a place to live.

"I moved here just a few weeks ago from Connecticut," I toss out. "Living with Rebecca is great."

"I'll take it. Just let me know what you need from me."

I sit with baited breath waiting to see what Rebecca will throw out as a response to that comment. I pull my gaze to her face and she's white as a ghost. Her hand flies into the air and she points at the back of the restaurant. "Fingers is here," she whispers in a not-so-muted tone.

Chapter 13

"Fingers?" Bryce can't hide the laughter in his voice as he glances past me.

I shrug my shoulder as I smile back at him. "She didn't mean to say that."

"I did." She jumps out of her chair. "I'll go get our check and we can get out of here before he notices you."

Bryce throws me a quizzed look but I don't respond. I desperately want to turn and look. I've never seen Nathan outside the hotel or the club. I don't know what he looks like in the light of the day, moving about in a regular place like this.

I'm instantly aware of how I'm dressed. Whenever I've been with him, I've always taken time to pick out a dress, to style my hair and to apply at least some make up. Today, I'm just wearing a white sweater, faded jeans and my hair is pulled back into a high ponytail. I know, from all the comments, I've heard throughout the years that I look like a teenager when I'm barefaced.

"Fingers is on the move," Bryce leans closer to me. "I take it you don't want to talk to him?"

I shake my head slightly. I don't. I don't want him to see me like this. Today I'm just Jess. I'm not the same Jessica who takes his body into mine.

"Jessica?" I cringe when I hear his voice next to me.

I keep my head tucked close to Bryce hoping that Nathan will think he's mistaken me for his Jessica.

"Jessica?" he repeats and I feel his hand brush against my shoulder.

I look up and I'm immediately taken back by the petite blonde woman standing next to him.

He smiles down at me before his brow furrows. "Who is this?" He gestures towards Bryce.

"Jess and I live together. I'm Bryce." He extends a hand in front of me and it feels like an eternity before Nathan pulls it into his for a firm shake.

We don't live together I want to say. He hasn't moved in yet and it's not like that.

"You live together?" There's a hint of surprise skirting around the edges of the question.

"I'm…I am…I'm Wednesday." I stammer as I hold out my hand to the pretty woman standing next to Nathan.

"Wednesday," she repeats back to me, her hand lightly touching mine.

"Are you Tuesday?" I ask before I realize what I'm saying.

"I'm Ivy," she corrects me. "Is your name Jessica or Wednesday?"

I breathe in a deep sigh. Why did I just call myself Wednesday? Why did I have to be in this restaurant, on this day? Now that I've seen him with another of his fuck buddies I can't look him in the eye.

"We're all set." Rebecca is back at the table, pushing some cash into her purse. "We're all settled up so we can take off."

I silently plead with her to get me out of that chair. I can't stay in this restaurant a moment longer.

"Let's go, Jess." She motions towards the door. "You too, Bryce."

He stands and I reach for the arms of the wooden chair to push myself up. Nathan's hand moves to grip my shoulder.

I slide back down, painfully aware that I'm not going to get out of this that easily.

"Jessica," he breathes across my exposed neck as he leans in close. "I'll see you tomorrow."

I turn to nod, but before I can his hand is on my chin, tilting my face into his. I briefly flash to the image of Ivy standing behind him before his lips glide across mine.

He moans into my mouth and I instinctively reach up to cradle the back of his head with my hand. His tongue pushes my lips apart, then circles mine in a primitive dance.

His breath hitches as I pull his bottom lip between my teeth. I drown in the feeling of his kiss. Everything else in the room melts away.

He pulls back slightly, his tongue tracing a path around my ear. My eyes drift open as I hear him whisper very softly, "don't fuck him tonight. Save it for me."

Chapter 14

"One could argue that it was territorial." I ease back onto the couch as I reach for the glass of amber liquid from his hand.

"Or one could say that he couldn't handle the idea of that guy's head between your legs." He raises the glass in his own hand before he downs half the bourbon.

"What if I was sleeping with him? What if we were dating and you just kissed me like that?" I took a small sip and recoiled at the taste.

"I knew you weren't dating." He takes another strong swallow.

"How?" I place the glass down on the table in front of me. Since Nathan's show of affection at the restaurant last night I've spent most of the day skirting questions from Rebecca about what was going on between the two of us.

"I saw him come in to the restaurant." He empties the glass before placing it down next to mine. "You didn't react at all when he sat down."

I'm immediately aware that he must have witnessed me coming in too. "How long were you there for?"

"Long enough to watch you laugh and play with your ponytail while you were talking."

"That's not fair," I shoot back. "You should have said something earlier."

"I was busy," he says flippantly.

"With Ivy?" I stare at him.

"She's an old friend." He stands and moves to the counter to pour himself another drink.

"You said there wouldn't be any complications." I pull on the bottom hem of my dress. "Last night was complicated."

"I admit I didn't react well." He takes another shot of bourbon. "Something just snapped when he said you lived together."

"You just said that you knew we weren't dating." I jump to my feet. "Which is it, Nathan?"

His hand is around my waist in a flash. I feel how aroused he is when he pulls me into him. "When he said you lived together I realized that he got to see you in ways that I don't. How could he not want you?"

"I don't even know him." I came to his hotel with the intention of not revealing more of my personal life to him than he already stumbled on. Now, I was confessing in ways I didn't want to.

"I fuck you here because it's just us. I don't have to think about you with anyone else. Last night, when I saw him look at you, when I watched him lean in to you, I felt something."

"You can't say that." I try to pull free but he only firms his grip on me.

"It's the truth." His voice is calm, the tone low. It infuriates me even more.

"You're not getting it." I stress the words. "You're just not."

"What am I not getting?" He pulls the glass in his left hand back to his lips and takes a small swallow.

"If I decide to go out with a man, and we're having dinner and I'm about ready to go home to fuck his brains out, you can't just waltz up and kiss me," I spit the words out harshly.

"Jessica." He leans down to place the now empty glass on the table. "If I ever see you with another man and I sense that at some point your beautiful mouth is going to slide over his cock, I'm going to do whatever it takes to stop that from happening."

"You're kidding, right?" I push my hands against his chest to gain distance but he circles my waist tightly. He seriously doesn't understand how fucked up this is.

"I'm dead serious." The intensity in his eyes says more than his words.

"Nathan. You fuck a different woman every night in this room." I gesture to the luxurious room we're standing in.

"Not every night." He corrects me with a glare in his eyes.

"Whatever." I push against him again and his grip only tightens. "The point is that if I saw you out with a woman who I assumed you were going to sleep with that night I wouldn't say a word. I'd respect your privacy."

"That would never happen." He leans in close, the alcohol on his breath skirting past my nose.

"You don't know that." I laugh. He's so arrogant. How did I miss that? I have to stop this now. I can't believe we're actually having this conversation. Maybe he isn't a lawyer after all. They're not this dense, are they?

"I don't go out in public with the women I fuck." He pulls each word across his teeth and spits it out.

I push against him with all my strength and it breaks his grasp. "Wow," I mutter as I search for my purse. "Wow."

"Where are you going?" He pulls on my arm but I yank it harshly back.

"Anywhere but here." I move to the edge of the couch to pick up my purse.

"Why?" He blocks the doorway. "You can't just leave."

"Why not?" I stand my ground, my arms folded across my chest. "Because I'm your Wednesday fuck and you can't wait until Thursday shows up to get your fix?"

"Jessica, don't," he sighs heavily.

"Don't what?" I try to temper my voice.

"Don't go." He takes a step towards me. "I'm not good at this. Let me explain."

"Why bother?" I ask hoarsely. "There are two sets of rules. One for you and one for me."

"I don't want that." He hangs his head down. "I don't want that anymore."

"What do you want, Nathan?" I push the words at him.

"You," he whispers softly.

Chapter 15

"You want me for tonight and then tomorrow night someone else will be listening to those same words." I take a step back to lean against the couch. I feel deflated, exhausted and worn out from the emotional tennis match we're in the middle of.

"No. There's no one tomorrow. "He moves away from the door and I realize that now is my chance to walk out of the room and his life. My legs don't budge. I can't go. I need to hear what he has to say.

"There will be next week and I'm fine with that," I say the words even though I'm not being completely honest. I've learned quickly how to block out images of him with anyone else. I have to for my own sanity.

"How can you be fine with that? Women aren't fine with that." He picks up my drink from the table and takes a mouthful of the bourbon.

"We agreed to that." I shrug my shoulders. "No complications. Just sex."

"Do you want more?" he asks the question so effortlessly.

"More?" I repeat back certain that I'm not understanding him.

"More than just a fuck buddy."

It takes me a moment to digest his words. He didn't ask if I wanted him to be more than a fuck buddy. He asked if I wanted more than a fuck buddy.

"Do you?" he presses.

"You're asking if I want a relationship with someone at some point?" I push the words back to him, trying to decipher exactly what he's asking.

"Yes." He empties the glass and sits down on the couch.

"Eventually, sure," I reply. I do want that. I thought I'd have that with Josh but it didn't work.

"You're just happy having one night stands right now?" His words bite into me. He has no idea that he was my one and only one night stand and unless I'm mistaken, the definition of that doesn't include an emotionally charged conversation like this.

"I don't sleep with random men." I don't want to sound insensitive, but I'm not going to lie. "You were my first and only one night stand."

He raises his eyes to meet mine and I see something flash in his expression. "Have you fucked another man since you met me?"

The question is so swollen with arrogance that I want to laugh out loud. His face is dead serious though and I realize that, to him, it's coming from a genuine place.

"No." I sit next to him. "No one."

"I can't explain it." He pulls his hands together. "There's something about you."

I want to feel elation at his words. There's something about him too. Something that stretches far beyond what happens in this room when he's helping me feel pleasure. I can't let myself feel the promise of the words. He sleeps with so many women. I can't forget that.

"Have you slept with other women since me?" I ask knowing the answer already.

He doesn't respond and any bliss that my heart felt quickly sinks. He's never going to want just me. That's not how this happens. I can't let myself think that's a possibility.

"Nathan." I pull my tongue across my lips. "We've had a lot of fun together. A lot."

He reaches for my hand pulling it into his lap. "So much fun, Jessica."

"I just can't do this anymore." I pull a weak grin across my mouth. "We agreed that it would be uncomplicated and just sex. Last night it crossed over to something more and I just don't think you understand that when there are boundaries, they have to be respected both ways."

"I can't see you with another man." He squeezes my hand. "You can't expect me to sit there and not do anything."

"You and I are not in a relationship." I move my hand in the air between us. "We have sex. Mind blowing, amazing sex. That's what this is."

"I don't want that to end." He shifts his body so he's closer to me on the couch.

I stare at his legs. They're so strong. Even beneath the fabric of his pants, I can see the definition of his thighs. I don't want it to end either. I'm addicted to his body. The way he makes me feel is like a drug. I can't get enough of it. I have to come several times a day by my own hand just to be able to focus on anything but his tongue, his hands and his cock.

"How is this supposed to work if you don't respect our boundaries?" I hear my voice asking the question. Why am I even entertaining the idea of letting this go on? There are plenty of men in Manhattan. Hell, there are a hundred downstairs in the club right now. All I need to do is leave him, go downstairs and I can be having a raging orgasm with someone else within the hour.

"I'll respect them." He traces his finger over my leg towards the hem of my dress.

"Can you honestly do that?"

"I crave your body. I can't give that up."

"You can't act the way you do when you see me outside of this room." I don't want to want him anymore but I can't stop.

"If I see you again anywhere but here, I'll walk away." His breath, hot and fast, races across my neck.

"I can't do this tonight." I cover his hand with mine, stopping it on its path up my thigh.

"I want you."

"Not tonight." I push his hand onto the couch. "I'm leaving."

Chapter 16

"Can I ask you something?" I peer over the edge of the counter at Cassandra.

She smiles as she watches me wipe Allie's face after our spaghetti dinner. "Sure, anything."

I wait until the nanny scoops the little girl in her arms and takes her out of the room. "Have you ever been in a relationship that wasn't really a relationship?"

She tilts her head to the side as if she's trying to translate the question into another language. "I'm not sure I'm following, Jess."

"It's so complicated." I laugh as I motion towards the coffee maker. "Do you want a cup?"

She nods. "Just spit it out. We're both adults. I can handle it."

"You're sure?" I cringe at the thought of asking her about this but Rebecca assured me that whenever she had an issue with a man, Cassandra was always the first person to dish out the best advice.

"I met this guy at a club." I realize how cliché that sounds. "We hooked up and it was supposed to be a random, one night thing."

"I'm following so far." She pours some cream into the mug before she stirs it.

"We kept meeting." I giggle before I continue, "the sex is ridiculous."

She winks. "So far, so good."

"We have our rules." I start tapping points out on my fingers. "No last names, no details about our lives, no seeing each other socially."

"So it's just great sex and nothing else," she says it so matter-of-factly. I wish it was as easy as it sounds coming out of her mouth.

"Until he saw me with another guy last week." I shake my head and roll my eyes.

"What guy? You're dating someone?"

"No. It's Bryce. That guy that moved in with Rebecca and me." I know she's met him. I heard from Bryce over dinner last night what a MILF Cassandra is.

"He's gorgeous." She laughs. "Young, but gorgeous."

I smile. "Anyways, the random sees Bryce and decides that he should kiss me to mark his territory."

"Wait." She bolts upright on the stool she's teetering on. "The random just kisses you in front of Bryce as if to say, hands off she's mine?"

"Pretty much."

"That's kind of hot, don't you think?" She takes a long sip from the mug. "This is great coffee, Jess."

I blush at the unexpected compliment. "I was really pissed at him."

"Why?" she shoots back. "He was jealous, no?"

"I don't know." I sigh. "I can't read him at all."

"Did you ask him about it?"

"He said he didn't want me fucking Bryce, yet he fucks whoever he wants." I laugh when I realize how ludicrous it sounds.

"He's falling for you." She points her finger at me. "The random is falling for you."

I want to believe that. She can't be right though. He told me he was fickle. He warned me that he likes variety.

"You know, he's never asked for my number." It's the first time I've shared that with anyone. I've been too embarrassed to tell Rebecca that detail.

"That's a complication to him," she states. "He doesn't want to have the responsibility of having to call the day after."

"Exactly. So why can't I just forget about him and move on?"

"You're falling for him too." She pats my hand. "If you don't want to get hurt, now is the time to bail out of this, Jess. Men like that never change."

I know she's right. My mind knows it. My body just isn't ready to accept it yet.

Chapter 17

"I was shocked you wanted to come here," Rebecca adjusts the neckline of the top she's wearing. "I thought you wanted to avoid Fingers like the plague."

I grin at the nickname. She refuses to call him Nathan and since I have every intention of steering clear of him in the future, I couldn't care less what she calls him. Taking Bryce to the club as a way to celebrate his arrival in Manhattan had been my idea. I wanted a bird's eye view of Nathan picking up another woman and sweeping her away to the eighteenth floor. I knew that if I saw it with my own two eyes, forgetting about him would be that much easier.

"I'll get us some drinks." Bryce calls to us as we exit the ladies' room. Although I'm still not used to the idea of a male roommate, having Bryce around had been fun. He was too much of a gentleman to try anything on either of us. Once we found out he was saving up to get his girlfriend back home an engagement ring, we knew he was the perfect choice to live with us. He had unexpectedly become something of a big brother figure to both Rebecca and I.

"Fingers at a distance." Rebecca taps me on the shoulder and I see Nathan out of the corner of my eye. He's chatting up a beautiful brunette, her hand resting softly on his forearm.

"That didn't take long." I try not to sound defeated. What was I really expecting? It was the exact way he picked me up. He trolls the club until he sees someone he wants to take up to his room, and he makes it happen. The mere fact that he has a fuck pad above a club says more than anything that could have come out of his mouth.

"Don't beat yourself up over it, Jess." My best friend hugs me from behind. "He's a man whore."

I laugh at the description. Maybe he was. Maybe he'd always be. Cassandra's words about men never changing ring loudly through my ears as the pulsing music shifts to a higher tempo. I want to dance. I search the floor for Bryce but he's still in the line for the bar. My eyes scan the room before they settle on a handsome man staring directly at me.

He nods in my direction and I smile back. Maybe the best way for me to get over Nathan is to just fuck someone else. Maybe I need to rid my mind and my body of the memory of his touch. I have to stop thinking about him. I have to stop wanting him so much.

"Dance?" The man with the brown eyes from across the club is beside me now, his hand resting squarely on the skin of my back. The sheer black dress I'm wearing is backless and the chill that races through me at his touch is unexpected, and welcome.

"Absolutely." I throw my hand into his and he leads me onto the floor.

The one glass of wine I had earlier at the apartment is now warming me from the inside out. I feel free and liberated.

"I'm Drew," he says into my neck as he pulls me closer. "You're beautiful."

"I'm Jess," I whisper back. I can be Jess with him. I want to be. Jessica is gone. I left her back in that hotel room.

He hand slides across my back and I shiver at the touch. I push myself into him. I need this. I need this distraction from everything. I don't have to sleep with him. I can just enjoy being close to a man. Being close to someone who isn't as fucked up as Nathan is exactly what will get me through this night.

"What do you do?" I love that he asks me that. He's interested. I don't care if it's small talk or if he's just asking to be polite.

"I'm a personal chef," I say with a grin.

"Seriously?" He stops and pulls back so he can look at my face. "I'm a chef too. I work at Axel NY. Do you know it?"

My mouth falls open at the mere mention of that restaurant. It's only the best dining experience in all of Manhattan. "Are you kidding? I have been dying to go there."

"You'll come." He pulls me back closer, his warm breath flowing across my neck. "You'll be my guest."

This is what it's supposed to be like. This is what it feels like to be with a man who sees me as an actual person and not just someone to fuck in a hotel room one night a week.

"I want your number before you drift away." He stops mid step to pull his smartphone from the pocket of his jeans.

I start to call out the numbers and he pushes the phone into my hand. "Put the number in yourself. I don't want to mess it up."

I feel giddy as I punch each of the digits into the phone and save my name in his contact list.

"I'm calling you tomorrow morning, just so you know." He runs his tongue over his lips. I soak in how striking he is. He's got a boyish charm that reminds me of home.

"I'll be waiting." I feel my heart leap at the fact that he didn't assume I'd jump into bed with him. He wants to get to know me.

"Jessica." I hear Nathan's voice to the left and my stomach drops.

I turn slowly. He's not more than three feet away, his hands tucked into his pants pocket. "What the fuck do you think you're doing?"

Chapter 18

"Did you fall asleep again?" I spit the words out him as I pace the floor in the lobby of the hotel.

"What?" He raises both his hands in the air.

"You had to have been asleep the last time we talked because you agreed to not interfere if you saw me with another man." I run my hand across my forehead in pure and utter exasperation.

"That didn't include you looking for a new fuck buddy right in front of me." His tone is hard and unyielding.

"You were doing the very same thing." I motion towards the entrance of the club. "When I got here, you were all over some brunette."

"I work with her, Jessica." He shakes his head slightly. "I was passing through the club on my way upstairs when I saw her."

"It's not Wednesday," I glance at the clock on the wall. "It's eleven o'clock which means it's fuck time. Why aren't you naked and in bed with someone else?"

"I was going up to get something before I went home."

I pause at the mention of his home. It always seems to escape me that he doesn't live here. He just stays here to fuck women. I wonder what his home looks like. I wonder what his last name is.

"I was just giving him my number." I know I sound bitchy, but I don't care.

"So he could call you?"

"Yes, Nathan," I seethe. "Normal people exchange phone numbers and then they communicate with one another."

"You're mad that I never asked for your number?"

"No." I turn to walk back towards the club's entrance. "I'm mad at myself for ever thinking I could do this."

"You can do this." He pulls on my elbow, stopping me in my tracks. "I can do this."

I don't turn. I can't. I don't want to look at him when he tells me that it will work and that we just need to go up to his room to talk it out. If we do that, I'll be on my knees with his cock in my mouth within twenty minutes. I have no barrier of resistance when it comes to him. His body is irresistible to me and the only way to stop wanting it is to walk away.

"I can't fuck you anymore," I whisper the words. "I just can't."

He pulls me back around so I'm facing him. "You don't mean that."

"It's just sex." I exhale sharply. "We had sex for a few weeks and now it's done."

His jaw tightens. "You can't end this. I shouldn't have acted like that with the other guy in the club."

I wince at his words. He truly thinks it's all just about how he reacts to other men. He doesn't understand that I'm becoming attached to him. That I want him in ways he'll never want me.

"It's not about the other guy." I feel spent. "We can't keep talking about this."

"What's it about then?" He pulls his hand through his hair and I realize he's feeling just as anxious as me.

"You can have any woman you want, any night of the week." I motion towards the club, its pulsing music drifting into the hotel lobby. "All you have to do is leave your suite, come down here, buy a beautiful woman a drink and you're in bed with her an hour later." I know I sound defeated but I don't care. "I came here that first night looking for exactly that. I just wanted a man for one night. Something anonymous and intense. I wanted what you gave me."

"I wanted that too," he offers meekly.

"Something changed between then and now." I feel my heart pound as the words leave me. "I don't know how to explain it."

"Try." He shifts nervously from one foot to the other. A group of women walk past us and his gaze is locked on me. He doesn't pull his eyes away from my face.

"I've never met anyone like you." I laugh at the broad scope of that understatement. "Before you, I hadn't ever been with a man who could make me feel so many things."

The edge of his mouth curls in a small smile and I curse inwardly. I don't want him to take pleasure in this. I don't want him to see our experiences together as some sort of accomplishment.

"I don't know anything about you. I don't know how old you are or your last name. I think you're a lawyer because you're wound up so tight," I pause to smile at him. "I have no idea where you live or what you like to eat for dinner or what makes you happy beyond coming in a woman's mouth. I know nothing."

He stares at me, not making any effort to respond.

"I moved here from a very small place in Connecticut. I loved the same boy for a long time and one day I woke up and realized that I needed more. I wanted more so I came here." I point at the floor as if my journey from home has brought me right to this spot in the universe. In many ways it had. "I can't keep riding that elevator every Wednesday night at ten o'clock to the eighteenth floor to get into bed with you."

"Jessica," he whispers my name and then silence fills the space between us.

"You get angry if you think I'm going to be with another man, yet you can't even share the simplest details of your life with me." I press my hand to my chest to quiet my pounding heart. "I need to move on."

"It's Moore." He approaches me.

"What's Moore?" I cock a brow in response.

"My last name." He crosses his arms over his chest. "My name is Nathan Moore."

"My name is Jessica Roth," I offer back.

"Jessica Roth," he repeats it. "I knew it was going to be something beautiful.

"It's just a name."

"How old are you?" He almost visibly squirms as he asks the question.

"I'm twenty-three." I don't hesitate. "You?"

"Thirty," he smirks. "Older, wiser."

"Not wiser." I shake my head slightly. "It's lovely to meet you, Nathan Moore."

"The pleasure is all mine, Jessica Roth."

Chapter 19

"So now what?" Rebecca pushes a piece of the frittata I made for breakfast onto a plate. "Are you two dating?"

"We're not doing anything, right now." I take a small bite of wheat toast.

"What? I thought he had an epiphany in the hotel lobby and you two were going to go steady." She throws me an exaggerated wink.

"I'm going to see him tonight to talk." I shrug my shoulders. Learning Nathan's name didn't offer much to me except for some extra information I garnered from Google after searching for him. He's a securities attorney, originally from Boston. There weren't even any images of him I could fawn over. The man still remained a tight lipped mystery.

"You want something more than what you have with him, don't you?" The question pulls me back from my thoughts about everything Nathan hasn't shared with me.

"I want to weigh all my options," I skirt the real answer. After hearing his name and seeing a flash of vulnerability in his eyes, I want everything. I want to be the only woman in his life.

"I'm going to throw a little welcome to the city bash for Bryce next week, on Thursday. You up for that?" She points to the expansive living room of our apartment. "We could host here and you could cook."

"I can't on Thursday. I've got to cook dinner for Cassandra and some of her friends. Some surprise birthday thing."

"That sucks." She takes a hearty bite of food.

"Move the party to Friday and me and my culinary skills are all yours."

She only nods in response as she finishes her breakfast.

***

"We're going to talk after." His hand cups my ass through the thin fabric of my panties. "I have to fuck you, Jessica."

"You're insatiable." I haven't been in the room for more than three minutes and I can already feel his erection straining against the fabric of his pants.

"I wanted to talk." My protest is marred by the moan that escapes me as his fingers slide over my cleft. I'm wet. He can feel it. He's known it since I walked through the door.

"I haven't fucked anyone since you were here." It's abrasive and bold, but coming from him it's a tender confession.

"Have you thought about me?" I tease. I want this too. More than I can admit. I ache for his touch. I long to feel his cock inside of me, pushing me to the edge. I have to come. I need to.

He glides his lips across mine and I melt at the taste of his breath. He's so greedy. His tongue pushes between my lips as his finger traces a path over my moist folds. He's going to bring me to the edge with his fingers again, just like that first night.

"Nathan," I whimper. I know the impact on him when he hears me say his name.

"Yes," he growls into my mouth as he pulls back.

I glance down. He's pulling a condom from the pocket of his pants.

"You were ready." I reach down to unzip his pants.

"I knew I'd have to be inside you the minute you got here." He pulls out his cock and it falls, full and heavy into my hand.

I groan at the feeling of it. I want to taste it. I want to bring him that kind of pleasure again.

He deftly pulls the condom over the thick vein before he rips my panties to the side. "I'm going to fuck you so hard. I want you to scream my name."

I suck in a deep breath as he glides the head over my clit. My hips buck against the wall, seeking more contact. Even if I wanted to pull back, I can't. His body is like a magnet to me. I can't resist him. I don't know how to.

He stifles a scream from my mouth with his own as he pushes himself completely into me. Hitching my right leg up, he moves swiftly to find his rhythm. I hold tight to his face, pulling his mouth into mine as he thrusts faster and harder. My head bangs against the inside of the door. We're both fully clothed but beneath his touch, with him inside of me I feel so open and bare.

His right hand moves to cup my ass, tilting my body slightly so the head of his cock hits that tender spot inside of me. I moan loudly at the sensation. I'm so close already. He can bring my pleasure to the surface so fast. It's confusing, and intoxicating all at the same time.

"Nathan," I whimper as I get close to the edge.

"Fuck, you're so sweet." He pounds harder, his hand cupping my ass tighter. "You have the perfect little body. Always so ready for me. Always so eager."

His words push me closer. "Please."

"Christ," he ups the tempo and my head slams repeatedly into the door. I can't register anything other than complete and total pleasure.

"Fuck." The word comes from a place deep within me. I can't control it. I can't control the orgasm that rushes through me. I cry out as he pumps harder, emptying himself as my name slides slowly over his lips.

Chapter 20

"I wanted to do that after we talked." I adjust the hem of the dress I'm wearing, hoping it will cover me now that I've lost my panties for the night.

"We're going to do that again after we talk," he says it so flippantly and with such a broad grin on his face that I almost melt at the notion.

"What are we now?" The question is awkward and misplaced.

"More than we were before?" It's not an answer and it does little to help me wade through all the cluttered emotions I'm feeling.

"What does that mean?" I don't want to sound needy or wanting but I also don't want to go back to taking an elevator up to his suite once a week and knocking on the door.

"It means that next Saturday night we're having dinner at Axel NY." He grins.

"No." I almost bounce into his lap. "How did you manage that?"

"My friend, Ivy. You remember the blonde from the restaurant." He cocks a brow waiting for me to respond.

I nod feverishly.

"Her boyfriend is a friend of the owner so she got us a table." He slaps his hands together. "I know you want to go there."

"How?" I search his face.

"The guy." He rolls his eyes. "You know that guy you were dancing with. I heard you talking to him."

I push back to that conversation. "How much of that did you hear?"

"Enough to know that you're a chef," he says smoothly.

I blush at the words. "Not a chef yet but I'll get there."

"You're going to accomplish anything you want." He taps me on the tip of my nose. "I can tell."

"What about this?" I motion to the air between us.

"What do you mean?"

"I know you don't do relationships." I pull a thin smile across my lips.

He sets his hand on top of mine. "I'm not good at them."

"No one really is," I say teasingly.

"I'll promise you this." He pulls my hand into his and traces a path along my palm with his index finger. "I'll try to be more open with you. I'll share more when I feel comfortable and you can do the same."

I nod and try to force a smile. I want to share everything now. I'd be willing to but I can tell he's not ready yet.

"I would like one thing." He pulls his phone from the pocket of his pants. "I'd like your number."

I feel a rush of happiness run through me. "You don't ask for numbers often, do you?"

"It's a big step." He laughs. "So are you going to give it to me or not?"

I recite my number for him as I watch him enter it into his phone.

"Did that guy call you?" He reaches to place his phone on the table. "The chef guy. Did he call?"

"No." I shake my head. "He won't."

"He will." He pulls me closer to him. "He wanted you. I could see it on his face."

"That was fear when you stood next to us glaring at him." I snuggle into his chest.

He reaches for my hips to pull me into his lap so I'm facing him. "When a man wants a woman it's there, in his eyes. The want and then need is there. I saw it on his face."

I pull my hips closer to him, my wetness sliding over his pants. "Is it on your face?"

"Every time I see you." He moans as he reaches to grab my thighs.

"The first night you saw me it was there." I push back and then pull forward again, tempting his erection through the material.

"It was there when you walked through the door of the club." His hands inch even higher. "I had to have two drinks just to calm my cock down."

"You knew you'd have me." I say it as fact. I know it's the truth. I remember exactly how he looked at me that first night at the club.

"I almost had to jerk myself off in the men's room. I couldn't control the want or the need." He moves his hands up my sides, pulling the dress with them. "That tight little body teasing me from across the room."

I lift my hands above my head and he pulls the dress over. "I wanted you too," I whisper.

"You came to the club to get fucked." He pulls the front clasp of my bra open. "You were made to be fucked by me."

He takes one of my nipples into his mouth, twirling his tongue around it. I throw my head back at the sensation and I feel his hand push down my belly.

"You're so wet and ready." He moves his finger quickly across my clit. The pressure is so light I can barely feel it. "Sometimes, at night, I close my eyes and think about how you taste and I jerk myself off."

I moan at the thought of him coming to any thoughts of me. I push his hand back down, towards my center. He pulls it back up as I moan in protest.

"I'm going to make you scream, Jessica." He holds my hips as he shifts his hips to the side, pulling himself down on his back. "You're going to ride my face until you can't take it anymore."

I feel him pull my thighs towards him and I eagerly acquiesce. I move my body so my core is right above his mouth. I feel so close already and he hasn't even touched me with his tongue yet.

He jerks my legs and I fall forward, my cleft meeting his mouth. He sucks the folds between his lips and I reach for his hair. I pull on it, looking down. His eyes bore into me as I feel the first orgasm wash through me.

"Nathan," I murmur.

"Again," he whispers before he claims me with his tongue. I groan at the intensity and rock my hips back and forth, using his tongue as a tool for my pleasure. His hands grip my thighs, pulling me tighter into his sweet embrace.

His tongue flutters over my clit as I push myself into him. I feel so wanton, so brazen. I'm perched above him, taking all the pleasure I can from him while he's fully clothed beneath me. I glance back and see his erection straining against his pants. I want to taste him too. I want to feel that.

I'm pulled back into the moment when he sucks gently on my clit. I'm so close to the edge again. I grip his hair, pulling it hard. His tongue spears into me and I fall into the clutches of an intense climax. I scream his name as I fall forward.

"Again," he whispers and I try to pull away. I can't. It's too much.

"No," I protest weakly as he grips my thighs even harder. "No."

He nods his head as I race to the edge quickly yet again when he sucks on my clit with reckless abandon. I feel so sensitive, so swollen. I can't take it.

Tears stream down my face as I feel the last orgasm rise from within. I curve my back, pull his head into me and let out a deep, intense and soul wrenching moan.

Chapter 21

"I'm sorry I didn't tell you about the address change until this morning." Cassandra pulls open the heavy door of an apartment building in midtown. "I was so busy planning the guest list and getting a gift that I completely forgot we were cooking at his place."

"His place?" I question. I overheard her talking about her ex on the phone last week. Now I'm wondering if part of the surprise involves him.

"My boyfriend." She blushes at her own words. "Is it possible to have a boyfriend when you're thirty-two?"

"I think it's possible at any age." I laugh as I stand next to her waiting for the elevator to reach the lobby.

"So it's a surprise for your boyfriend?" I'm trying to piece together exactly what we're doing here. Not that it really matters. The fact that she's given me a huge bonus to take care of this private dinner party for eight is really all the explanation I need. This money is going straight into my culinary school fund.

"It's his birthday." She reaches into her pocket. "I got him tickets to a Nets game." She proudly pulls them out and flashes them in the air.

"He's a big sports guy?" I try to keep the small talk going even though the box in my hand, that is filled with ingredients for the gourmet dinner I'm about to prepare, is so heavy that my arms are slowly going numb.

She nods as the lift arrives and we step in. "He's at the sports bar with his buddies almost every night. He knows I need my time with the kids, so it works out."

"Sounds perfect." I smile.

"How's it going with your guy?" She finally presses the button for the twentieth floor and I feel relief at the prospect of being able to put the box down within the next few minutes.

"Things are better. He's not trolling the club for ladies anymore, at least." I adjust my grip on the box.

"I met my guy at a club too." She fishes in her purse for something. "That club I went to with Rebecca, actually. You know the one. It's in that hotel in Times Square."

"I guess clubs are the place to find a man in Manhattan." I breathe a heavy sigh of relief as the elevator signals the stop and the doors spring open.

"This way." She points to the left as she pulls a ring of keys from her purse. "Thank god he gave me a set of keys last month or this whole surprise birthday party would have gone to hell."

I laugh as I follow her to a dark oak door marked with a number six.

She only struggles with the key for a moment before she pushes the door wide open. I step through and place the heavy box down on the floor. I shake my arms, hoping to get some feeling back in them before I have to start cooking the five course dinner that Cassandra requested.

"It's a gorgeous apartment, isn't it?" Her voice trails off as she disappears around a corner. "The kitchen is this way, Jess."

I grimace at the thought of picking up the box again. "I'll be right in."

I just need a minute to find some strength in my arms so I soak in the room. It's obvious it's a man's apartment as all the furniture is leather in deep, rich tones. An enormous television adorns the wall above a granite fireplace and a wall of photos leads into the hallway.

"What does your boyfriend do?" I call into the apartment. He has to be in real estate or maybe investments. This apartment, and its view of Central Park, had to come at a steep cost.

"He's a lawyer." She pops back into my line of sight.

"It's such a beautiful place." I try not to sound envious. I can't help but be. This is the type of place I hope to live in one day. A place I can call home based solely on my own hard work and determination.

"Look how adorable his niece and nephew are." Cassandra points to a framed picture of two young children adorning the fireplace mantel. "They're not as cute as Allie and Aaron, but it's close."

I laugh as I pull my eyes along the entire line of pictures. I lean closer when I reach a black and white photograph of a man and a woman.

A key rattling in the door, makes Cassandra jump. "Shit. What the hell? How can he be here? He was supposed to be in court until six. It's not even four."

I don't react. My eyes are still fixed on the picture.

I hear the apartment door open as she races towards it. I reach for the picture, pulling it into my hands.

"Why are you here?" Her voice is loud and demanding. "You're ruining my surprise."

"What?" His voice is low and calm. "What surprise?"

"My chef is cooking you a birthday dinner. I've invited all your friends."

I close my eyes. I can't turn around. I can't do it.

He said he doesn't do relationships.

She said she met him at the same club.

She has keys to his place.

I glance down at the picture again. Nathan's smiling face stares back at me.

"Jess, turn around." She calls across the room. "I want you to meet my boyfriend, Nathan."

PULSE
The Complete Series

Part Two

Chapter 1

There isn't a trap door in the floor of his apartment that's going to open up and drop me out of sight. I only have one choice. I have to turn around. I need to pretend that I don't know him even though last night I literally sat on his gorgeous face and had more orgasms than I can remember.

"Jess." Cassandra's tone is more insistent now. "Turn around."

I place the photograph of Nathan back onto the fireplace mantel before adjusting the collar of the chef's jacket that Cassandra gave me earlier. *"I want you to look professional for this, Jess. It's a very special occasion."* The words she spoke just a few hours ago ringing in my ears with more irony than she could have ever imagined. How is it even possible that the man I've been sleeping with is dating my boss? There are how many millions of people in Manhattan and I have to crawl into the bed of the one man I desperately should avoid? Idiot, Jessica. You are a grade A idiot.

I feel as though I'm moving in slow motion as I twist on my heel and spin around. I can't look at him. I'll just stare at her.

"Jess." She's motioning towards me with her hand. "Come over here."

My legs feel as though they're weighted with an extra ten pounds each as I drag my black flats across the hardwood floor.

"This is Jess." She wraps her arm around my shoulder pulling me into her body. "She's my chef."

"Jessica," Nathan says my name. The name he calls me when he's deep inside of me and I'm screaming out in pleasure. I wish I could pull my hands to my ears and block out his voice. I wish I could quit this job on the spot and tell Cassandra that her boyfriend spends every night at a club looking for someone to fuck.

"She likes to be called Jess." Her arm drops from me and she twirls around so she's facing him directly.

"Jessica," he ignores her correction." You're her chef?" The emphasis on the word *her* barrels through me like a freight train. Her, the woman he's dating. The woman he sees outside the hotel.

"Yes." Cassandra gives him a nod. "She's new. I wanted to tell you about her but..." her voice trails when the shrill sound of a phone ringing bites through the air. She fishes in her purse before pulling it out. "It's work. I need to take it."

"Go in the kitchen. It's private." He exhales in a rush.

"I'll be right back." She taps him lightly on the chest before she rushes down the hallway, chattering into the phone.

"Happy birthday," I drawl once I'm certain she's out of earshot. "You're how old now, thirty-one? That's how many in disgusting, cheating asshole years?"

"Stop it," he says huskily. "I'm not cheating on anyone."

"Your girlfriend would disagree with that." I shoot back. Does he seriously think I'm an idiot? Maybe he hasn't realized I have a brain since we haven't spent more than twenty minutes in total talking since we met.

"Cassie's not my girlfriend." His tone is clipped. "You don't know what you're talking about."

I squeeze my eyes shut at the mention of the endearment. *Cassie.* He calls her Cassie. Of course he does. She's his girlfriend. She's not one of the random women he fucks in his hotel suite. She's not like me.

"You're a fucking liar," I seethe through clenched teeth. "She's a good person and you're a cheating bastard."

"Shut up," he hisses at me. "Listen to me..."

"I should tell her." I turn on my heel, indignation racing through me. "I'm going to tell her what an asshole you really are."

"You're not going anywhere," he growls as he pulls on my elbow.

I spin back around, my hand slapping him so hard across the face that his head snaps to the left.

"What the fuck?" His hand darts to his cheek. "How the hell did you end up inside my apartment with her?"

"Fuck you." I bite back in a hushed tone. "Maybe it's because there's only six degrees of separation between your cock and every woman in Manhattan."

"What?"

I narrow my eyes at him. "There are more places to go to find a woman to fuck than just that club. You met her at that club, you met me there. You need to find a new place to pick up women." I feel sick to my stomach. I wish I hadn't stepped foot in that club.

"This is so fucked up," he says, his voice barely audible. "You've got it all wrong."

"Your girlfriend is my boss." I point out. "It's pretty simple."

"It's more complicated than that."

"I don't care what it is." I cross my arms over my chest. "All I care about is my job. I need to get out of this with my job." I have to. One lesson my past has taught me is that if you're the bearer of bad news, you always end up having to pay for it, in one way or another. If Cassandra finds out from me that Nathan is a cheating son-of-a-bitch, she'll hate me as much as she'll hate him.

"What about us?" He grabs me by my shoulders, shaking me slightly.

I shove back away from him so harshly I almost lose my footing. He's so much more imposing when I'm not wearing heels. He's almost an entire foot taller than me. "Us?" I sneer." There is no us. I don't care about you. I care about my job. I need this job." I desperately need the job. Cassandra pays me so well that I can cover my expenses and save for culinary school.

"That was a waste of time." Cassandra's voice calls as she rounds the corner from the kitchen. "Jess, bring that box in here, now."

I move to pick up the heavy cardboard box I placed on the floor just a few minutes ago when we arrived. I squat down and pull it into my shaking arms. I have to calm down. I have to get through the next few hours. After tonight, I never have to see him again.

"What's this?" Nathan reaches to take it from me, scooping it into his left arm.

"We're cooking you dinner." The delight in her voice is grating on me. She's so happy. Why shouldn't she be? She met him at the same club as I did and she's his girlfriend. She has a key to his apartment and knows his birthdate. She probably sleeps in his arms and hears stories about his day. She's oblivious to what he's doing at night. She has to be. There's no way she knows that he has a hotel suite that he uses just for sex.

"No. I don't want that," he says hoarsely. "You shouldn't have planned this."

"It's your birthday," she whines. "Your secretary said you'd be in court until six. It was supposed to be a surprise."

I feel his eyes bore into me but I don't shift my gaze from Cassandra's face. If I bolt right now and tell her I'm done, Rebecca will likely face the consequences of that too. My roommate needs her job as much as I need mine.

"Jessica." His voice is husky and strained. "I need a minute with Cassandra."

"For what?" She narrows her eyes at him. It's the same look she gives to Allie and Aaron when they're disobeying her.

"In the kitchen." He gestures over my head. "Now."

"No," she snaps. "Whatever you want to say, here is fine. Make it quick. Our guests are coming in a couple of hours and Jess needs to start cooking."

Shaking his head he starts down the hallway, the box still under his left arm. "You had no right coming here."

She pushes her hand into his chest stopping him in his tracks. "I have every right."

"We're on a break." There's a frustrated note in his tone. "We agreed to not see each other for a few weeks."

"It's your birthday, darling." The intimacy of her words jars me. I swallow hard to level my breathing.

"That doesn't make a difference," he says soberly. "We're not together right now."

"That's temporary." Her hands run up his chest. "Tonight is a new beginning for us."

I finally pull my eyes back to his face and he's staring directly at me. His right hand clenched into a fist by his side. "We should be having this discussion in private."

"What discussion?" She nuzzles her face into his neck. I know I should excuse myself and leave the room but I feel as though my feet are nailed to the floor. I can't move. I can only stand in stunned silence as I watch my boss fawn all over the man I've been fucking for the last few weeks.

"It's over." He pushes her away.

"What's over?" Her voice cracks before she clears her throat. "What are you talking about?"

"It's over," he repeats, his tone smooth and controlled. "Give me back my keys."

"You're just mad because I surprised you. We can talk about this," she's pleading.

"There's nothing to talk about." His gaze, clear and steady, is locked on my face. "I'm done."

"I'm not." Her mouth twitches. "You can't break up with me."

I pivot to face Cassandra. "I think I should go." The words come out of me with a shaky breath.

She turns her head to look at me. I wince at the sight of tears streaming down her face. "No," she whispers.

"I told you weeks ago I was done." He pushes past us both. "You didn't want to accept it then but it's over."

"Nathan. Don't do this," she says sniffling. "You can't."

"Stop prolonging the inevitable, Cassie." His tone is terse and decisive. "I met someone else."

"Are you fucking her?" The words tumble from her lips in a heated rush. I close my eyes pulling in all the strength I can find. I can't react. I can't let her know that it's me.

"Every chance I get," he says gruffly.

"You pig," she snaps. "I've been so torn up about us I haven't even gone on a date."

"Your loss," he quips in an even tone. "This is over. You need to leave now."

I stare at Cassandra as she walks past him, the only sound in the deafening silence the thud as she drops his apartment keys at his feet.

Chapter 2

"I have to go, Nathan." I yank on the handle of the door knowing full well that it won't budge since his back is pressed against it. "She's going to come back looking for me."

"Cassandra?" He throws his head back with a chuckle. "She's too self-centered to remember she even brought you here."

"You're wrong." I take a step back. "She's been good to me."

"You're a status symbol to her." He reaches out to stroke a finger along the collar of my jacket. "You're the cook she can use to impress her friends."

"They're your friends too," I bite back. I take a determined step backwards so I'm just out of his reach.

"No. I don't know her that well."

"You're her boyfriend." My gaze narrows. "She invited the friends you share to your birthday celebration."

"She invited her friends." His jaw tightens. "She wanted them here so she could show off my view." He gestures out the expansive windows.

"I want to go." I stare at the floor. I need to go. I need to process everything that's just happened.

"You're not leaving." He leans forward suddenly to run his hand down my cheek. "I can't believe you're in my apartment."

I feel an instant ache flow through me at the first hint of his touch. I can't still want him. He's Cassandra's boyfriend. I need my job. I don't need him. I have to keep telling myself that.

"I need to leave." My tone is insistent and firm but I know he can see through it.

"It's my birthday." His finger runs slowly over my jaw. "A kiss, Jessica. One kiss for my birthday."

"No." I pull back causing his hand to drop. "We're not doing that anymore."

"Why not?" His eyes open fully and bore into me. "Fucking you is all I want."

"You fucked her." I wince when I say the words. Oh god. He fucked her. He touched her the same way he did me. He licked her. He made her scream his name when she came with him inside of her.

"I screwed her twice months ago." He pulls forward so his breath courses against my ear. "I've never really fucked her."

"There's no difference." I take a heavy step back. I have to gain distance. I can't be close to him.

"I screwed her against the wall in her office one night and then again in the back of a limo when she dragged me to an event. Both times almost fully clothed. Both times just my dick inside of her. Briefly. I didn't even come the second time."

"Shut up." I cringe from the vulgarity of the words, from the confession. "Stop talking about her." I don't want to think about the two of them together. I can't imagine her feeling anything from his body.

He leans forward again, running the pad of his thumb across my lips. "I never fucked her mouth. I never wanted to be in her the way I want to be in you."

I recoil at the touch. I can't have this conversation with him. Cassandra has taken care of me. She's given me an opportunity when no one else would. "Don't say that."

"Don't say what." He surges forward grabbing my waist, pulling me into him. "That all I think about every minute of the day is fucking you? That I'm addicted to the taste of you? That I get hard instantly when I think about sliding my cock into your tight little body?"

"You dated her. You brought her here." I gesture to the room around us. This is the place he said he'd never bring a woman he fucked. "She had keys."

"I gave her those keys so she could sit and wait for the plumber on a Saturday when I was visiting my sister in Boston."

He has an answer for everything. It can't be that simple. Cassandra couldn't have misinterpreted their relationship that much, could she?

"I ended it weeks ago, Jessica." His hand slides across my hip. "I told her it was over, she wouldn't accept it. She wanted a temporary break instead. I gave her that to give her time to adjust."

"I can't face her." I pull my gaze down to my palm. "I can't believe I was sleeping with her boyfriend."

"Jessica." His finger brushes against my chin, tilting it up. "I didn't want her. I've never wanted her the way I want you."

"I have to go." I try and twist his body so I'm closer to the door but he's unrelenting in his stance.

"No." His lips glide over my forehead. "I'm not letting you go."

"I don't want this anymore," I say the words with purpose. I need them to sound genuine. "I can't see you again."

"You're a horrible liar." His hand slides up my hip to the front of the chef's jacket.

"I'm not lying." I swat his hand away. "I'm leaving."

He spins me around so effortlessly that I don't have time to react before my back is against the door. "Kiss me, Jessica. A kiss for my birthday."

I lean into the heavy wood of the door. I stare at his lips, watching his skillful tongue course over them, wetting them in anticipation.

"One kiss," I mutter before I feel his lips crash heavily into mine.

He groans into my mouth, his hands ripping the front of the chef's jacket open. His tongue slides next to mine, pulling it over his.

I try desperately to suppress a moan but my body betrays me. My hands jump to his hair, pulling the black locks between my fingers. I want this. I've wanted this since he walked through the door. He sensed it. He always knew.

His hand inches its way up the front of the white t-shirt I'm wearing. He growls as his finger slides over my now hard nipple encased in a lace bra. "Let me fuck you. God, I need to fuck you."

"Nathan," I whisper. "I can't."

"You want me." He pulls the front of my bra down, my left breast popping free. His fingers claim it, pulling and pinching it, the pleasure racing through my body.

"No," I whimper. I don't want to want him so much.

"No?" He pulls my bottom lip between his teeth. "You want me to fuck you. You're wet, aren't you?"

I pull the front of his shirt into my fists, pulling him into me. "Yes." I breathe into his mouth as a small whimper rises from deep within me.

"I'm going to lick you until you scream and then you're going to slide my cock between those perfect lips and swallow my load before I fuck you."

I moan at how raw the words are. I can't stop him. I just want to feel him in every part of me.

"In my bed now, Jessica." He picks me up, pulling my legs around his waist. "This is exactly what I want for my birthday."

"Jess." A heavy pounding on the door stops him dead in his tracks. I leap from his arms pulling the front of the chef's jacket around my disheveled body.

"Nathan, let me in." Cassandra beats the door harder. "Where's Jess?"

He pulls his hand across his brow, his entire body shaking as he sucks in a deep breath. "She left," he calls through the door. "She fucking left."

I'm shaking as I pull myself back together, adjusting my bra before buttoning up the jacket. I smooth my hair as I lift my gaze back to him. He's leaning against the door, his head resting in his palm.

"I've been waiting downstairs for her." She thumps her fist into the door again. "She never came down. Let me in."

I reach around him to yank the door open. He acquiesces without uttering a word.

"Jess." Mascara is running down her face. "What are you still doing here?"

"She was in the bathroom," he offers, his hand pressing against the bottom of my back.

"Let's go." She reaches for my hand and I grab it, squeezing it within my own. "I'm sorry you had to meet that asshole," she mutters as she pulls me towards the elevator.

Right now, in this moment, I'm sorry I met him too.

Chapter 3

"I need to cut back your hours, Jess." Cassandra ties a patterned scarf around her neck. "I just can't afford this anymore."

I take a deep breath. I've been waiting for the other shoe to drop. It's been four days since I followed her out of Nathan's apartment and now she's finally going to confront me. She must know that I'm the woman he was talking about. Wait. Am I the woman he was talking about? Maybe there was another woman he was fucking. He has a suite just for random sex. I can't shoulder all the blame for their broken relationship.

"Okay," I offer. What am I supposed to say when she's essentially telling me that my dream job is no more? Add to that the fact that I've been fucking her estranged boyfriend and my life can't get much worse.

"I'm humiliated." She turns to face me. "I can't believe I have to say this."

My stomach twists into a knot. She looks so worn-out. I heard her crying this morning when I got to her apartment. She misses him. I can't blame her. I miss him too.

"Just say it," I blurt out. I just want it over with.

"Nathan was helping me," she begins before taking a long pause. "Financially."

I look into her green eyes and I see a cast of worry over them. "I didn't know," I mutter. I couldn't have known. He didn't tell me that part.

"I was struggling when we met and he offered. No questions. I wanted it to be a loan, but he refused. He just gave it."

I can't respond. What am I supposed to say to that?

"He helped me for a few months before I asked him out. We went on a few dates." She inhales sharply. "The sex wasn't spectacular, but you can't have everything right?"

I feel a blush course over my face. The sex is spectacular. It's beyond that.

"I can't keep taking money from him after the other night."

"Yes," I mutter. Of course she can't. He dumped her royally on her ass right in front of me. How can she keep taking anything from him after that?

"I can give you two days a week." She shifts in obvious embarrassment. "If you find something better, I'll send you on your way with a great reference."

I nod. Two days a week? It's better than nothing.

***

"Is Mr. Moore in?" I quiz the gorgeous brunette sitting behind an almost bare industrial looking desk.

"Who are you?" She pushes the question at me without even the slightest hint of pleasantness.

"A friend."

"No." She taps a few buttons on a phone on her desk. "Your name? What's your name?"

"It's…" I begin before she turns her attention to the call.

"There's a girl here." Her deliberate use of the word *girl* isn't lost on me. "Name?"

"Jessica Roth."

"Jessica Ross," she snarls into the phone. Maybe she just has a lisp.

"Jessica." Nathan appears in the doorway of one of the many offices lining the area behind me. "What a surprise."

I walk towards him, my heart racing. Showing up unannounced at his office was bad enough. Trying to walk on this plush carpet in stilettos was making me feel not only unbalanced but awkward too.

"I just wanted to talk," I say wearily. It has taken all the courage I have to search for his office address, to get in a cab and to ride the elevator up, all without knowing how he'd react.

"Inside." He motions to the doorway of a large office with a glorious view of the city.

"I…" my voice trails as he slams the door shut behind me and pulls me into a tight embrace.

"I didn't think you'd ever answer any of my calls or texts," he interrupts, his eyes scanning my light yellow dress. "You're a vision."

"I came to talk about something." I look over his shoulder. It's a tactic I learned years ago when I didn't want to make eye contact with Josh.

"I've missed you." He pushes my hair back from my shoulder.

"No, please don't." I pull on my hair to move it back into place. "I can't see you anymore."

"Jessica." There's a slight pause. "I'm sorry about the Cassandra bullshit. I didn't want you dragged into that."

"Bullshit?" I push back from his arms. "It's not bullshit, Nathan. It's my life and it's her life."

"You've worked for her for what, two weeks now?" He turns back towards his desk. "Quit the job and move on if it's that bad."

"I'd rather quit you and move on," I state boldly.

"Quit me?" He doesn't turn back to face me. "What's that supposed to mean?"

"I'm not fucking you again," I say each word slowly, making sure it's loud enough that he can't question my intention. "I came here to tell you to stop calling and texting me. Leave me alone."

He shuffles through several papers on his desk before he finally turns back towards me. "It doesn't work that way."

"What?"

"You can't just decide that we're done." The cocked brow that accompanies the statement is clearly meant to intimidate me. It's working.

"This is so ridiculous." I pull a weak laugh through my lips. "You're already fucking other women. I'll be a distant memory by next week."

He charges towards me and heaves me against the wall with his hands. "You don't know what you're talking about."

"I know what you told me." My voice is trembling. I can hear it. He has to hear it too. "You said you were fickle and you liked different women. Don't pretend you haven't been fucking other women the entire time you and I have been sleeping together."

"That first night." His hand drops to my thigh. "When I finally got you into my bed," he whispers across my lips. "Do you remember that?"

I nod passively. I know I should push him away. I know I should tell him to fuck off. I can't.

"I licked you until you came all over my face." His tongue traces a pointed line across my jaw. "I've craved that taste since then."

My pulse quickens at the mention of his lips on my body. I can't think about that now. I came here with one purpose. I need to end this before any more damage is done.

"Then you came back and sucked me off." His hand inches higher towards my panties. "I can't stop thinking about you naked, on your knees, my cock in your mouth and you moaning because you couldn't get enough of it."

My body reacts and I have to take a heavy breath to stifle a moan. "That was then," I offer helplessly.

"This is now." His finger glides across the edge of my panties. "You're so hot and wet right now."

"No," I impulsively try and disagree. I don't want him to know what I'm feeling.

"Jesus, you're already ready. You want me to fuck you right now, don't you?"

"I….no…it's…" I groan as his finger slips under the fabric of my panties and across my slick cleft.

He's on his knees before I can react, my panties pushed to the side. "I've wanted this for days."

I bite my lip to hold back a deep, guttural moan as he claims my wetness. His tongue circles my clit before he pushes a finger along my folds. "You came here for this."

I push my head back into the wall, closing my eyes tightly. I didn't, did I? Does it matter that I bring myself to orgasm every morning when I wake up and think about him fucking him? Does it count that I can't stop thinking about how good it felt when he came down my throat?

"Nathan," I cry out as I near the edge already. I need to tell him to stop. I can't keep doing this with him. It's wrong. He's wrong for me.

"You're so good. You taste so good." He pushes his head hungrily between my thighs as he laps up my wetness, purring into my folds. "Come, Jessica. Come now so I can fuck you."

The promise of his beautiful, full cock inside of me pushes me into the middle of an intense orgasm. I almost cry out in pleasure but he's on his feet now, his damp lips pushing into mine, pulling my moans into his body.

I hold onto his lapel as I feel him lift me gently and push me back onto the corner of his desk. My body is so wanting. I feel so reckless. I can't control this need.

"I'm so hard." He pulls a condom from his desk drawer. "I'm going to come before I'm even inside your sweet little body."

I drop to my knees before he has time to respond. I whip my tongue over the head of his cock and I'm gifted with a single drop of pre-cum. I roll it over my tongue before I pull him into my mouth.

"Fuck. Jessica. Jesus," he hisses through his teeth. "It's too good."

I bob my head slowly up and down, pulling the length of him into me. It's so much. I want it. I want to taste it all.

He moves his hips in rhythm with my sucking, his hands lost in my hair, pulling at the roots as he races to the edge. "I want it to last. I can't. It's too fucking good."

I brace myself when I feel his balls constrict under my touch. I moan deeply as he pumps himself into me, emptying every last drop.

Chapter 4

"We can't do that again." I adjust the neckline of my dress before I pull one of my heels back on. "I came here to end things."

"We're going to do that again." He kneels to help me put on my other shoe. "You're not ending anything."

"Cassandra cut my hours." I don't see any reason to keep avoiding the subject I came to his office to talk about. "She told me about the money."

He stops and looks up at me and I see something flash over his face that I haven't before. It's softness, kindness, just something that's too fleeting to place. "She was short for a few weeks, so I helped her out."

"There's more to it than that." I step back and slide my hands over the skirt of my dress. "She was depending on you."

"I'll keep helping her if it helps you." The words are genuine. I know that he means them. I know he'd help me too if I asked him. I can't. I came to Manhattan to make it on my own and that's what I'm going to do.

"I've got an interview lined up already." I do. I finally texted Drew back, the man I was talking to at the club before Nathan pulled me away from him. He's a chef at one of the best restaurants in the city and he managed to land me a meeting with someone there for a sous chef's position.

"Where?"

"Just a place." I don't see any reason to go into details about my life. This one night stand had gotten so far out of hand that I couldn't see any way to reel it back in other than walking away. I was getting too emotionally invested in him.

"Jessica. Where?" He pushes my hair away from my shoulders so he can adjust the straps of my dress.

"Axel NY," I say meekly.

"That creep from the club works there, doesn't he?" His eyes scan my face. "You're not working there."

"Excuse me?" I feel instantly assaulted by his words. "He's not a creep and yes, he works there."

"Have you seen him?" he growls. "Have you seen him since that night at the club?"

I still. I stare intently at his face. Is he fucking kidding me? Is he acting territorial over a random guy I saw once at a club who is now helping me find a job? "You're insane."

"I'm what?" He grabs my arms.

"You can't tell me what to do." I pull free of his grasp. "We have sex. Correction, we used to have sex."

"We're more than that." The way he tosses the words so easily at me, irks me.

"Are we?" I push back. "Do you still have your fuck pad?"

"My what?" he chuckles as he asks the question.

"Do you still have that suite at the hotel that you take women to when you're going to fuck them?" I tilt my head to the left waiting for an answer that I already know.

"That's irrelevant." He reaches to straighten his tie, the entire time his eyes are locked on me.

"This is irrelevant." I slide my hand in the air between us. "We've gone over this too many times already. You don't own me. You don't control me. You fucked me. Just like you fuck countless other women every month."

"Jessica." My name breezes across his lips just as I walk through his office door.

Chapter 5

"What's going on with you and Fingers?" Rebecca stops at the corner to wait for a passing taxi before she steps onto the uneven pavement.

"Nothing," I call over the blare of a car horn. Midday traffic in Manhattan wasn't the perfect backdrop for any conversation, especially not one about the mutual lover I shared with Rebecca's boss.

"You're not sleeping with him anymore?" She tosses me an evil grin and I can't help but giggle.

"That ship has sailed." I mean the words. It's been more than a week since I walked out of Nathan's office. "I deleted his number from my phone and I haven't looked back." I have looked back. I conveniently left out the part about putting him back into my contact list. I know his number by heart. I can't get it out of my mind.

"Are you fucking Drew?"

I stop mid-step and I'm almost bowled over by a group of tourists heading up Broadway. "What?"

"The guy that got you the interview at the restaurant." She pushes her hand towards me as if the motion will spur me on. "Are you sleeping with him?"

"I didn't realize you knew his name."

"He's hot." She stops to adjust the strap on her shoe. "I never forget a hot guy's name."

"I'm done with men." I push against her trying to help her balance. "I think you need a new strap on that."

"New shoes would be better." She winks. "So are you?"

"Am I what?" I can't follow the conversation. I'm still stuck back where she told me she knew Drew's name.

"Fucking the chef?" She enunciates every syllable, her voice a pitch louder than everyone else on the street.

I pull my hand to my mouth to stifle a loud laugh. "Scream it for the entire city to hear," I tease. "I'm not sleeping with anyone. I'm done with men."

"Famous last words." She scoops her arm through mine as she pulls me across Amsterdam Ave in search of a bistro for lunch.

***

"I don't even know how I got the job with zero training." I tap on Drew's chest. The two martinis I've had since we arrived at the restaurant are definitely going to my head.

"Hunter loved you." He finishes his glass of beer.

The fact that I got to meet, Hunter Reynolds, the owner of Axel NY didn't hurt my chances at all. When I mentioned that I had met Ivy, Nathan's friend, his face lit right up. Apparently she was dating his best friend. Sometimes, even the smallest connection can make a world of difference in a city like New York.

"I can't believe they offer tuition for culinary school." I almost bounce off the bar stool into Drew's lap.

He nods as he motions to the bartender to bring another round. "That's how I got my training. I worked at another restaurant Hunter's family owns and they paid for everything."

"I'm so excited." I empty the martini sitting in front of me in one small sip.

"It's going to be so fun working together." He laughs as he pulls some bills from his wallet to hand to the bartender. "I think after this round I need to get you home."

"The night is still young." This is the first time in weeks that I've felt happy. I'd start my new job at the restaurant next month which meant I could quit working for Cassandra right away. I'd finally stop feeling awash with guilt every day I went to her apartment.

"Are you seeing anyone?" The question feels misplaced. This wasn't supposed to be a date. We agreed on the phone that Drew would take me to my interview and then we'd go for a drink afterwards if I got the job. I wasn't interested in anyone after the never ending one night stand fiasco with Nathan.

"No. Why?" I wince after I ask. Why did I just ask him that?

"Do you want to go out sometime?" He stares straight ahead as he asks the question.

"Are you asking me on a date?" The martini has apparently

removed any filter I had. There's nothing like cutting to the chase, Jess.

"I'd like that." He traces a path across my arm with his finger. "You're a lot of fun."

I smile at the compliment. It's so simple and sweet. Just like him. "So are you."

"Let's get you home."

Chapter 6

"Whoever you are, I'm going to kill you for forgetting your key." I swing open the door of the apartment. The incessant knocking started just as I was getting into bed.

"Jessica." Nathan's hand is resting against the door frame, his dark hair falling casually onto his forehead. The jeans and sweater he's wearing don't match the seriousness of his expression. "How do you know where I live?" I start to push the door shut without thinking. I don't want him here. It's taken every ounce of strength I have not to think about him constantly.

"Is he here?" He pushes past me into the dimly lit room. "Where is he?"

"Bryce?" I stare at him as he shuffles through the apartment, moving quickly from room-to-room. "Why do you want to talk to my roommate?"

"Not him." His gaze pierces through me. "That guy, Drew. Is he here?"

I pull on the sash of my robe to tighten it. "What?" Why is he asking me about Drew?

"He brought you here, didn't he? Where the fuck is he?"

"How do you know that?" I spit out. Drew dropped me off ten minutes ago.

"Did he leave, Jessica?" he says the words slowly as if I'm unable to comprehend them at a normal pace. "Is he coming back?"

I study his face. His eyes are dark and focused and his hair a mess. "Why are you here?" I demand. "What are you doing here?"

"Where's Drew?" He pulls on my arm so hard I wince.

"That's not your business." I'm so confused. I don't understand why he's here. Why is he asking about Drew?

"Like hell it's not. You were all over him at the bar."

His words barrel into me. *At the bar.* He saw me with Drew at the bar? "You were spying on me." My voice cracks with the realization.

"I was walking past and saw you through the window." His face flushes.

"No." I take a heavy step back wanting to distance myself. "You followed me."

"Don't flatter yourself." He pulls his hand through his hair, pushing it off his forehead. "I saw you through the window. You were unsteady on your feet so I wanted to make sure you got home safely."

"You watched me with him." I breathe sharply, suddenly feeling faint knowing that he saw me and Drew come into the building together. "You followed me here."

"Where is he?" He pushes again. "He didn't leave through the front door."

"He…he…" I stammer. "He went out the back exit. It's closer to the subway." I point meekly in the direction of the street.

"He's not coming back?" I can hear the relief skirting the edges of the words.

I shake my head.

"Promise me you're not going to sleep with him." His face is emotionless. "Tell me he's never going to have this mouth." His thumb traces a path across my bottom lip. "It's going to kill me if he does."

"You have to stop." I push his hand away. "You can't tell me what to do when you're sleeping with other women. It's not fair. You can't."

"Don't fuck him." His tone is pleading. He pulls me into his chest. "Promise me you won't and I'll give up everyone else."

***

"How many men have fucked this sweet body?" He pulls on my hair from behind, pushing his cock deeper into me. I push my head into the pillows on my bed wanting to skirt the question. I can't talk about other men when I'm so close to the edge of an orgasm.

"This feels so good," I exhale. "So good."

"Tell me, Jessica." He reaches his other hand around so it's resting on my mound. I whimper knowing that he's going to circle my clit with his finger. He's going to push me even closer to the edge. "How many men have been inside of you?"

"I can't." I moan deeply as his fingers glide effortlessly through my wet folds.

"You can't remember?" He pushes his cock deeper into me, filling me fully. "You can't remember how many men have slid into you? Have taken you?"

"Don't." I push back onto him, wanting him to fuck me harder. He's torturing me and he knows it. He's withholding until I answer his question.

"Don't what?" He almost pulls himself entirely out of me. "Don't stop fucking you?"

"No," I cry out as he pulls back harshly, his cock falling from my body. "Nathan, please, just fuck me."

"Tell me." He pulls so hard on my hair that I whimper. "Tell me how many men you've let fuck you."

"No." I won't. I can't let him have this much control. I don't want him to know.

I feel the bed shift behind me and I tremble with a veiled sob. He's going to stop just because I won't tell him how many lovers I've had?

I almost scream when I feel his tongue race over my folds. "You want to come so badly." His voice is loud and commanding. "You're so close. Look how swollen and ripe you are. "

"Yes." I push back on my knees, trying to find his tongue. I need to find it. I need him to suck on my clit until I come.

"Tell me how many men you've let inside this perfect little body." His tongue traces a slow and almost painful path over my clit. It's so light I can barely feel it, but my entire body trembles.

"Lick it, Nathan," I coax. "Just lick it."

"Like this." He laps greedily at my folds before pulling my clit into his mouth. He sucks his cheeks in. The intensity is overwhelming. I feel a rush begin deep within me.

"Like that." I groan.

"Tell me." He pulls back again and my body's left helpless. I'm on fire, aching and so close to coming.

"Three," I whisper. "Three."

"Three," he repeats back as he glides himself fully into me with one swift movement. "Not one of them has fucked you the way I do, have they?"

"God, no," I scream as I grip the pillows tightly in my hand as he pounds his cock into me.

"Tell me how good it feels." His voice is a deep growl. "Tell me how much you like being fucked by me."

I almost come from the words. "So much."

"Jessica." He leans over me, his lips trailing a path down my neck.

"So good," I cry out as I feel my body tense with pleasure.

"So fucking good." He pumps himself harder into me before he screams my name.

Chapter 7

"Just so we're clear, Jessica." He pulls the sweater over his head. "You're not going to hang out at bars with random men anymore."

"Just so we're clear, Nathan." I mimic back, tucking the blanket from my bed around me. "You're the one who hangs out at bars picking up random women."

"Touché." He dips his chin in my direction. "I'm willing to give that up for you."

"You'll forgive me if I doubt that's real." I pull a thin smile across my face.

"You can ask me if you want." He buttons his jeans before he pushes his feet back into the leather loafers.

"Ask you what?"

"How many lovers I've had." He sits on the edge of the bed.

"I don't think my brain can process a number that high," I tease, even though the thought pulls my stomach into a tumbleweed of knots. It has to be in the hundreds. Maybe it's even in the thousands.

"One." He leans forward to brush his lips against mine. "One."

I furrow my brow at the response. "One?"

"I've fucked a lot of women." He closes his eyes briefly as if he's trying to hide behind the reality of that statement. "Having a lover is different. It's more about what's in here." He pulls my hand to his chest.

"Don't say things you don't mean."

"I never do." He nuzzles his face into my hair. "You smell so good right after I've fucked you."

"So you were serious then?" I pull back. I want confirmation that what he said right before he carried me to my bed is real.

"Serious about not sleeping with anyone else?" He pushes a stray hair from my forehead. "Dead serious, Jessica."

"You're going to give up the hotel room?" I push the issue. If he doesn't, I'm not going to agree to anything. I don't see him as a one woman type of man.

"I gave it up after I saw you in my apartment." A vein in his neck pulses. "Seeing you there, that changed everything."

"It blew up your relationship with Cassandra." I pull my legs closer to my chest.

"No." He glances down at the sheet. "You belonged there. You looked so perfect standing there by the mantel when I walked in. I couldn't stop staring at you."

"You seriously think you can settle for one woman?" I raise a brow. I want this so much. I want him. I just don't want to toss all my hopes into a basket that he's holding only to find out he's lying to me.

"I can't stand the thought of you with anyone else." He pulls my hand into his lap. "When Drew walked through the front door of this building holding your hand, I almost lost it. In my mind you were on your knees with his cock in your mouth. When he didn't come back down I thought he was buried inside of you listening to you come."

"So you want us to be exclusive so I don't fuck anyone else?" I ask the question slowly. "That's all this is about?"

"I'm not all roses and romance, Jessica." He stands and pulls on the hem of his sweater to straighten it. "Don't expect that from me."

"I'm not." I feel slightly embarrassed that I assumed that was part of it.

"I want this all to myself." He runs his hand over my leg before he brushes his lips across my forehead. "If that means I have to make sacrifices, I'll do whatever it takes."

Chapter 8

"So you two are going steady?" Rebecca takes a perfume sample card from a young woman in the aisle of Macy's.

"I think my vagina and his dick are going steady." I shrug. "I can't say anything about the rest of our bodies."

Her head rolls back in laughter. "He's a sex fiend, isn't it? It sounds like all you two do is fuck and I mean by sounds, I heard the screams coming out of your room last night."

"He's amazing in bed." I feel my face flush. "I'm addicted to that. I really am."

"I would be too." She stops to admire a row of handbags. "I just don't know how a man like that gives up all his other women."

I close my eyes to shake off the image of Nathan at the club. He promised me he gave up the room. I need to believe him if this is going to work.

"I'm sorry, Jess." She brushes her hand across my arm. "I didn't mean it like that."

"No." I turn away from her. Of course she meant it like that. She knows how I met him. She knows that he kept a room above the club just for fucking different women.

""I just meant that a man like that gets bored easily regardless of how hot the woman he's sleeping with is." Her words are meant to console me, but they only thrust me into more sordid thoughts of Nathan and his insatiable libido.

"I have to find a way to trust him," I say it as if it's an easy endeavor. I've already doubted him since he's taken most of the day to return a text I sent him this morning.

"I wouldn't worry about it." She picks up a bracelet and holds it up to the fluorescent lights in the store. "Enjoy the sex while you can and then when it's over you won't be too invested."

"I wish it was that easy," I mutter under my breath as I glance at a showcase filled with earrings.

***

"Push back." His hand pushes lightly on my mound as I stretch back in the bathtub, pulling his cock deeper within me.

"Like this?" I grab hold of the sides of the tub, arching my back away from him.

"I love when I'm that deep." He rests his head on the back of the tub, his other hand lazily running a circle over my throbbing nipple.

"Do you like me?" My throat tightens as I ask the question.

His eyes dart open. "Do I like you?"

"Yes." I push back again, pulling his cock even deeper within my body. "Do you like me?"

"I love your body." He jerks my hips down into his lap, causing his cock to plunge to its depth inside of me.

I let a slow, low moan escape through my lips.

"I've never fucked anyone so perfectly made for me." He moves to grab my breast, cupping it in his hand. "Everything about you is what I crave."

I push down setting a rhythm between us. "You like my body."

"No," he interrupts, his finger rising to my lips. "I love your body."

"Do you like me?" I ask again, my eyes boring into him under heavy lashes. The heat in his bathroom and the two hours we spent in bed before the bath has pulled every ounce of energy from me.

"Jessica." He stops and pulls his cock from me. "Jessica," he whispers into my mouth as his lips float over mine.

"Tell me you like me." I breathe into his kiss.

"I'm crazy about you." He leans back, cupping my cheeks in his hands. "You're remarkable."

"In bed?"

"No." He runs the pad of his thumb under my eye. "In bed you're fucking spectacular."

I pull a small grin across my moist lips. Of course he'd say that. He loves what we do in bed.

"Out of bed, you don't know me," I say it. It's been skirting across my thoughts for weeks, dancing at the tip of my tongue.

"I want to know you." He kisses the tip of my nose. "I'm going to know you."

I lean forward and rest my head against his chest. I hope that's true. I want him to know me, everything about me.

Chapter 9

"I didn't think you'd be able to pull yourself out of bed." He looks up from the desk in his guest room. "Do you want me to call down so the doorman gets a cab for you?"

No. I don't want that. I want him to tell him that I can stay the night. I want him to at least acknowledge that I'm leaving with more than a quick call to someone else to arrange my transportation home.

"I can hail a cab myself." I sling my purse over my shoulder. "Thank you for today."

"Thank you for today?" He playfully throws the words back at me.

"Yes." I stand in front of him, absentmindedly playing with the hem of my skirt. I regret being so vulnerable in the bathtub. Rebecca was right. I can't get too invested in him. He's not a man you can trust your heart with.

"Thank you for fucking you?" He's on his feet now, strolling towards me. "Thank you for making you come so many times?"

"Sure," I toss back. "Although, I do know how to come myself."

"Next time you're going to show me that." He brushes his lips across my forehead. "Get home safe, Jessica."

I feel my body heave a heavy sigh as I watch him walk back to his desk and take a seat. His eyes instantly focus on his laptop as he places a call on his cell.

I turn and walk out of the room in silence, wishing I could redo the entire day from beginning to end.

***

"I can't believe today is your last day." Cassandra pulls me into a warm embrace.

"Me either." I mean the words on the surface. Truth be told, I'm breathing a heavy sigh of relief that I don't have to face her every day. Even though she's never realized that I was the woman

Nathan was talking about, I haven't felt settled working for her since then.

"You're going to go work at Axel NY?" She claps her hands together in delight. "Do you think you can get me a table?"

"I have absolutely no pull over there." I smile. "I doubt at this point that I can get a table."

"I think I'll see you there sometime." She pinches my side. "I'm dating someone new."

The instant the words leave her lips I feel as though a boulder has been lifted from my shoulders. "You have? Really?" I know I sound excited. Maybe too excited but I don't care. I want her to be happy. I want her to find a man who can fill the void she's long felt in her life.

"A guy from work." Her face brightens. "It's really new and early but he's crazy about me."

I feel a stab of longing when I hear those words. He's crazy about her. He's probably wild about more than just her body.

"I hope it works out," I offer. I genuinely mean it. I want her to get a guy who will treat her with the respect she deserves. "Maybe he has a friend he can introduce me to."

"Things aren't going good with the random?" She reaches to touch my wrist. I smile at the subtle sign of affection.

"It's going okay. Better, I guess." I'm honestly not sure how to answer her question. "I just have this nagging feeling."

"What feeling, Jess. Spit it out." She reaches to push a piece hair back behind my ear. "What are you feeling?"

"I feel as though he's only in it for the sex." I shrug my shoulders. "He asked for my number but that's it. He never asks about my life unless it relates to the possibility of another man getting in my pants."

"So he's jealous but disinterested?" She cocks her head to the side.

"Exactly."

"Maybe he just likes the sex so much that he wants to keep you to himself but he's not interested in a real relationship."

"I think you just defined him to a tee." I reach to give her a quick hug. "Keep in touch."

"Come by and visit the kids whenever you want and Jess, watch out for your heart."

Chapter 10

"This is so much fun." Rebecca literally screams over the hum of the crowd, the drink in her hand very close to spilling all over the front of her white dress. "We haven't partied this hard in years."

Correction. She hasn't partied this hard in years. I'm drinking a virgin margarita and feeling absolutely no buzz at all. I have an early prep shift at the restaurant and I can't be cloudy for that. I want to make the best impression I can. Going with her to this new club opening is simply a favor. As soon as she finds someone to latch onto, I'm going to catch a cab to go home.

"We should dance." She pulls on my hand forcing me to leave my drink on the bar as I join her on the crowded floor.

"This is fun." I call over to her as the pulse of the music races through me. I close my eyes, losing myself to the rhythm. I don't want to care about anything right now. I don't want to think about the fact that I called Nathan twice today and got absolutely no response. Tonight isn't about him. It's about me having fun.

I feel a hand on my side and my eyes pop open. A tall, blonde man is dancing next to me. I know I should push him away but it's just dancing. I'm not doing anything wrong. I'm having fun.

"What's your name?" he asks over the music.

"Jess," I almost scream back.

"Pretty." He smiles before he snakes against mine. I don't pull back. I'm coasting to the sounds, the smells, the feeling of the club. This is a place where I don't have to answer to anyone. I can be who I want to be and just enjoy knowing that other men want me.

I close my eyes again, not caring that his hands are now both on my waist. I can feel his pelvis gyrating against me. He's aroused. He's so wanting. If I met him the first night I trolled the other club, he would have been the man I fucked. It would have been one night. Simple. Over and done with.

The tempo changes and he moves closer. He shifts his hand from my waist to my hip. I push against him as he breathes even heavier on my neck.

Suddenly there's another set of hands on me. These are more aggressive, pulling me harder. I push against it, but I can't stop the grip. The hands pull me away from the blonde man and deeper into the crowd.

I feel a rush of hot breath on my neck and a hand pressing hard on my stomach. I push myself into the man behind me. I'd know his scent and touch anywhere. He must have listened to the voicemails I left him telling him where I would be. "When other men touch you, you think about me," he whispers. "Your body can't deny it."

"Your body wants me more, Nathan." I push back against him, feeling the strain in his pants. "You want to fuck me right here. Right in this middle of this dance floor."

"I'd fuck you anywhere." He turns me around quickly, pushing his full lips into mine. "I don't watch you for one night and you're in a club, dry humping a stranger."

"You should keep better tabs on me." I run my hand down his pants, outlining his rigid cock beneath the material.

"Tell your friend you're leaving right now."

Chapter 11

"Goddamn it." He exhales sharply as I pull my teeth across the tip of his cock. "You're so greedy tonight."

I nod before taking the head into my mouth again, pulling my tongue over the sensitive tip while my hands glide down the thick root. "Your cock is beautiful."

"It's the only cock you want." He tugs lightly on my hair, causing me to moan in protest. "Take it all the way in, Jessica. Suck me off until I shoot it all down your throat."

I adjust myself so I can run a hand between my legs. I need to come too. He teased me with his fingers in the taxi on the short trip from the club to his apartment, but he didn't get me off. I'm so close. I want it so much.

"Harder, baby. Suck it harder." He pushes himself farther down my throat and I feel him swell. I want to please him but I'm so close.

I suck slowly as I finger my own clit. I feel his body tense as I look up. His eyes are glued to my naked body and my hand skillfully working towards my own release.

"Holy fuck," he moans loudly. "Jesus."

He grabs hold of my head with both hands and starts fucking my mouth slowly, his cock gliding effortlessly between my lips. I trace my tongue around it, while I circle my center. I've never felt so much all at once. I'm so close.

"Christ. You're so hot." He pumps harder. "Touch yourself."

I only can nod in response as I eagerly push myself closer to the edge.

"Fuck." He strokes his cock as I suck just on the tip. "This is too good."

I feel the edge of the orgasm race through me and I reach to pull more of him into my mouth as I moan around his core.

"Ah, Jessica," he screams through clenched teeth as he plunges his cock into my mouth, his hot desire rushing over my tongue and down my throat.

***

"I should take you to the club more often." He pulls me into the crux of his arm. I settle my head next to his chest.

"You didn't." I laugh. "I went. You followed me there."

"I didn't follow you anywhere." He grazes his lips over my cheek. "You shouldn't go to places like that without me."

"You should answer your phone when I call." I trace a path across his chest, my fingers playfully running through the hair.

"I was in court." It's the same response every time I ask him a question about his day.

"Was it interesting?" I push for more. I want to know more. I want to know everything there is to know about his life.

"No." He doesn't offer anything beyond that.

It's time for a new approach. "Do you like being a lawyer?" Maybe if I get him to talk about something he actually takes pride in, he'll want to share more.

"It's alright." Mission failed. He doesn't say anything more on that subject.

"Do you have plans for the weekend?" I'm not giving up. I'm not leaving here without at least some new tidbit of information about him tonight.

"I'm going to Boston to visit my sister and her family."

"Does she have kids?" I'm finally making headway.

"We should get you home." He kisses the top of my head before he pulls away. "It's getting late."

Chapter 12

"Let's say you were having great sex with a guy…"

"I wouldn't be sitting here talking to you." Rebecca twirls a forkful of spaghetti in the center of her plate before she pulls it into her mouth. "This is so good, Jess."

I smile at the compliment. I'll never get tired of people telling me they like my cooking, even if one of those people is my best friend.

"Let's say after you finish your spaghetti, you were having ridiculously good sex with a guy and that's all he ever wanted to do."

"Where's the question?" She pulls more food into her mouth through a twisted smile.

"What would you do?" It's awkward. I'm not presenting it correctly but I just want her opinion.

"I'd thank my lucky stars and I'd take vitamins, lots of them."

I snicker and drop my fork onto my plate. "No. I'm not explaining this right."

"Fingers is just not that into you, is he? I mean other than the places he can stick his big dick?" She waves her fork in the air.

"Why does that bother me so much?" I cringe when the question leaves my lips. "Why do I give a fuck if all he wants to do is fuck?"

"Here's what I think." She gulps down a hearty swallow of red wine before she pulls a paper napkin across her lips. "It's like he wants you to see him exclusively but you don't get to have all the dating and fun bits that usually come with that. All you get is the crazy hot sex."

"When you put it that way." I shrug my shoulders before I continue, "I guess it's not that bad."

"Jess. You feel used, don't you?" She winces at her own words.

"I think so." My mouth purses. "I guess I do."

"Tell him." She stands to clear both our plates from the small dining table. "Or go back to just being random fuck buddies until you do find someone who sees you as more than that."

***

"Jess?" A vaguely familiar voice bolts out of the darkness as I leave the restaurant after my Saturday night shift. I'm exhausted and seeing anyone I know right now is not something I want. What I do want is a nice hot shower, some popcorn and a good movie I can get lost in. I've texted Nathan twice today to see how his train ride to Boston was and I've got nothing back in return.

"Jess?" The voice is louder now and I feel a pit in my stomach when I realize who it belongs to. It can't be. He can't be here.

"Josh?" I turn slowly. He's right behind me. The man I spent three years of my life loving is standing on a crowded New York City sidewalk staring right at me.

"It's you." He rushes to me and envelopes me in a hug. I melt into his arms. This is what home feels like. This is what it's like to be wanted.

"What are you doing here?" I sob into his shoulder. I'm so overcome with emotion. I can't think straight. All the pain that swallowed me up before and during our break up is now a distant tug at my heart. I can't pull it back to the surface. All I can feel is relief at the familiar feeling of his strong arms around me.

"Things between us ended so badly, Jess." He runs his hand up and down my back. It's the same comforting gesture he always did when I had a bad day or when life got to be too much.

"I'm sorry for that." I pull back from his embrace and gaze up into his face. It's the same face I left just a few weeks ago. The same deep brown eyes and dirty blonde hair. His open grin sends a course of regret through me. He was so upset the day I left. His entire face pulled into a painful grimace as I told him it was over and I was moving away.

"You had every right to leave." His eyes stare at my chef's jacket. "Jess. You're a chef." He picks me up and twirls me around on the crowded Manhattan sidewalk.

"No." I sigh when he places me back down. "I'm a sous chef in training which just means I cut potatoes and peel vegetables all day but it's a start."

"Can we go somewhere to talk?" His expression seeps of expectation. I can't disappoint him. I need him right now just as much as he needs me.

"Come home with me." I reach into my purse to send Rebecca a quick text warning her that I'm bringing Josh by. I search the new messages and still nothing from Nathan. "I'll cook you something."

"I've missed you, Jess." He wraps his arm around my shoulder.

"I've missed you too."

Chapter 13

"That was great, chef." He pushes himself away from the small dining table and pulls himself to his feet. He's so tall. Somehow he seems taller than I remember.

"Come, sit with me." I pull him by his hand to the small couch in the corner of the living room. Rebecca must have ditched when she read my text about Josh coming over. The last time he was here visiting, we were still together and they didn't see eye-to-eye. Josh's idea of an ideal life for me was being a paramedic's wife with a few kids by the time I was thirty.

"I can't believe you live in this great apartment." He soaks in the wide space. "You live here with Rebecca?"

"We have another roommate," I offer, even though my interactions with Bryce are typically limited to a passing glance in the hallway or a quick hello over a morning cup of coffee. "Bryce is his name."

"Is he your boyfriend?" The question is swollen with indignation. Josh's hair trigger was one of the reasons we were constantly in conflict. I had to temper almost everything I told him when we were living together.

"No. He has a girlfriend back home." I don't want to argue with him. I just want to enjoy a small reminder of what I left behind.

"Do you have a boyfriend?" He must have read something between the lines in my reaction to his question about Bryce. Nathan isn't my boyfriend. Boyfriends encompass more than a few sex fuelled hours a couple of times a week.

"I don't." I don't expand my answer. Nathan is away for the weekend and if Josh's EMT schedule is still the same, he's due back in Connecticut for a shift on Monday morning.

"How are you feeling about things?" My stomach drops at the broad scope of his question. He's going to bring up the one subject I can't bear to talk about. I don't want that. I don't want to hear him mention his name.

"I'm good." My reply is rushed and forced. "It's all good."

"It's not getting any easier, is it?" He's going to push this on me. I can't believe after the blow up we had right before our break up that he would drag this subject back into the light of day.

"I don't want to talk about it." I stand. I need distance. I need to get to the other side of the room.

"He died, Jess. Not talking about it isn't going to change a thing."

I feel the room spin at the mention of his death. I can't do this. I won't. "I'm not talking about this. Is that why you came here?"

"No. I came to see you. I wanted to see how you are." He stands and walks towards the door. "We're going to talk about this one way or another. You can't keep running from it. You have to face it at some point."

I push my back against the wall as the apartment door closes behind him. My knees buckle and I slide to the floor.

I need you. I really need you, Nathan. I type the words into my phone and press send.

Chapter 14

"I've been thinking about you all weekend." Nathan pulls me into his apartment and into a tight embrace.

I slap his hands away once I realize he's pulling on the hem of my sweater. Seriously? He thinks I'm going to fuck his brains out right now even though he ignored my text messages pleading with him to call me?

"What's wrong?" He nuzzles his face into my neck.

"Is your phone broken?" I push back and stare at him.

"It's fine. Why?"

"It's fine?" My stomach cramps with the simple and straightforward understanding that he simply chose to ignore all of my pleading texts and voicemails.

"What's with you?" He walks across the room to pour himself a drink and motions toward an empty glass.

"I don't want anything." I can't drink. I can't even think straight right now. "Why didn't you call me back?"

"I knew I'd see you today, Jessica." The carefree lilt in his voice is grating on me. He doesn't care that I called him and left sobbing voicemails. It doesn't faze him at all that I sent him a flurry of texts.

"Do I mean anything beyond a decent fuck to you?" I pull my hands across my chest. This is it. I'm not investing anything more in this ridiculous excuse for a relationship.

"What's got you so tied up in knots?" He scans his phone, only further pushing me over the edge.

"Did you get any interesting messages tonight?" I know I sound like a bitch. I am a bitch when I'm dealing with a man who can't seem to think beyond the scope of his cock.

"Work stuff." He tosses the phone on the couch. "I missed you."

"Shut up, Nathan." I spit out, the stress from the last few days boiling over. "Shut the hell up. Did you think I was coming over here so you could fuck me?"

"I hoped you'd want to fuck me too." The words pierce through my skin like a needle.

"You're serious, aren't you?" My voice trembles. I'm unable to hide my anger.

"What the fuck is wrong with you?" He finishes the glass of bourbon before he takes a seat on the couch facing me. "Sit down."

"No." I won't submit to what he wants. "I'm leaving. This is such utter bullshit."

"You just got here. Sit the fuck down, Jessica." He doesn't move to stand or to stop me.

"Fuck off, Nathan." I turn to leave.

"What's your problem?" He's finally on his feet, racing to block me from the doorway.

"You." I push a finger against his chest and it barely moves. "You're the problem."

"What the fuck did I do?" He grabs my hand and clenches it within his fist. "I've been away for three days and I come back to this."

"You didn't think at some point this weekend that it might be a good idea to return one of my messages?"

"You're upset about that." He pulls a thin grin across his face. "I'd rather talk to you in person."

"You're such an asshole," I shout. "Just a narcissistic asshole."

"Watch your mouth," he says tightly. "Don't say things you're going to regret."

I pull my palm across my face to smear the tears that are now streaming down my face. "I regret everything. All of it. I regret ever meeting you. All I am to you is a convenient fuck and for some reason you don't want me to fuck anyone else so you pretend that we're in a relationship." I pull the last word heavily across my lips.

"We are in a relationship, Jessica." I can hear the impatience in his tone and it only spurs my emotions more.

"People in relationships help each other." I pull my gaze to the floor. I can't look at him. I know that being vulnerable with him is a mistake. He doesn't care. All he cares about is coming inside of me.

"What do you need?" he asks it so calmly. How can he do that? How can he react so impassively knowing that I'm such an emotional wreck?

I push past him and grasp the door handle within my palm. "To leave," I whisper.

"Talk to me." He pulls my hand away from the handle and into his. "Tell me."

"I told you in my text messages. I cried about it in my voicemails."

Panic skirts around the edges of his eyes and everything suddenly makes sense. He hasn't read any of the messages. He hasn't heard one of the voicemails. He just didn't care enough to check.

"Since you obviously didn't bother to check the messages I left you, I'll recap them for you. My ex-boyfriend came to visit me to remind me that I killed a man when I lived in Connecticut." His hand drops mine and without looking at his face, I open the door and slip into the hallway.

Chapter 15

'You didn't kill anyone." Rebecca runs her hand down the side of my cheek. "Josh can't keep telling you that, it's wrong."

"I let him die. It's the same thing. "I close my eyes tightly. The memory of that night in Connecticut washes over me again. It's become an endless loop that I can't escape from. I thought running from my life there would block out the pain. The heavy reminders that Josh brought back with him, can't be chased away with a simple change of scenery.

"You did your best." She moves closer to pull me into a tight embrace. "No one can fault you for that."

"It's not like that. I was trained to know what to do." I can barely say the words. I studied to be a paramedic. I know what to do when someone stops breathing, yet I let Josh's grandfather die in my arms.

"Jess." She sits upright on the bed now, her hands on her knees. "You listen to me and you listen good."

I stare at her. She's rarely this impassioned about anything that doesn't include designer fashion or men. "He was old. He had a heart attack. You did what you could and he died. End of story."

"Josh blames me." I pull my teeth over my bottom lip. "He'll never stop blaming me."

"Josh is fucked up." There are tears in her eyes. "You gave up everything because his grandfather died. No one could have saved him. He was too…"

"Josh could have saved him." I cut her off. "He's stronger than me. He could have done CPR longer. I tried." I had tried. I had done CPR until the moment the EMTs arrived. I'd done everything I was trained to do. I just didn't do it well enough.

"People die, Jess. He was visiting you two. He would have died at your place, or back at his place. It wasn't anything you did." She grabs my hand. "Please let this go. Please."

"I wish I could do it again," I whimper into my pillow. "I wish I could have that day back."

She curls up next to me on the bed. "You can't. It's over."

***

"I was wrong." The words float through the air behind me as I walk the four blocks back to my apartment from work. "Jessica, I was wrong."

I stop at the sound of my name. *Jessica*. Only one person calls me that.

"I can't believe what an ass I was." He's behind me now, his hand resting on my shoulder. "You had every right to be pissed off at me. Hell, you had every right to fucking leave me."

"You were such an ass." I volley the words into the air. "You are an ass."

"You're going to forgive me." He traces a path across my exposed neck with his finger. "This is the first step."

A flourish of pink roses appears in front of me. I feel his other hand wrap around my waist. "I told you I don't do romantic but this isn't romantic so don't get your panties in a knot and expect this all the time."

"My panties in a knot?" I whip around and face him.

"I can't tell you how badly I feel." He pulls a finger across my nose. "I haven't slept since you railed on me. I listened to the messages."

"You should have listened to them when you were in Boston." I tap my foot on the sidewalk. I hate when I'm wearing flats. I'm so small compared to him. He feels even more empowering to me like this.

"I don't look at my phone when I'm there. I need to explain that to you."

I nod slowly. "You do and I need to explain some things to you too."

"I know a good lawyer." He points a finger at himself. "For that small issue you've got going on back in Connecticut, Jessica. If that's your real name."

"We'll get to that one day." I reach to take the flowers from his hand. "I'm going home. Thank you for these."

"You're not coming home with me?" He pushes his hands in the pockets of his pants. "I thought you'd come home with me."

"Never assume anything, Nathan." I turn to walk down the street. "A good attorney never does that."

Chapter 16

"I shouldn't have to beg you to read text messages I send you." I glance at the roses that are now sitting next to my bed, slowly wilting.

"I shouldn't have to wait almost a week after giving you flowers to hear from you." He sits on a chair next to the bed, his legs crossed, his suit jacket hanging open.

"I needed time to think and to deal with things."

"What things?" he pushes the question back at me so quickly. What happens if I open up to him and we end up back in the same spot we're always in? In bed with no connection to one another beyond that?

"I think we should cut out the exclusive part of our relationship." I don't see any reason to beat around the bush. I don't want to keep having false expectations when I know he can't possibly emotionally deliver on them.

"Why would we do that?" He moves to the edge of the bed. "There's someone you want to fuck?"

"How do you get through your workday when all you think about is fucking?" I ask half-teasingly. It's a question I've long wanted an answer to. I've never met anyone who talks about sex or thinks about sex as much as Nathan.

"You're diverting." He traces a finger over the pattern on the cotton blanket. "Who do you want to fuck? I need to know."

"Right now, absolutely no one, present company included." I don't show any emotion with the statement. I don't want to. I can't fall back into this knowing that he only sees me as someone who can get him off whenever he wants.

"You didn't call me over here to fuck you?"

I stop before I answer. I exhale sharply thinking carefully about how I should respond. "You like fucking me, don't you?"

"I love fucking you." The smile that crashes over his lips makes him devastatingly handsome. Only he can say the word *fuck* so effortlessly and yet with so much raw desire.

"We need to get back to that." I slide the words over my lips, thinking about how amazing it would be right now to just let go and let him claim me again.

"I'm all for that." He eases his suit jacket from his shoulders, letting it fall to the bed behind him.

"Sit here." I pat the area where my pillows are. "Rest your back against the headboard."

He stands and quickly starts unbuttoning his shirt.

"Clothes on, Nathan," I command. He really only has a one track mind. It's becoming clearer to me each time we spend a moment together.

He kicks off his shoes before he sets himself at the head of the bed. I crawl into his lap, pulling the skirt of my sundress around my thighs.

"I really like you." I lightly graze my lips across his. "I've never met any man like you before."

His heavy lashes close slightly as he breathes in the scent of my skin. "I've never met anyone like you before, Jessica." He pulls me closer, the stubble on his skin, grazing my cheek.

"Sex with you is so good." I kiss him lightly. "I love it. I really love it."

"Me too." His hands inch up my thighs and I don't stop him. I don't want to stop him.

I pull my panties across his pants, feeling his swollen cock straining against the fabric. "You and I just need to fuck and nothing else."

"I want to fuck you so much." His hands skirt the edges of my panties, playfully pulling at them.

"You think about fucking me all the time," I whisper into his cheek. "That's what you picture when you think about me."

"It's all I think about." He groans as his finger slides over my cleft. "You're just so ripe and ready for me. You always are."

"If I let you fuck me now, you'd like that," I tease.

"I'd love that." He pushes a finger across my moist folds and I have to bite back a moan.

"Don't you wonder…" I let the words trail as he circles my clit with his finger.

"Wonder how good you're going to taste when I eat you?" He deftly pushes a finger inside of me.

"Wonder what happened to me in Connecticut." I pull back and stare at his face.

His eyelids close briefly before he pulls his gaze to mine. "You would tell me if you wanted me to know."

I shift my body to try and move from his grasp, put he slides another finger into me.

"You don't want to know." I bite back all the emotions that are racing through me. I want to hate him for not caring. I want him to push me back and lick my wetness until I'm screaming his name. I want him to react. I want him to feel something besides unadulterated lust for me.

"Don't play games with me, Jessica." He pushes his fingers farther into me until I can't help but release a small moan.

"I'm not." I push back on his legs, trying to disengage myself from his body but he's unrelenting. "Don't act like you don't want me as much as I want you." He twists his fingers within me as his thumb settles on my clit.

"I don't want you," I lie through clenched teeth. I don't want him just like this. I want to mean more to him than a fuck. I have to mean more than that.

"Stop lying." He leans back and pulls on my thigh with his free hand. "I'm going to make you come with my fingers, just like that first night. You're going to scream my name by the end of tonight because your body craves mine."

"No," I push back against him. "I won't scream your name."

"When you're in this bed at night, you touch this." He nods to his fingers. "You pull your fingers over your clit while you think about my tongue."

"Don't say that." I feel so shameless. I wanted to seduce him into admitting he only wanted me for sex. I wanted to make him see that there was more to me.

"You're getting close. You're so swollen and ready." He pushes another finger into me, stretching my pleasure. "I should fuck you right now."

"I'm…" my voice trails as I feel an orgasm wash through me. I pant, biting my lip to hold back the quiver that is rushing over me. "Nathan," I say his name in a breathless whisper. "Nathan."

He pulls me into his chest, resting my head against his cheek. "I wanted..." I don't know what I wanted but he knew what I needed.

"Jessica." He cradles the side of my head as he whispers softly in my ear. "You grew up in Bloomfield, Connecticut. You're a registered EMT. You were living with a jackass named Josh Redmond who fucked you over so badly because he made you believe you were responsible for his grandfather's death. You ran away from all of that and you fell into me. I've got you. I'm not letting you go."

I pull my head up and stare at his face. I can't form one word in response. I can't process everything that just came out of his mouth.

"You didn't really think I just spent the last week of my life jerking off to memories of you, did you? I had to fill in my time somehow."

"I don't know what to say." I feel my lips tremble.

"Don't say anything." He pulls my head back into his chest. "This isn't romantic. Don't take it that way. You can't tell a lawyer you killed a man and expect him not to want to know more. "

I smile softly as I pull my arms around him.

Chapter 17

"Are you going to tell me about Boston?" I offer him a bite of my baked pretzel and he pulls off a large piece.

"What about Boston?" He chews on it before reaching to take the plastic cup filled with lemonade from my grasp.

My eyes follow a nanny with her two young charges as they race towards the entrance of the Central Park Zoo. "You said you'd explain why you don't look at your messages when you're in Boston."

He pulls the remaining pretzel from my grasp. "I'm starving. We should have gone for a sandwich."

"Don't divert." I push at him. "Meeting in the park at noon was your idea, not mine."

"I wanted to see your face." He taps me on the nose. "Work is a bitch right now."

I nod. "Boston." I push again.

"Boston." A slight grin pulls at the corner of his mouth. "This is why I ignore everything when I'm in Boston."

I watch in silence as he pulls his wallet from the inner pocket of his suit jacket. He carefully opens one of the flaps to reveal two small pictures. He holds them up for me to gaze at. "This is Madison and this is Mackenzie."

I smile at the glowing faces of two children. "Your niece and nephew." I recognize their images from the picture that was in his apartment when Cassandra took me there. "I saw a picture of them on your mantel."

"The day Cassie took you in?" He drops his gaze to his pants, pulling softly on a loose thread.

"Yes." I wish I hadn't brought it up. I don't want to talk about her anymore. I don't want to talk about anything but the two of us.

"I don't miss her at all." His voice is quiet and raspy. "If you left me, I'd miss you so much."

I turn sharply to look at his face but he's staring into the distance. "I'm not going anywhere."

"I'm serious, Jessica." He pulls his eyes shut for a brief moment before he turns to look at me. "I'd miss you too much. You get that, don't you?"

"I get that," I reply quickly. "I do."

"Come over tonight." He pulls his lips across the bare skin of my shoulder. "I need you."

He's never said that. He needs me? "What's wrong?" I need to ask. I have to know. He doesn't open up like this. There aren't any small cracks in Nathan Moore's demeanor.

"Be there at eight. I'll be waiting for you." He reaches to pull my palm across his lips.

***

"Nathan," I gasp as he plunges his tongue inside of me. "Please. It's too much."

"Never." He cradles my ass off the bed, his mouth deftly close to coaxing yet another orgasm from deep within me.

My body is trembling, I'm covered in sweat, my hands gripping his bed sheets. "You have to stop."

"I can't stop." He angles my body higher so his tongue can probe me deeper. "I love the taste of you."

"I can't breathe." My hands dart to his hair, pulling on the soft strands. "Let me suck you off. Please."

"You're going to suck my cock." His breath tickles across my overly sensitive folds. "You're going to suck me until I come all over your body."

The raspy sound of his voice pushes me closer to the edge. I almost whimper from the sensation. I can't keep up. I can't do this. It's so much.

"You're the sweetest little thing." He laps lazily at my clit, pulling it softly between his teeth. "I can't wait until my cock is buried inside you and you're clawing at my back."

I race over the edge at the thought of him inside of me. He hasn't fucked me in so long. It feels like so long.

I feel the bed heave beneath me as he moves his body from it. I close my eyes knowing he's getting a condom. He's going to fuck me when I've already come so many times.

"Nathan," I whisper his name through heavy lips. I feel so spent. I feel as though his mouth pulled every ounce of strength from within me. How can he make me feel so much?

"Jessica." He breathes into me as his lips skirt softly over mine. "Spread your legs. I have to fuck you now."

"I can't." I lift my hand and rest it against his chest. I feel the fine mist of sweat that is glistening over his skin. He worked so hard to make me come so many times.

"Feel it." He pulls the heavy weight of his cock over my cleft and I moan loudly at the sensation. My hips buck in reflex. My body wants him even if I can't handle the idea of any more pleasure.

"Oh god, "I whimper. "It's so much."

"Today, in the park." He eases himself slowly between my folds. "The sun caught your hair. So pretty, so beautiful."

I moan loudly as my hips shift to take in the full length of his cock.

"You'll never get enough of my cock." He glides his lips across my cheekbone as the words skirt across my skin. "You looked so perfect today. Not just like a woman I couldn't wait to fuck. It was more."

I clench my hands around his back as he pounds into me. "Nathan, it's so good."

"So good, Jessica." He strokes into me, his cock pushing deeper with each thrust. "I love how you feel. You're always so ready for me. Your body. My body."

I feel my pulse race at the words. I want to belong to him. I want him to want me that way.

"Fuck." The word escapes my lips from the deepest part of me. The part that is inextricably linked to his pleasure.

He ups the tempo, his cock vibrating within me. He's close to pulling another orgasm from my body and I can't wait to rush over the edge.

He lets out an animalistic growl when I clench my sex around him as I near my release. My fingernails dig into his ass, pushing him to his limit, pulling him into me.

"Jessica," he cries out as a vein is his neck pulses. I feel his body contract with desire just as my own orgasm crashes through me.

Chapter 18

"Stay."

It's a single word. One small word isn't supposed to hold so much emotion. He doesn't understand that. He can't understand what he's asking of me.

"You want me to stay?" I pull the dress I was wearing when I got to his apartment over my head and onto my body.

"Yes." Another simple word. There's no inflection is his tone. I can't tell if he's being serious.

"Nathan." I reach down to pick up my panties and toss them aside once I realize he ripped them in his haste to get me naked beneath him.

"I can't let you go tonight." There's no mistaking the ripe emotion rippling through the words. "Get back into bed. I need you here."

I yank the dress back over my head and ease back beside him. He pulls me close, his arm circling my waist.

"Jessica." His breath runs hot against my back. "Listen to me."

I try to turn so I'm facing him but he holds steady to my body. I feel his breath catch when I reach back to run my finger along his thigh.

"Listen," he repeats the word. "I can't handle you with anyone else."

"I know." I breathe in a heavy sigh. We're going to circle the subject of my not having sex with anyone else again even though I haven't contemplated the thought in weeks. I even turned Drew down when he asked me out to a movie with him and some friends of his.

"No." His body is trembling. I can feel it reverberate through me. "You don't understand."

"I do." I try to reassure him. He's probably freaking out over the fact that the man I bought the pretzel from at lunch winked at me. I should confess that he winks at every woman who gives him a dollar tip.

"I feel things." His voice cracks and my breathing stalls. "Things I don't know how to feel."

I can't move. I can only listen and feel his emotions race through me.

"I fuck women." I sense the stubble of his chin on my cheek as he shakes his head slightly. "I used to fuck women and I didn't think twice about them. I couldn't tell you their names or what they looked like anymore."

I don't respond. I can't say a word. He's being more open right now than he's ever been. I can't derail this.

"I can tell you that the second tooth on the upper left side of your mouth is slightly crooked. Not enough that anyone would notice but it makes your smile more beautiful."
I feel my eyes swell with tears as I listen intently to his words.

"I can tell you that when you laugh you pull your hand to your face to cover your perfect mouth. Every time you laugh. I first noticed it when you were at the restaurant with your roommates. It's adorable."

I nod. I do that. I know I do that. I've always done that.

"I can tell you that you say my name unlike anyone else on the planet and I live for the sound of it. Sometimes I just close my eyes and imagine the word rolling from your lips. I could listen to it forever."

"I don't say it differently."

"Say it now."

"Nathan."

"Like that." He pulls my body into his. "Just like that."

I smile at his reaction.

"I can't stand the thought of another man knowing any of this." His lips push into my shoulder. "Promise me you won't let anyone else see this part of you. Promise me."

I nod my head in silence. I don't know what to say. Something has shifted between us. That small crack that I saw within him has split wide open.

Chapter 19

"I'm going to Boston next weekend. Are you working?" I love how casually he shares information about his life. It's been a week since his tender confession in the bedroom and I've spend every night tucked into his bed and his life.

"Just on Sunday." I sigh. "I have Saturday off. Bryce's girlfriend is coming to town so we're going to hang out."

"That'll be fun?" It's more of a question than a statement and I can't help but laugh.

"It will be." I push back against his chest. "I haven't met her yet, but I hear great things about her whenever I catch Bryce long enough to talk to him."

"You'll have a good time." His hand drops to stroke my thigh. "Are you taking her to your restaurant?"

"No." I shake my head slightly. "Somewhere simple and then to a movie."

"What about Rebecca?"

"Hot date or something." I shrug as I run my hand down his chest. "Or maybe it's just an excuse because she doesn't want to hang out with me."

"How could anyone not want to hang out with this?" He pulls the blanket off of both of us with one swift flick of his wrist.

"You're such a charmer." I push my back into the sheets, pulling my hand over my breasts. "You know just what to say to a girl to make her wet."

"Make her wet." His full lips graze over mine with a heated touch. "You're always wet for me, Jessica."

"Always." I let the word flow between my lips slowly as my fingers part my folds. He's right. I'm always wet for him.

"That very first moment when you walked into the club, I knew you were made just for me." He eases his body slowly on top of mine. I hear the sound of the condom package in his hands. His eyes never break my gaze as he pulls it over his cock.

"I was made for you." I circle my hips on the bed when I feel his cock skirt across my clit.

"I chased after you the next night because you slipped away when I fell asleep." His lips part slightly as he pushes just the head between my folds.

"You were so sleepy." I kiss the side of his cheek before my breath rushes at the feeling of his full length pushing into me.

"I woke up in a panic." He adjusts his hips so he can claim me with long, leisurely, painfully delicious strokes.

I smile at the tender confession. We've never talked about that first night. The night he drifted into a peaceful sleep when I took forever to calm my nerves in the bathroom.

"I couldn't work the next day." He reaches to grab both my hands, pinning them to the sheets. "All I could think about was how badly I fucked up. How you'd gotten away from me forever."

I try to push back against him, but his grasp is too tight. "I want to touch you," I whimper.

He only shakes his head slightly in response. "When I saw you the next night, I almost came right there. I couldn't believe it was you. I wanted to pick you up and throw you over my shoulder on the spot."

"You practically did." I moan when he shifts his hips and pushes deeper still.

"I was going to have you. I wanted you more than I've ever wanted a woman." His lips brush against mine in slow, easy strokes. The tempo matches his cock. He's taking me so slowly tonight. I almost can't bear the measured drip of pleasure.

"Faster, please," I beg, my hips pushing into him.

"I want this to last." He digs his feet into the bed, pushing for more leverage. "I can't fuck you when I'm in Boston. I need this to hold me over."

I close my eyes and drop my head to the side. It's almost unbearable. The way his cock fills me completely. The scent of his skin mixed with my own. The pleasure in knowing that he's taking as much from this as he's giving to me.

"Nathan," I moan under his heated touch. "Just fuck me."

He rallies on his heels and lets out a deep guttural groan as he offers me my reward for the sweet torturous tease he's inflicted on me. In one deft movement, my hips are off the bed, and he's pulling me into him, crashing my body against his.

I scream at the depth of his cock. The pain mixed with unbearable pleasure pushes me over the edge almost instantly. I can't see beyond the feelings. I close my eyes as I course through an intense orgasm.

"Jessica," he calls into my skin as he pulls me into his lap. "Christ." I feel his cock constrict inside me and his body convulses as he clings desperately to me.

Chapter 20

"Are you expecting a call, Jess?" Bryce's voice snaps me out of the daze I've been floating in since Nathan left for Boston late last night.

"No." I smile up at him. "I was just checking my messages."

"Trudy's ready to take off if you're up to it." He points to his girlfriend who is sitting in the living room, thumbing her way through one of Rebecca's fashion magazines.

"Sure. Where do you want to eat?" I can't stifle a yawn as I pull myself up from the chair next to the table.

"Maybe you should be napping instead of hanging out with us?" It's a question that is ripe with suggestion.

"Am I being a third wheel?" I lean in close not wanting Trudy to hear me. "I can stay here while you two go do your own thing."

"Just for dinner?" His face brightens at the idea. "I just haven't seen her in weeks and it would be good to catch up."

"Go." I try to veil a heavy sigh of relief. "Take her and have fun."

"Maybe we can catch a movie tonight?" I feel as though he's throwing me a bone since he knows that Nathan has skipped town for the weekend.

"I'm going to nap. We'll figure it out later or not." I tilt my head to the side. I'd actually give anything to just have a quiet night tucked into my bed with no distractions. I've been working so much lately that it was all catching up to me. I needed a decent night's sleep and I wasn't finding that in Nathan's arms. We couldn't keep our hands off each other.

I watch them head out the door before I turn to check my phone again. Still nothing from Nathan. That's two text messages that he's probably not going to see until he's back in New York on Monday morning. I have to give up the notion that he's going to respond to me when he's with his family. He's already made it clear that they're his priority when he's there.

I turn to head down the hallway towards my bedroom when I hear a key in the apartment lock. I don't want to entertain anyone. Maybe if I can get behind my closed door and into my bed before they notice me, I'll be home free.

"Jess." Rebecca's voice calls to me just as I have my bedroom doorknob in my grasp. "What's going on?"

"Naptime." I smile through gritted teeth. We haven't spoken much more than a few words to each other in more than week. With our conflicting work schedules and my routine of staying at Nathan's every night now, we just didn't connect anymore.

"Make it a siesta. We're going clubbing tonight." It's a statement, not a question and I'm not amused.

"We're not." I stress the words across my lips. "I'm so drained. I'm going to stay in and sleep."

"Bryce and that boring girlfriend of his are going with me. You should too."

"I don't feel up to it." It's only a half lie. I know Nathan wouldn't want me hanging out in a club when he's away. He's told me as much more than once.

"Just call Fingers and tell him. You can skip the guilty conscience that way."

"He…" my voice trails as I realize I can't confess that he doesn't respond to me when he's away. She won't get it.

"I'll come for a couple of hours," I acquiesce. If I just go, I won't feel as badly the next time I blow off a dinner invitation with her for a night with Nathan.

"Go to bed." She pushes me through the doorway into my room. "I'll wake you when it's time to get ready."

***

I know you won't see this but I'm going clubbing with my roommates. Don't freak out.

I press send and toss my phone into my purse as the taxi pulls away from the curb in front of our apartment.

"Did you send a message to the old man telling him you were out having a life?" Rebecca's comment pulls a giggle out of both Trudy and Bryce.

"I did." I can't shelter a smile as I realize that I've missed hanging out with her. She knows what I need and one night with friends is exactly what I want right now.

"Coincidentally, we're going to start at the club where you met Fingers."

"Fingers?" A wide smile covers Trudy's face. It's the most emotion I've seen her express since she arrived.

"It's a name we call her boyfriend." Rebecca rolls her eyes as she motions in my direction. "Don't ask."

"Why are we going there?" I whine into her shoulder. "I hate that place."

"You hate that place because his fuck pad is there." She doesn't try and temper her tone at all.

"He gave that up."

"Don't be so sure, Jess." She cocks a brow. "Remember how I told you men like that never change."

"He's different," I say glumly. Why did I agree to go with them back to that club? I don't want to think about how many women Nathan fucked in that room when he's been so open with me lately. He may not tell in so many words, but I can feel his resistance slipping away. I know within me that he's falling for me as fast and hard as I'm falling for him.

"You're second guessing him, aren't you?" I'm thankful that she whispers the question into my ear. I don't need Bryce and Trudy witnessing all the self-doubt I'm suddenly feeling wash over me.

"No." I wasn't. I didn't doubt him at all. He told me he gave up the fuck pad and he'd done nothing since that moment to make me doubt that.

Chapter 21

"He's in Boston, Jess." I can smell the tequila on Rebecca's breath even though she's three feet away from me.

"I know he is." I shoot back. I want to leave. I hate being in this place. Every time I pull my gaze up I see a beautiful women and I instantly wonder whether Nathan's fucked her at some point.

"You keep looking for him." She takes another shot. "I see you looking around the room for him."

"That's not it," I argue. "It's these women."

"What women?" She almost screams the question over the noise of the crowd.

"He's fucked some of these women, don't you think?" I lean forward to temper my tone. I don't want to announce to the entire club that I'm the woman Nathan takes to his home. I don't want to know anything about any woman he's ever touched.

"Most of them." She shrugs her shoulder as she nods her head.

"I can't be here." I hop from the barstool to my feet. "I want to go home."

"No." She pushes me back down. "We're staying."

"Rebecca." I raise my voice slightly to get my point across. "You can stay. I need to go."

"You're just scared." The words tumble out her too quickly. "You're scared he's still fucking women upstairs, aren't you?"

I am. She's right. Ever since we stepped foot back in the club I've been thinking about that. I'm wondering whether the room is rented to someone else right now or if he's still holding onto it.

"Let's go see." She pulls on my arm, steering me towards the entrance to hotel Aeon.

"What are you talking about?" I down the shot the bartender placed in front of Rebecca just to calm my nerves. I recoil at the heat of the tequila as it courses down my throat.

"We go upstairs, we knock on the door and we see who answers." She pulls on my hand yet again and I don't stop her this time. I race behind her until we're in the lobby.

"It's a stupid plan," I spit out in a muted tone. "It's not going to work."

"You don't want it to work." Her words are slurred. "You don't want to know that he still has a place because then you have to kiss him and his big cock goodbye."

"He doesn't have a room." I know I sound too insistent. I'm not just trying to convince her. I'm trying to steel my own doubts about him.

"We're doing this, Jess." She points towards the bank of elevators. "You remember which room it was, right?"

I nod my head in silence. I can't move. I can't go up there knowing that there's a very slim chance that no one will answer the door and I'll be cursed with the knowledge that he may be lying to me about holding onto the room.

"Let's do it already." She jerks my hand so hard that I almost fall forward. She's not going to give this up. She won't.

We ride the elevator up to the eighteenth floor in silence. I fish in my purse, pulling my smartphone into my palm. I scroll through my new messages and there's nothing from Nathan at all. Absolutely nothing for over a day now.

I pull Rebecca down the dimly lit hallway to the doorway I remember. She knocks softly and we both perch our ears to the door. Nothing.

She knocks again and we both wait for what feels like endless moments.

"No one's here." She cocks a brow and leans against the door jam." Now what?"

Now I breathe a sigh of relief. He's not in the room. My heart told me he wasn't. I knew he was telling me the truth.

I scroll my thumb over my phone's screen and type a message to Nathan.

I miss you so much. I can't wait to see you when you get back.

I press send and I turn to walk towards the bank of elevators hoping Rebecca will give up her useless mission to trap Nathan in a lie.

The unmistakable sound of a not-too-distant cell phone chime breaks the silence in the hallway.

I stare at my phone.

Call me as soon as you're back from Boston.

My hand shakes as I type out the message before my thumb hits send.

The same chime rings through the air.

"His phone is in that room," I murmur, my voice shaking as intensely as my hands.

Chapter 22

"Do you see what I mean?" Rebecca giggles as the elderly security guard presses his ear to the door, listening to Nathan's phone ringing. "My friend left her cell phone in there when she was visiting Mr. Moore."

I throw her a small smile, grateful that she's pulled out the composure to lie for me.

"We just need a minute to get it back. That and her bra." She practically yells the last word at him and it definitely has the desired effect.

"I...uh…" His face flushes a deep shade of crimson at the mere suggestion that I left lingerie in a room. "I'm not supposed to let people in."

"I know." Rebecca pats him on the back. "The thing is, she and Mr. Moore had a fight and she can't talk to him right now. She's really emotional because it's that time of the month."

I grimace at the words. He does too and I can tell that she's pushing every single one of the buttons that make him incredibly uncomfortable.

"Let me see if he's here." He pulls a radio out of his belt and punches in Nathan's room number. We all listen intently at the sound of the room's phone ringing beyond the barrier of the wooden door.

"He's out." Rebecca leans close to him. "Probably chasing another skirt."

I roll my eyes in her direction but she's solely focused on her mission to get this poor man to open the door and break every rule he's ever been taught.

"You've got two minutes," he whispers as he pulls a master key card from his pocket and swipes it. The green light shines as he pulls the doorknob down, pushing the door open just enough so I can sneak in.

Rebecca nods to me as she starts chattering to him about how brave he is and what a selfless job he's doing protecting all the patrons of the hotel.

I slip into the darkened room and fumble with the light switch. As the small lamps on the table flicker on, I'm overcome with a rush of emotions. It's exactly the same as I remember it. This is the room. The same room that Nathan fucked me in and promised he gave up for me.

My eyes dart to the counter near the bank of windows. Everything is in its place. It's obvious the cleaning staff have gone through the room recently. The glasses are all spotless and lined neatly in a row. The trash is cleared.

I move quickly to the bedroom, realizing that I won't have much time if Rebecca runs out of steam. I push the call button for Nathan's number on my phone again and hear his ringing near me. I flip the light switch and instantly see the lighted screen of a phone dancing in the dim light. It's sitting on the top of bed.

I reach for it and see my number flashing back at me. I pull my thumb over it and my breath hitches. I lean back against the bed, my knees giving out.

I close my eyes and pull in a deep breath.

I scroll silently through the messages.

There's the five I've sent since this morning and so many more...

I miss you sweetie. When are you going to fuck me again?

I can't wait to have your cock back in my mouth. Call me.

Thanks for yesterday. I'm still thinking about your tongue.

It's been awhile, Nathan. What does a girl have to do to get laid by you?

They're endless.

Each more intimate than the last.

All from different numbers.

My thumb hovers over the contact list.

Hundreds of names.

All women.

I scroll to the J.

Click on it once.

Scan the names until I find Jessica.

Jessica A.

Jessica C.
And me...
Jessica R.

PULSE
The Complete Series

Part Three

Chapter 1

"I can't wait to get out of these clothes." Her voice is sweet and high. She's probably gorgeous and already half naked. He's pouring himself a drink. I know he is. He drinks too much, he fucks too much, and he lies way too much.

I glance back down at my phone to the text message Rebecca sent me ten minutes ago. She convinced the security guard to take her to the lobby when she told him she was feeling sick so I could have more time in the room. Who knew she had such mad acting skills? Who knew within minutes after she walked away Nathan would glide through the door with another of his fuck buddies? Now, here I am, stuck in the bedroom of his hotel suite while he gets ready to fuck someone else. Great, Jessica. What are you going to do now, hide under the bed? It could be an option if I wouldn't end up with a concussion from the mattress banging me in the head when he's ramming whoever the hell he brought in here with him.

There's no time like the present. I take a deep breath, pick up his smartphone, adjust the hem of my dress and walk out the bedroom door.

"What the fuck? Jessica?" It doesn't take him more than a second to see me. He's standing next to the bar with a drink in his hand, his suit coat already off. A suit on a Saturday night? Fucking lawyer.

"Nate, what's wrong?" The brunette standing next to him grabs hold of his arm. At least all of her clothes are still on. Jeans and a t-shirt? Where did he meet this one? At the drugstore when he was picking up his monthly supply of five hundred condoms? Would that even be enough? I'd guess a thousand to be safe.

"Jessica…" That's it. Nothing else comes out of his lying, cheating, bastard mouth than that.

"Nate," I'm not going to give him the satisfaction of saying his name the way he likes it. I'll just follow the lead of the condom clerk. "Aren't you going to introduce me to your friend?" Very adult of you, Jessica. Asking to meet the next passenger on his never ending fuck train shows just how mature you really are.

"I'm not his friend…I'm," she's stammering. Of course she is.

I take a step towards them. "I'm not his friend either," I offer. "I'm just a random fuck too."

"Shut up," he snaps. He's pissed. Well, good for him. "What the fuck are you doing here?"

"What the fuck am I doing here?" Seems like a good place to start. "What about you? Last time I checked this isn't Boston."

The brunette is pulling on his arm. "What's going on, Nate?" Her eyes are glued to his face but his gaze never breaks mine.

"I'll tell you what's going on." I dangle his smartphone in the air. It hangs precariously between my index finger and thumb. "Nate has a few dozen calls he needs to return and a few hundred text messages he should read from all the women he's been fucking."

"Shit." His breathing stalls as his eyes hone in on the phone. "How the hell did you get in here? Who let you in?"

I cock a brow. Thank God I had that shot of tequila before I came up here. I can feel a tiny buzz racing through me, that and more anger than I've ever felt before. "Like that matters," I spit back. "Why the hell do you still have this room?" That's a stupid question. That beautiful brunette standing next to him is one of the many, many reasons he lied about giving up his suite.

"We're not doing this right now." His tone is clipped and terse.

"Are you talking to me or her?" I wave a finger in the air towards what's-her-name who pulls the half empty glass of bourbon from his hand and downs it in one shot. "Good call, girlfriend. You're going to need that if you're hitting the sheets with this one." I nod toward Nathan.

He pulls the glass from her hand and slams it with a vacant thud onto the bar. "You have to go."

"Gladly," I scoff. "Consider me gone."

He's rigid as his icy blue eyes stare into me. "Not you. You're not going anywhere."

"You're not serious?" I challenge. "I'm not hanging out here to watch the two of you go at it."

His face is expressionless as he reaches in the pocket of his pants to pull out a set of keys. "Take these. Go to my apartment for the night."

The brunette reaches for them casually as if it's second nature to her. She's been there. She's been inside his apartment just like I have. "What about..." her voice trails when there are three soft knocks on the door.

It's Rebecca. She's come back looking for me. Nathan takes a heavy step towards the door but I'm faster. I bolt across the room and swing the door open wanting to leave this room, this man and this nightmare behind me.

"Hey, you're Jessica, aren't you? I'm Travis." He's wearing a ball cap pulled low over his forehead. Curly blonde locks spill from the sides.

"Travis," I repeat his name because I have no idea what else to say. Who the hell is Travis and why is he standing in the doorway of Nathan's hotel suite with two suitcases in his hands?

"We're going to Nate's place." The brunette is calling from behind me. What kind of kinky threesome did I stumble on?

"She looks exactly like that picture you showed me on your phone." Travis is a chatty one. Whose picture on whose phone?

I twist around to look at Nathan. He's holding *a* phone in his hand. I'm holding *his* phone in my hand.

"I took this picture of you when you were at the restaurant with your roommates." He holds up the phone and there's an image of me from the side talking to Bryce. I look like I'm eighteen-years-old. It was the day I saw him with his friend, Ivy.

"But this is your phone." I dangle the phone in my hands.

"No," he corrects me with a cock of his brow. "This is my phone."

"We should go, babe." The brunette is inching towards the door teetering a bit as she scurries across the carpeted floor. It's obvious that bourbon has done her in for the night.

"I'm Sandra, by the way." She holds her hand out diminutively. "I'm Nathan's sister."

Chapter 2

"You could have stopped me at some point."

He takes a heavy swallow of the drink he just poured before he finally turns around. "What the fuck are you doing in this room?"

"What?" I bark back. "Why don't you tell me why you still have this room?"

He walks past me to sit down on the couch. "Give me the name of the person who let you in."

"You're seriously worried about who let me in to your precious fuck pad?" This is ludicrous. It's so past fucked up that I can't wrap my brain around it.

"Why are you dressed like that?" He tilts his chin at me. "You were downstairs in the club, weren't you?"

My legs are shaking so hard I have to sit on the edge of the coffee table. "Don't change the subject, Nathan."

His eyes blaze down my bare crossed legs. "Were you down there looking for someone to fuck? Did you sneak in here so you could use my room to screw someone else?"

My stomach roils at the suggestion. "Don't do that. Don't."

"Don't do what?" His tone is clipped and harsh. "I leave town and come back early to find you, dressed like that, and smelling like tequila. What am I supposed to think?"

"You?" I bolt to my feet. "What are you supposed to think? What the fuck am I supposed to think about this?" I sweep my arm around the suite. "And this?" I toss the smartphone I found on the bed at him.

He catches it deftly and rests it on his thigh. "What about it?"

"What about it?" I'm yelling and don't give a shit if everyone on the floor hears it. "What about explaining what the fuck is going on?"

"I paid for the room monthly." He runs his hand over his face. "It's not mine anymore after Tuesday."

"You said you gave it up." I can feel the fury building within me. I'm so close to exploding.

"I haven't fucked anyone here, Jessica." His tone is biting. "No one has been in that bed since you."

I wonder in that instant how many women he fucked in this room before me. How many of those women on that phone stood in this exact spot waiting to get their turn. "What about the phone?"

"I don't use this phone often." He qualifies, "It's a phone I used to use in Boston. I got a new number when I moved here last year."

"What?"

"I rarely check it anymore," he says it so flippantly, as if that's going to explain away all the names, numbers and illicit messages sitting on that phone.

"My number is in that phone." I raise my voice even louder. "I'm just one of the Jessicas you have in there. How do you keep us all straight?"

He closes his eyes briefly as if to temper what he wants to say. "You're overreacting. You need to sit down so I can explain."

"I'm not sitting down." I can barely breathe. "You can't explain that." I reach for the phone but he snatches it up before I'm even near it.

"I will explain it." He's so arrogant and smug. What an asshole.

"Start with the thanks for yesterday text. That woman can't get enough of your tongue."

He picks up the phone and runs his thumb across the screen before his eyes scan the messages. "That's Sarah. I haven't fucked her in more than a year."

I shake my head at the illogical response. "Nathan, yesterday doesn't mean a year ago."

"She was thanking me for helping her out of a legal bind." He shrugs his shoulders as if that's magically going to make her tongue comment disappear.

"What the fuck does your tongue have to do with her legal issues?"

"She wanted me to fuck her again. Actually, she wanted me to eat her out so she kept talking about my tongue but it hasn't gone anywhere near her in a long time." He smirks at his own words. He actually thinks this is funny.

"You expect me to believe that?" My foot starts tapping. There's no way he's telling the truth. His head was probably buried between her thighs last night when he got to Boston.

His jaw tightens. "It's the truth, Jessica."

"Bullshit," I spit out.

Cursing under his breath he runs his thumb over the screen of the phone again. He taps it lightly and the room fills with the sound of a phone ringing. He's calling someone, right in the middle of this.

A woman's voice flows over the speakerphone. "Nathan? Is that you?"

"It's me." His tone is unreadable. "How are you, Sarah?"

What the fuck.

"Horny." She giggles. "Are you in town?"

"No," he says gruffly. "How did that issue with your sister turn out?"

"What?" He's caught her off guard. She's not going to be part of his rouse. He's about to get busted.

"Sarah," he exhales harshly. "That advice I gave you last week, did you take it?"

Silence fills the air and then she finally speaks again. "I got her to call your lawyer friend. It helped her a lot. Thanks again for arranging that for her."

He cocks a brow at me. I don't respond. So what if he helped one of his fuck buddies with something? There's still that small issue of his tongue and her body.

"When's the last time we fucked, Sarah?"

She practically moans. "Do you want to do it now? I can come to wherever you are. Just tell me where."

"When is the last time we fucked?" he repeats, stringing out every word.

"The last time we fucked?" How many goddamn times do I need to be reminded that he fucked the woman on the other end of the phone? "I don't know." Her breathing stalls for a few seconds. "It was before Labor day last year, so I guess a little more than a year ago?"

He ignores her response and stares straight at me.

"Do you want to meet up or not?" I can hear the expectation in her voice.

"No."

"Maybe tomorrow then?" she asks quietly.

"Never." He looks down at the screen. "Don't call my office again and forget this number."

"What?"

"Forget you ever knew me." He ends the call with a quick tap of his thumb. "Happy now?"

Chapter 3

"Enough." Why the hell was he doing this? He'd now called three more women and grilled each of them about the last time he'd had his dick in them. "I don't want to hear anymore."

"Do you believe me that I'm not fucking anyone else?" The question is meant to challenge me. "If you don't, I'll call every woman on this phone. I have all night."

"Why do you still have it?" I stand and cross my arms over my chest. I wish I hadn't worn such a low cut dress.

He straightens so he's sitting upright, his arm casually thrown over the back of the couch, his legs crossed. He looks so at ease. "I told you I rarely look at it."

"It's almost fully charged and it was turned on when I found it." I'm not backing down from this. I refuse to. He thinks that by calling a handful of the hundreds of women on that phone and asking when he last banged them, that he's off the hook. Not so fast, Mr. Moore.

"So?"

"So?" That's his retort and he calls himself a lawyer. "If you didn't care about any of those women and you weren't planning on sleeping with them, why keep the phone?"

"Your number is in there." He means it as a compliment. It's a backhanded, disgusting and degrading reminder that I'm just another random fuck.

I swear I almost physically recoil from the comment. "Why isn't my number in there?" I point to the other smartphone, the one that he showed me earlier that has my picture on it.

"Jessica." The calm exterior that he's trying to maintain is quickly melting away. "You're taking this all wrong."

"I'm taking this at face value." I try and stay composed. I have to. I can't fall into a driveling mess at his feet. I refuse to even though everything inside of me is breaking into pieces.

"You're the one who broke into my room." The amusement skirting the statement pulls at my anger.

I dart my hand towards him. "Give me the phone."

"What?" He cradles it in his hand. "Why?"

"Give me the goddamn phone, Nathan."

He leans forward to offer it to me. "What are you going to do with it?" The question irks me even more.

"Does it matter?" I step out of his reach, pulling my thumb across the screen.

"No, it's…it's just that I," he stammers as he stares at my finger tapping.

"Cat got your tongue, Nate?" I glance up from the phone. "Or maybe one of these women has a tongue you can't resist?"

"No," he scoffs. "I told you I'm done with them."

"You're done with me too." I toss the phone at him and it bounces against his chest. "I deleted my number."

"What?" He's on his feet now, his voice husky and edging anger. "Why?"

"Why?" I parrot back. Is he seriously asking me why I don't want anything to do with him anymore?

"Jessica." He takes a step towards me and I teeter on my heels in an effort to get out of his reach. I grab for the bar, holding on to the edge to get my level footing back.

"Leave me the fuck alone." Any barrier that I've had up until now is gone. It's crumbled beneath the slew of half-truths and realizations about how many women he's actually slept with. "I'm going home."

"I'll take you." At any time before tonight, that would have been an offer I saw as sweet and endearing coming from him. I would have jumped at the chance to take him home into my bed.

I shake my head. "No." It's all I can manage. I just have to get out of here.

"You can't just leave," he pleads. "We can talk about this."

I hold my hand up as he approaches, warning him off. "I'm done."

Chapter 4

I can't believe you just bailed on him." Rebecca flips her damp hair back as she pulls the hairbrush through it.

My lips twist into a scowl. "What was I supposed to do?"

"You think he's still screwing them all?" She almost visibly winces when she asks the question.

I shrug my shoulders. "Don't know and don't care."

"Oh, you care, Jess." She pulls herself up off my bed and throws the towel she had her hair wrapped in, into my laundry hamper.

"I don't," I scoff. I can't, I want to say. When I held that phone in my hand and read all those messages I felt devastated. I can't explain to her that I was falling for him. Who the hell falls for a man they met in a club who fucks women in a room right above it? I'm too humiliated to admit I was developing feelings for Manhattan's biggest man whore. Correction. Boston and Manhattan's biggest man whore.

"Liar." She leans back down on the bed. "So you're done with Fingers for good?"

"Don't call him that," I whine. I don't need the constant reminder that Nathan fingered me to orgasm the first night I met him. My fate was sealed then. Why did I ever let Rebecca convince me to go back to that club the next night? "This is all your fault."

"My fault?" She smiles. "How is it my fault that your boyfriend is trying to set a world record for banging?"

"You're the one who dragged me to that club."

"I didn't throw you into bed with him. He's the one who worked his magic on you." She leans her shoulder on me. "You're spending too much time mourning the loss of him and his big dick."

"What?" I smirk.

"Get back in the saddle." She props herself up on her knees and whirls her hand above her head as if she's casting a lasso in the air. "Go out and find a new guy. Once you fuck him, Fingers will be a distant memory."

"It doesn't work that way." I laugh.

She flashes me a smile. "You won't know until you try. When you have a night off, we're going out dancing and I promise we won't go near his club."

***

"What's going on with you, Jess?" Drew taps me on the shoulder as I'm walking out the employee's exit after my evening shift.

I turn to briefly glance at him. He really is attractive, in a cute boy next door kind of way. Why hadn't I met him first before I fell into Nathan's bed that night? "Nothing. I'm good," I lie. I'm not good. It's been almost a week now since I had my face -off with Nathan in his hotel room and he hasn't come looking for me. Why do I care? Why do I want him to? It's not as though I want to climb back into bed with him. I just want the satisfaction of knowing he still wants me.

"You're feeling okay?" That's never a good question to ask a woman. Obviously, he thinks I don't look okay.

"Sure." Sure? You need something better than that, Jessica. He's cute, he's interested and some time with him would help erase Nathan from your mind. Just listen to Rebecca. Live a little.

His face comes into full view as he takes a step around me. "I want to kiss you."

I didn't hear that, did I? "Did you say you want to kiss me?"

His lips glide across mine in response. His hands jump to cradle my cheeks, tilting my head. I open my mouth, and a small moan filters out. He groans in response and pulls me tighter into his body. He's aroused, already. This sweet, uncomplicated man wants me just from a kiss.

"You're beautiful, Jess." I hear the words as I feel them on my lips.

"I'm not," I whisper back. I'm really not.

"Take me home with you." It's a breathless request that will chase away not only the ache in my heart, but the one that's consumed my body for the past week. I want to feel him. I want to know what it's like to be with a man who isn't focused on so many others. I just want to forget Nathan.

"I can't." The words betray my body. I can. I really can I want to say. I want to.

He lunges for me again and this time his kiss is heated, wanting and aggressive. His hands glide down my body, cupping my ass, pulling me into him. I try not to react to the feeling of him pressing against me. His cock is so hard. It would be so easy to just take him by the hand, and pull him into my bed and my body.

"Soon." It's a promise in a kiss. "I'll take you to dinner on Friday and then you'll decide."

I run both my hands up his lean, muscular chest, grabbing onto the collar of his chef's jacket. "It's a date."

Chapter 5

"Explain to me how you can be in Manhattan less than two months and have two hot guys falling all over you and all I get are the geeks from the tech department at work chasing after me?"

"Tech guys have mad oral skills," I offer. "You should check them out."

"It's your tits." She squeezes her breasts together and stares down at her less-than-ample cleavage. "If I had your tits, I would be beating men away with a stick."

"If you can afford this apartment," I begin as I swing my hand around her spacious bedroom. "You can afford big tits."

"You didn't buy those." She nods towards my breasts which are on full display at the moment in a pink lace bra.

"True, but everything has a price." I point towards a short red dress she has hanging in her closet. "Maybe that one?"

"That's not your color." She bounces off her bed. "Blue is better."

"Blue it is." I hold the short, blue halter dress she hands to me in front of myself as I look in the mirror. "He'll like it, right?"

She pulls my hair back over my shoulders as she stands behind me. "Use him, Jess."

I turn around quickly. "Use him?"

"Drew." She raises both brows. "Use him to forget about Fingers."

I frown at the mention of not only his nickname, but of him. "This has nothing to do with Nathan."

"It has everything to do with him," she corrects me. "You need to wash the taste of him away. This is your chance. Don't fuck it up."

***

"Do you always open your door dressed like that?"

I can't respond. What am I supposed to say? I swung the door open without checking who it was because I'm waiting for Drew to pick me up.

"Where are you going?" He pushes past me and darts into the apartment before I have a chance to stop him.

"Nathan," I say his name knowing it will hurt when it leaves my lips. I know that he's going to take some satisfaction in hearing it.

"Jessica, why are you wearing that?" It's too personal and harsh. I feel assaulted by his presence. I feel exposed. I didn't want to see him again. I sure as hell didn't want to see him when I'm wearing a dress like this.

"You need to go." My voice is so faint. "I have plans."

"Are you fucking someone else already?" There's no mistaking the frustration in his tone.

I start to move towards the door. I need him gone before Drew comes up to get me. "It's none of your business." I want him to believe the words. My life isn't his concern anymore. It never really was in the first place.

He catches my wrist in his grasp. "Like hell it's not my business."

I can't do this. I can't deal with him right now.

"I need to be inside you, Jessica." His eyes sweep over me. "I'm aching for you. Tell me how I can fix this."

"You miss having sex with me?" I ask, not because I need to know the answer, but I need to hear it, from him. I need the confirmation that all he misses is fucking me.

"More than I've missed anything in my life." He steps closer and touches my shoulder. "I think about the way my cock stretches you as I'm fucking you. I think about your beautiful mouth and what it feels like to shoot down your throat."

I don't move. I can't. Why aren't my feet listening to my brain?

"Do you know what I think about most of all, Jessica?" His fingers jump to my thigh. "I think about when I'm sucking on your sweet little, swollen clit and you come hard all over my face."

"No." I swat his hand away. Please, no.

"No?"

"Don't." I swallow past a hard lump in my throat so I can find my voice again. "Don't say that."

"It's all true." He leans in and his breath skirts over my neck. "I need you, Jessica. Tell me what to do. I'll do anything."

"Leave." I step back and look down at the floor. "Just go."

"I'm not going anywhere." His tone is measured and calm. "I've given you almost two weeks to come and talk to me and you haven't. You think I'm going to sit and wait forever?"

He was waiting for me? "You shouldn't have waited." I want to sound genuine. I want to sound as though I don't give a fuck if I ever talk to him again.

"What else am I supposed to do?" He reaches to touch me again and I take another step back. I'm running out of room to avoid him.

"You have a phone full of women lining up to sleep with you." The words startle me as they leave my own lips. I've tried so hard not to think about that phone and all those numbers. "Call up one of them if you need to get off."

He sighs heavily before pulling his hand across his mouth. "I threw that phone away. I don't have it anymore."

My heart leaps at the announcement but any joy is quickly replaced by the realization that my number never made it into his actual phone. He filed me in with all the other hundreds of women he fucked. "Why was my number in there?"

"It's complicated." He runs his hand through his hair, pushing it back from his forehead. "Your number is in here too." He pulls a smartphone from the pocket of his jeans. "You can check." He holds out the phone for me.

I don't reach for it. I can't. I can't start investing myself in this again. "It doesn't matter." I shake my head slightly trying to ward off any thought that this could actually work. "You should leave."

"Jessica." He leans forwards until his lips are hovering close to mine. "Let me make this right."

"You can't." I take in a deep breath. I have to calm down. "I can't do this anymore."

"Why not?" He reaches out and scoops my hand in his.

I feel weak from the contact. I can't want him still. Why does my body still react like this? "I saw that phone. I saw all those names." I'm instantly assaulted by the wave of pain I felt when I was scrolling through his contact list. "I'm just one of the Jessicas." I hold up my index finger. "Just one. Jessica R. That's who I am to you."

"That's not who you are." His hand squeezes mine. "Christ, please."

"I'm nothing." The words sound pathetic and pitiful. I don't want them to. I don't want to be that girl who cries because the guy didn't give her all the attention. We were just fuck buddies. That's how it started. That's all it ever was to him.

His gaze darts over my face. "You're everything. Don't you know that? You're fucking everything to me."

Chapter 6

"I'm not." The words leave my lips before I have time to temper the emotion that is coursing through them. They're true though, I'm not. I'm not everything to him.

"Jessica." His body stiffens as he scans my face. "You know how I feel."

I raise both brows in response. I know how he feels? Him? What about how I feel? "I know that you enjoy the company of a lot of different women. Everything on that phone just proved that to me."

"Fuck that phone." His soft tone tears into me. I'm raging inside. Everything that I'd held in for the past two weeks is rushing to the surface and he's standing here acting so calm and collected. I want to reach out and slap him across his unshaven face.

"How can you say that?" I bite past all of the emotions. "Do you know what it felt like? Looking at all those women's names? All of those messages?"

"It kills me that you saw that." His eyes pierce through me. "I keep thinking about how I'd feel if I found a phone filled with guy's numbers and messages talking about how they want to fuck you."

I rally some inner strength before I speak. "You'd never find that. That's not who I am." The words are meant to sting. That's why I shot them at him.

"I'm not that person anymore." He shields his mouth with his hand as if he's warding off something. Maybe a grimace or a wince? Maybe he's still proud of all his conquests and he's aching to crack a smile.

"When did you last sleep with a woman?" I don't want to keep beating this issue into the ground. I want him to finally admit that what he said in the bed that night when he told me I was different was just a litany of bullshit meant to convince me not to fuck anyone else.

"Right before I left for Boston." His tone is steady, and his gaze is unwavering. "When I fucked you slowly and you came all over my cock."

I resist the urge to moan right there on the spot. God, that was amazing. I've thought about that moment every day since I walked out of his hotel room two weeks ago.

"Before that? When?" I push. I want him to just admit that he's been seeing other women this entire time.

"It was the day before that when you sucked me off and I shot my load all over your beautiful breasts and then you rode my dick until you screamed my name."

I'm so aroused. My body is aching for his. Even knowing that he's been with that many women, I still want him. What the fuck is wrong with me?

"The time before that," he begins before he steps closer to me, "was on the kitchen table in my apartment. I bent you over and rammed my cock balls deep into that tight, sweet little body of yours. You couldn't even hold on. You came almost instantly."

I had. I remember. I'd gone to get a glass of water and he was right behind me, pushing me down, pulling up my dress and just taking me.

"When's the last time you fucked someone else?" I look up from the floor and directly into his eyes. "Don't bullshit me. Tell me when."

I see a flash of panic wash over him and my heart drops. Please don't say since you said all those beautiful things to me in your bed. Please don't let it be since then.

"When, Nathan." I push. I just want to know. I just want it to be over with.

"Cassie." He closes his eyes briefly before pulling them back up to lock on mine. "It was with Cassie."

Chapter 7

It's a lie. It's a goddamn, straight-in-my face, unbelievable lie.

"You're a fucking liar." I push my finger into his chest and he doesn't budge. "You know that's not true."

He pulls my hand into his in one swift motion. "Don't call me a liar," he seethes. "Ever, Jessica."

"You. Are. A. Liar," I spit the words out one-by-one, letting them roll off my tongue with languid grace. "A fucked up liar."

"You don't know me," he bites back. It's harsh, the tone petulant and rage filled.

"Exactly," I snipe. "All I know about you is that you're incredibly good in bed and you've been with more women than I can count. So many women that you can't even remember them all. "It's razor sharp and meant to pierce through him.

It does. He takes a step back as if I've physically struck him. "Enough." His hand darts up to ward me off.

"Enough?" I mimic him. "Enough, what? Enough of your goddamn lies? Why the fuck can't you just leave me alone? Why can't you just call another random and fuck her brains out so you forget about me?"

I see pain wash over his expression. His hand jumps in the air as if he's about to grab hold of me, but his jaw clenches and his hand freezes. "Jessica." It's barely a whisper. I can hear something skirting the edges of it. I can't tell what it is.

"Nathan, we're so far past being done with this." I move to the door but he's on me before I have time to react.

"Jessica, please." His voice cracks and a small part of me feels sympathy for him. I can't do that. I can't let him get to me that way. It's all about actions. Everything he's ever said to me stands in the shadow of that hotel suite filled with liquor and condoms and that phone. That goddamn phone that was bursting with endless pleas begging him to crawl back into bed. All those women, all that sex.

"I'll never forget what I saw on that phone." I close my eyes as if that will shudder away all the memories of those names, of the numbers and of the painfully intimate messages.

"I can't change my past." His eyes narrow. "This is killing me. You have to let me back in."

"Back in?" I exhale sharply, my pulse racing. "Back into this?" I pull my hand over my body.

"No." His tone is icy, hard and calm. "Back into here." He pushes a finger against my chest. "You were feeling everything I was."

I can't respond. He's right. I was feeling everything he said he was. I was falling for him at breakneck speed until I crashed into that hotel room and everything changed.

A knock at the door jars us both. Drew's timing couldn't be any worse. He's waiting for me. He's waiting to take me on a real date. He's waiting to take me to bed at the end of the night. He's going to help me get over Nathan once and for all.

"I need to…"

"You're going out with him, aren't you?" He cuts me off, his voice is even and tempered. "It's the chef, isn't it?"

I nod. "Drew asked me… well, he asked me," I stutter unable to clearly say that I'm going out on a date with another man.

"Have you fucked him yet?"

"No." I shouldn't have answered. This isn't his business. Anything I do with Drew tonight isn't about Nathan. Except it all is. I'm only going on this date to forget the way it feels when Nathan kisses me, when he's inside of me, and when he says things that make me believe I'm special.

"You want to?" The question is ripe with pain. Not only for him, but for me too. *I don't want to sleep with Drew* I want to say. I want Nathan to erase everything I saw in that room from my memory so I can feel like I did two weeks ago. I want to float back into his bed and his arms and feel like nothing exists but the two of us.

"Don't ask me that."

He steps towards me until his breath is skirting my forehead. "If I would have found you first, I wouldn't have fucked any of them. Don't use his body to get back at me."

Chapter 8

"That guy that was at your apartment is intense." Drew takes a leisurely drink from the wine glass in front of him. "He was at the club the first night I saw you. What's his deal?"

"He's a lawyer," I jeer. I don't want to talk about Nathan right now. When I'd opened the door to greet Drew, Nathan had pushed past him and didn't look back.

He surveys my face as if he's trying to read between the lines of what I'm saying and feeling. "Did you hook up?"

Of course he'd ask me that. Why does it seem as though every man in Manhattan has to know about the sex life of every other man? "A few times." I don't see any reason to lie. It's not as though it matters at this point.

"Is that still going on?"

Why the inquisition I want to say. We're out on our first date, enjoying a pre-dinner glass of wine and Nathan is already spoiling the evening for me. "That's over," I say it clearly.

"What was he doing at your place?" He tips the glass in my direction before he takes another sip.

"Just talking." I know I shouldn't be irritated by his questions but I am. We're not twenty minutes into our evening and he already knows way too much about my personal life.

"I don't share, Jess." The words are misplaced.

"You don't share?" I repeat them back hoping I misheard them. Who does he think he is? The second coming of Nathan Moore? Why do these men insist on marking their territory before I'm ever served an entrée?

"If we're going to do this." His hand waves over the table. "You can't be around a guy like that."

I'm insulted, I haven't even finished my first glass of wine and he was setting ground rules. "We're just out having dinner."

"You know I want to sleep with you." Sex. Do men in this city do anything other than live, breathe and talk about sex?

"I was hoping we could get through our dinner first," I say it half-teasingly. "Why are you being so serious?"

"My last girlfriend fucked me over pretty good." He downs the rest of his wine. "I'm not going down that road again. I don't want a woman who isn't ready to be exclusive."

Shit. He's been hurt and now I'm going to pay the price for that when all I wanted was to use him to get over my last relationship.

"I don't want anything serious." I exhale. "I'm just looking for some fun."

"Fun?"

"Just fun," I offer. What am I supposed to say to him? I want to make you come inside of me so I can chase away each and every memory I have of Nathan's cock?

"I'm looking for more than fun. I don't share." He doesn't temper his intentions at all. I wouldn't be surprised if he dropped to his knee and pulled an engagement ring out of his pocket right now.

"I'm sorry I didn't know," I wince when I say the words. How could I have known? He kissed me the other night like a man hungry for my body. I thought he wanted to fuck. I thought we'd jump into bed together, roll around a few times and I'd get over my Nathan hurdle.

"If you cut him off, I'll be waiting." He doesn't even glance in my direction.

"I'm not hungry anymore," I say in a breathless whisper.

He motions for the waiter. "I'll take you home."

***

"He wouldn't fuck you because you wouldn't be his girlfriend?" The words sound just as ludicrous coming out of Rebecca's mouth as they sounded in my mind.

"I guess." I shrug my shoulders. "It was humiliating."

"I'll be his girlfriend." She winks at me. "Hell, I'll marry him and have his babies if he goes down on me. Have you seen his lips? Christ, they make me weep every time I see them."

"Every time you see them?" I cock a brow. "How often do you see them?"

"Only twice." She taps one finger. "That first time at the club when he was grinding on you and then two nights ago after he dropped you off."

"You took the time to study his lips?" I almost laugh out loud.

"Don't say you didn't notice them, Jess." She tips her head to the side. "Unless you were still thinking about Fingers."

"He was here." I point to the floor of the apartment. "Right before Drew showed up."

"No way." She doesn't even try and temper the shock in her voice. "What the hell? Why?"

I shrug slightly as I shake my head. "Trying to convince me that he's changed."

"He'll never change." She bolts out of her chair. "We need to change though. We're going clubbing tonight."

"No." I feel bone weary from my shift earlier today. It had taken every ounce of strength I had to avoid looking at Drew for the entire eight hours. He's attractive and he wants me. Maybe I should just be what he needs so I can get what I need from him. That's not fair though. I know it logically, but my body has other ideas.

"Yes." She pulls my hand into hers. "Tonight is the night Fingers becomes a distant memory."

Chapter 9

"There was this moment, when you first walked into the club, and I swear I felt like I'd been holding my breath forever waiting for you."

I imagined that. I've had two drinks and my pulse is racing from the vodka in the spritzers. My hair is damp from dancing. My dress is so tight. I don't know why I chose this one. It's black, short, and cut way too low. My breasts are round, plump and practically spilling out of the top of it. I'm doing everything in my power to forget Nathan, yet I can hear his voice in my head, saying the things I long to hear him say.

"Jessica. I was empty until then."

His voice sounds so soft, so close. Why can't I just forget him? Why can't I make it all stop so I can move on and pretend it never happened?

"I think about your body all the time. It was made to be fucked just by me."

I close my eyes and feel a hand curve around my waist. It's strong, big, and it's pressing on my stomach. I'm being pulled into a man. I can feel his chest. He's muscular, large, and much taller than me. He's aroused. I can feel his rigid cock pressing into me from behind. He's going to help me. He's going to make me forget.

I turn quickly and his lips are on mine. He's greedy. His kiss is soft, and sensual. His tongue is coursing over mine with a heated touch. I feel his hand on my thigh. I don't flinch. I want this. Even in the middle of this crowded club, I want these hands on me, taking me to the edge, showing me how much I'm wanted.

"Christ, I have to taste you." His voice is in my ear. "Now, Jessica."

My eyes fly open. I can't see his face. It's buried in my neck. "No, please," I say it without any meaning. I want this. I want to feel his body. I want to taste his skin, and his arousal. I don't care. I just want.

"This way." He pulls his hand around my waist. We weave through the crowd, the lights flashing, the music pumping, my heart racing.

Suddenly we're in a corridor with so many doors. He opens one and we slip in. The music is tamed, the lighting is dim.

"Goddamn you." His words bite through me as his hands pull on my dress, inching it up my thighs. "Fuck you're so hot."

I'm against the wall and he's on his knees before I can react. I slam my head back and push my hips towards him. I have to tell him to stop. I need him to…

"Christ, you're incredible." His tongue runs hot over my folds and I feel a moan stretch through my throat. It's just sex, Jessica. Just take it. That's all it is.

"Lick it," I demand. "Lick me."
He dives in and pulls his tongue across my wetness, moaning into my flesh. "Ah, fuck, Jessica, fuck."

I tangle my hands in his hair, pulling on the locks, guiding his mouth over my core. "Make me come, Nathan." I pull his name across my lips, slowly, carefully, knowing that it will spur him on.

He nods just as one finger slides into me. "Take it," he whispers." Use me."

I buck at the words and the sensations. I pull harder on his hair, wanting him to consume me. I haven't come in so long. I've thought about his mouth for days. I can't stop thinking about it. I'll never stop.

"Like that," I purr. "Lick it like that."

He eagerly acquiesces and laps at my clit. He traces his tongue over it and I slam my head back. Nothing feels as good as this. Nothing will ever feel like this.

"You're so good." His voice is barely audible. "I'll never get enough of you. Your body is perfect. I can't wait to slide my cock into you and fuck you until you scream my name."

I come at the promise of his beautiful, wide cock inside of me. My orgasm is fast and violent. My body bucks against the wall and into him. He sucks, licks and pulls at me until I feel another slower climax roll through me.

Chapter 10

"You're a lightweight." He traces his hand across my forehead.

"The doctor says I weigh a little too much for my height." I shrug my shoulders. "I like cake though."

He laughs so hard that his head rolls back. "You're hilarious."

I blush at the compliment. "I'm not a lightweight."

"How many drinks did you have?" He adjusts the blanket around my body.

"Maybe two?" I swallow. "Maybe more?"

"Maybe a lot more." He smiles down at me. "You need to sleep it off."

I nod. I do need to. I'm already feeling a headache barreling down on me. "Can I ask you something?"

He moves the glass of water he got for me closer to the edge of the nightstand so I can reach it. "Sure. What is it?"

"It's about the club." I need to ask. The question has been almost dripping off my tongue ever since we got in the taxi to come back to the apartment. I waited until he got me into my bed before I found the courage to ask.

"What about it?" He cocks his head.

"I think something happened." I felt it. I know I came when he was licking me. I know it was real. Why does it all seem so hazy now?

"Like what?" The grin on his face isn't helping.

"I think I did something." That's vague. God, that's way too vague. I'm so embarrassed. I should just say it.

"Something?" He's not going to make this easier for me. I'm going to have to spell it all out.

"I..I…" My head is pounding. I hope the aspirin he gave me a few minutes ago is going to curb this headache or I won't be able to drag myself out of bed tomorrow.

"Something did happen," he says it so quietly. He must know my head is about to explode.

"With you and me?" I hold my breath waiting for him to answer. I never saw his face. I just felt. It was so much.

"No." He turns the small lamp on my bedside table off. "It wasn't me, Jess."

"Bryce," I call as he stands to walk out the door. "Was he there?"

"He was there."

***

"Jessica Roth," I repeat. "It's not Ross. It's Roth." I pull my tongue between my teeth to accentuate the sound.

"Jessica Ross is here."

Bitch. Why the hell won't she say my name right?

"Jessica," he calls from the door of his office.

I curse under my breath as I walk past the receptionist towards Nathan. Why does he look extra hot today? His hair is falling onto his forehead, he hasn't shaved. Christ, why am I thinking about how great he looks when I should be thinking about how I'm going to ask him if he went down on me at that club?

"You look beautiful." He closes the door behind me. "To what do I owe the pleasure?"

Pleasure. Is that a hint? Is he hinting that he rocked my world in the club last night?

"I need to ask you something?" I push past him to sit in one of his office chairs. My legs are trembling, I have to gain some emotional traction or I'm going to skid out of control.

"Anything." He leans against his desk. This isn't working. His crotch is right at my eye level.

"It's just that…" I toy with a loose thread on the seam of my jeans. How am I supposed to bring this up?

"Are you feeling better?" There's a hint of amusement in the question.

"Better?" I parrot back. "What do you mean?"

He kneels down slowly so his face is right at my level. I don't move. I can't. His icy blue eyes are staring directly into me. "You know what I mean."

"I don't." I can't look at him. His lips are so perfect. They're so soft and pliable. I wonder if he uses lip balm. Jessica, shit. Focus.

"Jessica." He leans forward to grab both arms of the chair, trapping me in place.

I look down. "What?"

"I haven't washed my face since then." His breath wafts over my neck. He's so close to me now.

"Since when?" I can't look up. I won't.

His finger glides softly over my jaw as he tilts my head up until our lips almost meet. "Since you came all over my face last night. Twice."

My breath hitches. "That was real," I whisper.

"That was real." He shifts so his lips are hovering over mine. "I ate you right there in the club. You came so hard. You wanted me so badly."

"I don't…" What don't you, Jessica? You don't know? You don't remember? You don't know how to resist him? Bingo. That's it.

"Why were you there?" I look into his eyes. He was there trolling for someone and saw me. He was there looking for a woman to fuck. He was there because he'd given up on me.

His mouth twitches slightly but his gaze never leaves mine. "I followed you there."

My brow pops up. "No." I shake my head. "You were there looking for someone and saw me."

He moves closer still and I'm locked within his arms. I can only lean back into the chair. "I was coming to your apartment and saw you getting in a taxi with your friends. I followed you to that club, I watched you grinding all over other men. I saw you trying to drink away the memory of my touch and then I took you in that room to make you come because I've been aching to taste you for days."

I swallow hard. I can't rid myself of the lump at the back of my throat. "Nathan, I can't do this."

"You can't be away from me." His lips barely touch mine. "You were begging me to fuck that sweet, tight little body right there in that room. You were clawing at my pants. You couldn't get to my dick fast enough."

I blush at the words. I can't remember. I don't know. Did I do that? "I don't remember," I confess breathlessly. I can't think, let alone breathe, when he's this close to me.

"As badly as I wanted to fuck you right there, against that wall. As much as I wanted to hear you scream my name when my cock stretched you to your limits, I couldn't do it." His tongue glides slowly over his bottom lip.

"Why?" I have to literally hold tight to the arms of the chair to restrain myself from locking my hands around his neck and kissing him.

He exhales and his sweet breath rushes across my cheek. "When I fuck you, Jessica, every time I slide my cock into you, you're going to remember it."

My sex clenches at the words. I have to close my eyes to let the feelings course through me. I swear I could come just from listening to him talk about fucking me.

"Do you want me to fuck you now?" His lips skirt softly over mine and my eyes dart open. He's so close.

Yes, yes please. "We can't," my goddamn mouth says.

"We can't?" His finger runs a path across my collar bone before dipping into my cleavage. "Be more specific. Why can't we?"

I pull my hands up to rub my face. Maybe I'm back in my bed and this is some kind of hangover, erotic dream. Although if that were the case, he'd be telling me that he wants his cock in my mouth by now.

"I would give anything to slide my cock between those perfect pink lips." Wait. What?

"Nathan." It's less of a statement than a request.

"You're scared," he whispers into my lips. "You're scared I'm going to hurt you."

I nod. I am scared of that. I'm scared I'll let him back in and he'll fuck me over and not in a good way.

"Do you remember what I said to you at the club last night?" He runs the pad of his thumb across my lips.

"About waiting forever for me?" My voice cracks. I've replayed those words in my mind since I heard them.

"They're true. I've waited forever for you."

"You say things like that, but…" my voice stops. But what?

"I can't fuck anyone else." The words are abrasive and bold. "That isn't going to happen, Jessica."

"You don't mean it." I push back against him. I need to leave before he convinces me there's more to him than a man after a piece of ass.

"I mean every word."

Chapter 11

"So you're saying Fingers is a one woman man now?" Rebecca stares at me across the table in the crowded diner she chose to meet at for lunch.

"So he says," I try not to sound discouraged. When I left his office an hour ago I didn't stop to turn back around to look at him.

She takes a bite of the sandwich she ordered. "This is delicious. Not as good as what you make, but second best."

I smile at the awkward compliment. "There's just so much about him I don't understand." Understatement alert. That doesn't even begin to cover how confused I am about him. I have so many questions but the minute I start asking them, I'll be reinvested in the relationship and with his track record and the line of women he's been through, the effort just isn't worth it.

"So he went down on you at the club?" The words are muffled as she chews through another bite of the sandwich.

"What?" I almost drop the spoon of soup I'm holding near my mouth. "How did you know?"

"I saw him pulling you into one of the private rooms," she says it so nonchalantly as if it's an everyday occurrence in her world.

I shake my head to chase away the thought of Nathan on his knees, his face buried between my thighs. "Private rooms?"

"Did Fingers pop your private room cherry?" The fact that several people turn to look solidifies my first thought that she's talking way too loud.

"You practically screamed that." I point out. "I've never been in a private room before." I've never heard of a private room before. I feel like I lived in a cave before I landed in Manhattan.

"All club members have access."

The words hit me with the full force of a baseball bat. "Members?"

"You get special perks if you're a member of certain clubs." She stares down at the rest of her sandwich. I can tell she's having an internal dialogue about whether or not she should devour it.

"He had to be a club member to get in that room?" The gravity of that statement is sinking in slowly, coursing over my brain and seeping into my heart.

"You need a key card." She picks up her oversize purse and starts rifling through it. "See." Her face lights up as she pulls three separate cards from her wallet. "I'm a member of all three of these."

"Nathan had to be a member to get into that room last night?" Why am I asking her that? I know the answer.

"Absolutely." She picks up the sandwich. "That club just opened. I'm not even a member of it yet."

***

"Why are you such an asshole?" I ask it without any emotion. At least I don't think there's any emotion in it.

"Is this a trick question?" He swings the door of his apartment open wider so I can walk past him.

I survey the room. The last time I was in here, I felt safe, adored and special. Now I just feel like Jessica R again. "It's not a trick. You're an asshole."

He rubs his temple with his index finger. "Jessica. Do you want a drink?"

The question feels completely misplaced. "I have a hangover."

"Right." He taps the tip of my nose before he pours himself a glass of bourbon. "So you think I'm an asshole?"

"You took me into a private room last night." I'm just going to launch into this without a parachute. Bombs away, Jessica.

He takes a heavy swallow of the liquid. "Don't tell me you didn't enjoy it." The smirk that accompanies the statement pulls at the edges of my anger.

"That's irrelevant. We're talking about the private room." I need him to stay focused on something other than sex for twenty seconds.

He scratches his forehead. "Jessica, what's this about?"

Why does he have to say my name like that? Why didn't I tell him my name was Jess? If I had done that it wouldn't pull up so many feelings each time he said it. "You have a key card to get into that room, don't you?"

He studies my face. His expression is so indifferent. I can't read it at all. "I do, yes."

"Nathan." I feel my knees buckle slightly so I lower myself to a chair. "Nathan," I repeat his name.

"No." His voice is serious, the tone uncompromising. "Jessica, no. Don't think that."

"Think what?" I can feel my stomach knotting. "You have a key."

He slams the glass down with a thud on the bar before he's in front of me. "Jessica, listen to me."

I want to cover my ears. I don't want to hear another lie seep out of his mouth. "I just wanted to know if you had a key." It's the truth, that's all I came here for. I just wanted him to acknowledge that he had a key because he takes women in there to fuck them when he's at that club.

He moves swiftly to where his suit jacket is hung by the door on a coat rack. I watch silently as he rummages through the inner pocket, pulling out his wallet. "I need to show you this."

"You don't have to show me anything." I'm on my feet. I have to walk out of his door and never look back at him again. I can't keep doing this to myself. I can't keep circling back thinking he's going to magically change into a decent human being.

"God, this is so fucked up." His voice is barely recognizable. There's so much raw emotion in it. "Jessica, wait."

"No." I brush past him and reach for the doorknob. "I'm going."

"Look." He shoves a key card in my face. It's so close my eyes can't register anything beyond the blue and yellow hues of the card. "Take it. Just look."

"I don't want to." I turn the door handle. "You're never going to change."

"Look at the god dammed card, Jessica." His hand covers mind and twists the door handle back into place. "You're not going anywhere until you look at it."

Chapter 12

"You joined the club yesterday?" The details don't register. Why did he join yesterday?

"Jessica, fuck, please understand this," he's pleading. His hand is pulling on the hem of my sweater. "I can't resist you. I literally almost come when you walk in a room. I'm hard all the time when I think about you."

"Yesterday?" I repeat again.

"Shit." He moves away from me and starts pacing. "This is going to sound so fucked up."

"What?"

"I've come every day since you were in the hotel suite. I've jacked off thinking about you." He nods towards my body. "I'm so hard right now, Jessica. I can't control it. Tell me you get that."

I shake my head. "No. I don't."

He bows his head and pulls in a heavy breath. I can see his chest heave under the fabric of his light blue dress shirt. Small beads of perspiration are gathering on his forehead.

"Tell me," I spit out. "Nathan, say it."

"Your body is like a drug to me. Christ, it's like I'm fucking addicted to everything about you. The smell of your skin, the taste of you, how tight you are when you're gripping on my cock and I'm pumping myself into you." He leisurely runs his hand along the outline of his erection. "I could jerk off right now. Seriously, you make me so hot."

"The room." I want him to explain. I need that.

"You're going to hate me." His voice wavers with the confession. "You're going to walk out of here if I tell you."

"Nathan." My voice cracks. He's going to tell me he fucked someone else yesterday in that room after I left because he was thinking about me.

He reaches behind where he's standing to lower himself onto the arm of a chair. "I came to see you at your apartment. Remember I told you that?"

I nod.

"I spent all day in bed before that. Stroking, thinking, coming. I had to get you out of my system. I couldn't help myself."

"What did you do?" Why does it matter to me? Wasn't the phone proof enough that he can't keep his cock out of commission for more than a few hours?

"I don't know how many times I came but it wasn't enough." He pulls his hand over his face. "This is just so fucked up."

I rest my face in my palms. I need to walk out of here. I need to end this right now.

"I got that room at the club so I could fuck you there." The words spill out so quickly they fall into one another in a twisted heap.

"What?"

"Jessica, please." His voice is soft and tempered. "Don't hate me for this."

"You got that room at the club to fuck me?" My eyes widen. I can feel them. I'm pulled back to the club in that moment. Pulled back to when he reached around to grab my waist. My body knew it was him. My body wanted him just as much as he wanted me.

"I signed up for the membership when you were dancing." He pulls his large frame up so he's standing again. "I just wanted to pull you into a room and slide into you. I needed to feel you around me. I haven't been able to focus or think straight in weeks."

"You knew you'd have sex with me there?" I'm both appalled and aroused by the epiphany.

"When you walked out of your apartment in that dress, Jessica." His breathing stalls. "I almost lost it on the street."

"I just went there to have fun. I wanted to forget…" I can't confess that to him.

"You wanted to forget me?" There's no surprise woven into the question. He knows that's what I've been trying to do for weeks.

"I can't deal with this." I pull my hands to my mouth hoping that will stop the rush of emotions I feel. "You can't do things like this."

"Jessica." He's right next to me now. "I can't stop what I feel."

"It's all just sex." I want him to see that. I need him to see that everything between us centers on sex.

"You're wrong." His stance hardens. I've offended him. I can tell.

"I'm right," I counter. I look up into his face. There's so much emotion in his eyes. I can't read it all. I can't grasp what he's feeling.

"If it was all about sex, I would have hiked that tight dress up, slid my cock into you and fucked you hard until you screamed over and over again."

I take a step back out of sheer need. My body betrays me when he's so crude and direct. I know my breathing has increased. I can feel my pulse racing.

"You did have sex with me." I push back. "You licked my…"

"I wanted to hear you come. I crave the sound of that. There isn't a sweeter sound in this entire world than you when you're on the edge of an orgasm. I would kill to hear that." His breath catches before he continues, "I knew in that room after I heard you come twice that it was all I needed. I didn't need to get off. I didn't need to shoot my load between these perfect lips." He lazily runs the pad of his thumb over my parted lips. "I didn't need to feel my cock sliding into you. I knew then that the craving, the addiction, this never ending need that I have here…" He hits himself squarely on his hard chest with a fist. "Isn't about my cock. It's not about my need. It's all about you."

Chapter 13

"You've seen him again, haven't you?" Drew hands me another tray of carrots to peel. Before our awkward almost date he told me that he was recommending that I be moved up to dessert prep. My refusal to be exclusive with him meant that I'd be cleaning vegetables for the foreseeable future.

I toss the peels from the last batch into the bin for composting. "We're not going to talk about him." We aren't. The mere fact that I can't even wrap my head around what's happening with Nathan and I, is enough to keep me from trying to explain it to anyone else.

"You know that he's always at the clubs, right?" The words are meant to hit me bluntly in the face. They do. I don't turn to look at him. I can't. I'm certain right now my expression is a mixture of anger and disappointment.

I slowly slide the peeler across the carrot. "You don't know him."

"I saw him at the club for months before I met you there." If his comment is meant to enrage me, he's hit a home run.

"Drew." I turn around and dangle the carrot only mere inches from his nose. "What's your problem?"

He bats it away and we both watch it tumble to the floor. "Guys like that are bad for girls like you."

I feel like I'm listening to my father give me *the talk* before I went to high school. "I'm a big girl. I can take care of myself."

He smirks. "You're just like all the rest of them."

"The rest of who?" My eyes briefly land on the peeler in my hand. If I don't start getting along with him, I'm never going to move up the internal ladder in the kitchen of Axel NY.

He reaches forward to run his hand down the front of my chef's jacket. I don't miss how his hand lingers a touch longer than it should near my breasts. "Jess. I'm saying this strictly as your friend."

I nod. "What is it?" The carrots unfortunately aren't going to peel themselves and I'd like to take a break sometime this year so I need him to spit out whatever vile thing is sitting impatiently on the edge of his tongue.

"You're like really..." His nostrils flare slightly as he leans in very close to me. "You're really ripe. You have this aura that screams, I want you to fuck me."

I push back away from him so harshly that I almost tumble backwards into the large sink I'm assigned to work at. "You can't say those things to me."

"He fucked you because your body was asking for it." His tongue glides slowly over his bottom lip. "It was screaming the same thing to me when we danced that night and when we had a drink after I got you this job."

There it was. The icing on the Drew cake. He thinks I owe him because he set me up for an interview.

"You know this is completely inappropriate, right?" I glance behind him to where the kitchen manager is standing, staring at us.

"I know that once he's done with you and he's moved on to someone new, you're going to come crawling back to me."

"Don't bet on it," I mutter under my breath as I turn back around.

***

"Who knew Drew had it in him?" Rebecca turns the corner and almost walks face first into a man walking briskly down Broadway.

"He's a creep." I pull my hair into my hand. The wind today isn't making it easy to get around Manhattan on foot. I shrug. "It's weird. I swear he has this inner issue with Nathan. Like he's completely pissed off with him over something else and he's projecting that onto me."

She stops dead in her tracks. "When did you become Dr. Phil?"

I laugh at loud at the comparison. "I don't have a moustache." I push my lips out.

"You should find a new job." She weaves her way through a throng of school kids walking towards us.

"No way." I raise my voice so it carries over the traffic noise. "I need that job and he can go fuck himself."

"I'll volunteer. He can fuck me. I'm totally into hard-ass, arrogant, douche bag chefs."

Chapter 14

"Christ. Jessica. Jesus." The words tumble from his mouth and into mine. "I swear to God I could come right now."

I lean back and ram my hips down onto his cock. A small moan ripples through my body. "Only this one time, Nathan."

"Sure, whatever the fuck you say." He raises his arms above his head to grip the back of the couch. The sight of his biceps flexing only pushes me closer to the edge.

"You work out." I don't mean to say it out loud. Why would I say that?

"I do." His eyelids flutter open briefly to soak in the sight of my naked body. "Fuck me harder."

I don't need the coaxing. I push my body forward and grab the couch too. I slide my hips back and forth along him, gliding his cock into me. "I can't believe it feels this good."

"Believe it." His hands jump from the couch to my thighs. "You're so wet. Christ, so wet."

"You know I came here just to fuck." The words are raw and unapologetic. They're true. After listening to him tell me on the phone how he was going to fuck me if he ever got the chance, I got in a taxi and knocked on the door of his apartment. Now, twenty minutes later, I'm on the brink of my third orgasm.

"I don't give a shit why you came here." He smiles through clenched teeth.

I groan as he pushes my body back so he can run the pad of his thumb over my clit. "It's only this one time."

"It's not." He pushes his hips up from the couch in a lazy circle. "I'm so fucking deep right now."

"So deep," I repeat back. "I can't fuck you again."

"Shut up, Jessica." His hand bolts to my head and he pulls my lips into his. "Shut up and fuck me."

I raise my hips at the sound of the challenge. I push back down, hard and fast and he moans so loudly, it reverberates through me. I push back and then forth again clenching my sex around him.

"Christ, this is my heaven." He throws his head back onto the couch again, his eyelids closing.

I lean back, resting my hands on his powerful thighs as I glide my body back over his. I pull myself up and then drive myself back down over and over again.

"I'm going to come." His breath is barely more than a whisper. "I'm going to fucking come so hard."

I still as he pulls tightly on my hips, pushing his body deeper into mine. A deep, guttural groan flows out of him as he clings tightly to me.

"Please, Nathan." I grasp onto his shoulders. "It was one time."

"Like hell." He pulls me quickly from him, pulling the condom off with deft ease. "You're going to come until you see that you can't live without this."

I pull away. "I came. Twice, please."

He picks my body up so effortlessly, twisting it around so I'm kneeling on the couch. I feel him slide to the floor on his knees behind me. "I'm going to eat you until you come over and over again."

"Nathan." Why am I pretending to resist him? I'm the one who came here for this. I'm the one who can't stop thinking about that night at the club.

"I love this body. I love you." He plunges his tongue into me just as the last word leaves his lips. He didn't say that. No. He couldn't have said that.

Chapter 15

"You're sure he said it?"

"I heard it. I'm sure." I toss some mixed greens into a bowl. "He said he loves me."

She points towards a package of cherry tomatoes. "Use them all. I love those little things."

"See that's my point." I wave the large knife in the air.

She ducks in mock fear. "Hey, watch it. That point might kill me."

"Sorry." I laugh. "See how you love the little tomatoes." I toss a bunch in a bowl and rinse them under cool water. "He loves me like that."

"He loves you like a tomato?" Her face twists into confusion. "That's strange, even for Fingers."

"No," I snicker. "He just said it in the moment. It wasn't based in reality. I mean you're not in love with the tomatoes."

"Why are you trying to convince yourself that he doesn't love you?"

I feel the weight of the question bore into me. "Men like that don't fall in love. They just don't."

***

"This isn't a date." I feel the need to qualify it.

He stares at me over his wine glass. "Christ, you're full of bullshit lately."

"Shut up." I take a big swallow from my own glass before I realize I better slow down. "I can't drink too much."

"Because you'll end up sitting on my face in the cab on the way back to my place?" He raises his glass before he takes a sip.

I pull my hand over my mouth to stifle a laugh. He's likely right though. "No. I just want to stay clear minded. We have to talk about a few things."

"Do I still have to pay for this even though it's not a date?" He raises a brow playfully.

"I can't afford to eat here."

"You work here."

"I can barely afford to eat sandwiches on what they pay me." I glance back towards the kitchen. I didn't bother to check the schedule to see if Drew was working tonight. I'm hopeful he's got the night off too. I don't want to have to listen to him tell me why I shouldn't be seeing Nathan.

"What is it, if it's not a date?" He takes a bite of the overpriced salad the waiter just placed in front of him.

"Two people, who are kind of friends, talking." That seems about right to me.

"So talk, friend." He motions towards me with his fork.

"Why did you take your sister to the hotel suite that night?" I want to start at the beginning, or at the very least, the beginning of when things fell apart.

"Why do we need to talk about that?" He takes another hearty bite of the salad. "Do you make this when you're working?"

I shake my head. "I prep the carrots that are in the salad."

"They're the best part."

"You left for Boston and then you suddenly came back with your sister." It's not even a question. It's a lame statement.

"Why do you think I brought her here?"

"Stop being a lawyer."

"I can't." He pushes the plate away. "This tastes like dirt. Not the carrots though."

"Why, Nathan?" I need to know. Other than that brief exchange in the hotel room when I thought she was his next conquest, I've heard nothing about her since.

He reaches for my wine glass after downing what's left in his. "I can't believe I have to say this."

"It's the truth, right?" I feel the need to stress that.

"Christ, Jessica." He leans across the table to put his hand over mine. "I don't lie to you. Get that, okay?"

I don't respond. I just want the answer. I raise my brow in expectation.

"I brought them here to meet you." His voice is soft and sullen. It's hard to distinguish each word within the hum of the busy restaurant.

"No, don't say that." I push back from the table. Please don't say that. It means I fucked things up worse than I imagined that night.

He leans back in his chair and pulls his hands over his face before he lets out a deep sigh. "I couldn't shut up about you. I just wanted them to see you in the flesh."

"So you brought them back to New York?"

"I did," he says it with finality as if that's supposed to be the end of the conversation.

I push the plate of salad that's in front of me away. I have absolutely no appetite. I study his face, trying to read him. There are so many things beneath the surface and I can't place any of them.

"Jessica." He taps his finger on the table. "Listen to me."

That's all I've been doing all night. It's all I want to do. I want to listen until I hear him say he loves me again.

"I took them to the hotel so they could stay there." He reaches across the table to cradle my hand in his. "I was going to come to your place to take you home with me for the night. But then you did that whole breaking and entering felony thing and everything went to shit."

"You wanted me to meet your family?" I whisper the question.

"I needed you to meet my family." He motions to the waiter to refill both of our now empty wine glasses.

"Why didn't you tell me that?" I sit expectantly waiting for an answer while the waiter slowly pours the wine.

The dim hum of a cell phone breaks the silence between us. Nathan reaches inside his suit pocket to retrieve his phone. He doesn't even glance at the screen before he quiets it. "I'm crazy about you." He pushes the phone aside before he takes my hand again. "I don't know how to do this the right way." His free hand waves in the air over both of our heads. "I wanted my sister and Travis to see what I see in you. Simple."

It wasn't simple. None of it was.

Chapter 16

"You told me you only let three men fuck you." His voice is low and raspy.

I nod.

"How many cocks have you sucked?" He pulls lightly on the roots of my hair. "Christ, slow down, Jessica. Slow. It. Down." I lean back on my heels and pull my tongue over the wide crest of the head of his cock. I lap at it, listening to him spurring me on.

"Who could ever give this up?" He leans back into the mattress with both hands still nestled in my hair. "I'll never let this go."

I move my head down swiftly, pulling the length of him into me. I'm rewarded with a deep growl.

"You know exactly what I need," he pants. "Stroke it."

I wrap my left hand around the thick root, stroking it slowly and methodically as I suck just on the head. "It's so beautiful."

"You're so beautiful." His hips snap back as a single drop of pre cum seeps out. I twirl it over my tongue and run it along my bottom lip.

"Jesus." He stares at me. "I could come just from watching that."

I moan as he pushes my head down again and I glide my lips over him. I snake my hands up and down slowly, milking him as I pull him in and out of my mouth.

"I can't stand it," he growls. "It's so fucking good."

I pump harder, wanting him to find his release. My tongue soaks in the taste of him, my eyes glued to his face.

"I'm going to come." His body stiffens and I brace myself for it. I love the taste of him. I love how it makes me feel when I feel it inside of me.

I moan as he yanks me up with both of his arms. "Nathan, please." I want to finish. I need to.

"I can't." He flips both of us over effortlessly until he's hovering above me. "Christ, I want to fuck you so much right now."

I shake my head. "No condom." I can't. I just can't. Not after seeing the phone. I can't let him inside of me like this.

He leans back on his heels and I know he's going to get up from the bed. "I'll get..."

"Nathan," my voice is soft and gritty. My hand is gliding over my wet folds. "Please."

"Fuck." He leans back and strokes his cock while he watches me circle my clit with my own finger. "Touch yourself, baby. Do it."

I close my eyes and let my head fall to the side as I feel the pleasure wash through me.

"Open your eyes, Jessica," he demands. "Open them."

I push them open and I'm rewarded with the sight of him hovering over me. He's so beautiful. So strong, so steely.

"Nathan." His name escapes my lips. "Nathan."

I feel the tip of his cock touch my clit and I push my hips back into the bed.

"No." I shake my head.

"I won't." His lips melt over mine. "Trust me."

I moan through him when I feel the very tip of his cock circle my swollen bud. "Oh, God, please." I buck my hips closer. I need to feel more.

He strokes his heavy cock in his palm as he slides it over my cleft. "You're going to come like this."

I'm so close. I try to push my hand down to take over. I need to come now.

"No," he commands. "Don't touch yourself. This is all for me."

I gaze into his eyes as his cock rubs my clit, over and over, faster and faster. "I'm going to..." the words stop as the orgasm races through me. I reach out to grab his shoulders, pulling on him.

He pulls back harshly, lets out a deep, animalistic growl and finds his own release all over my body.

Chapter 17

"Why did you put my number in your fuck phone and not your regular phone?"

"My fuck phone?" He cocks a brow as he massages my foot. "Is that what we're calling it now?"

I lean back on the bed and cradle my head in my arms. "It's like a super hero phone for douche bags."

He cocks a brow as a slight smile grazes his lips. "One point for Jessica."

"Why did you do it?" I close my eyes. His hand moves up my leg, massaging the back of my calf.

"Do you have a few hours so I can explain it?" His tone is raspy and quiet.

"Yes." I nod without opening my eyes.

His hands leave my leg and I feel an instant loss. I sigh when I feel him pull himself up the bed so he's resting next to me.

"Turn over." His hand glides to my hip as I turn to face him. "Listen to me."

I nod.

"When I lived in Boston I was…" He stares into my eyes and I can see the reservation there. "God, Jessica, I was such an asshole."

"I know," I say under my breath.

"You know?"

"You're still an asshole. It only stands to reason it started there." I tap him on the tip of his nose.

"Two points for Jessica."

I smile. "Once upon a time, Nathan was an asshole…"

"Right." He tilts his chin. "Nathan was an asshole who fucked anyone he could get his hands on."

The words bite right through me. I pull my gaze down to the bed. Why did I ask such a stupid question? Why do I open myself up to this much pain?

"Jessica." His lips course hot over my cheek. "Listen, you have to listen. No lies, remember?"

"No lies," I repeat back. I'm getting too deep again. I just wanted to use him for pleasure. I thought I could separate my lust for him and my real feelings.

"I started randomly fucking women so long ago I don't remember when." He reaches to grab my hand and pull it to his lips. "Don't freak out. Please, don't."

"I'm trying." I am. I'm trying to understand. I want to understand.

He kisses my palm lightly before placing my hand on his cheek. "I had to get away from there. I had to leave. "

"Boston?" I question. He's never explained to me why he moved from there to New York. I've always wondered given that he races back every other weekend to see his sister.

"When you fuck that many women, you start to hate yourself." He pushes my hand into his face as he closes his eyes. "I wanted to start fresh here."

"In New York?"

"I took a demanding job because I knew it wouldn't leave me any time to fuck around." He moves his hand to drape it over my shoulder. "Then I met Cassie. She had kids, and a good job and needed me. "

I cringe when he says her name. I still think about the look on her face when he broke up with her in this apartment. When he blatantly announced that he was fucking someone else.

"It was boring. Christ, she was so fucking boring." There's nothing apologetic about the words. He said no lies. He's being direct. This is what I wanted. It's what I always hoped for.

"God, Jessica." His hand leaps to my waist as he pulls me into his naked body. I can feel every muscle on his strong chest. I can sense that he's already semi-hard again. "Then I saw you."

"At the club?"

"Everything inside of me shifted at that moment in time." He nuzzles his face into my forehead. "It's as if the world stopped and I finally got on it. A world that made sense. A world that I finally wanted to be in."

My breath stalls at the words. How can he do that? How can be such an utter asshole one second and so soft and endearing the next? It's no wonder I feel as though I can't breathe whenever he's in the same room with me.

"I've never felt these things before." He pulls his hand from me and taps his own chest. "I've never missed anyone this much when I was away from them for ten minutes. I've never craved a woman's body this way. I've never ached inside."

"Nathan…" I can't really form anything in my mind to say. My heart is in control right now and if I allow it to have its way it's going to make me say things I'm not ready to say.

"There was that one night." He pulls back so he can look at me directly. "Do you remember that night?"

I search his eyes for a clue. "What night?"

"You were dancing with the chef," he groans. "I saw you across the club. You were so gorgeous. Fuck, just so beautiful." He grazes his lips across my forehead. "I felt things I never felt before. I couldn't stand the idea of you being with him. I almost took him outside."

"He only wanted my number."

"No, Jessica." He shakes his head. "He wanted to fuck you. He wanted to be inside this tight little body. He was practically drooling over you."

I chuckle at the visual of that. "It wasn't like that."

"You can't see it." He pulls back and grabs my shoulder in his hand. "You can't see what you do to men."

"Just to you." I roll my eyes. "Drew didn't want to fuck me. Well, he did technically, but…"

"You don't understand." He studies me. "Men want you. How can they not?"

I reach to embrace him. "You want me. Don't think that means other men do too."

He grazes his hand over my bare back. "I can't take that chance. That's why I wanted your number."

My heart dips at the words. It's not from elation, that's not it. I'm disappointed that once again he's confessing that he wanted my number to keep me from sleeping with anyone else. "You asked for it that night because you felt threatened by Drew."

His body tenses beneath me and I immediately know I've struck a nerve. "Not threatened," he corrects me in an even tone. "That's not what it was."

"What then?"

"I asked for it because I realized that if I didn't, you were going to slip away from me."

I jerk back so I can look into his eyes. "You put my number into your fuck phone." It's meant to sound hostile. It's an insult, regardless of how he spins it.

"I've never been in a relationship, Jessica." He bows his head as if he wants to run from the truth.

"Are you serious?" The question sounds so much more callous than I wanted it to. "How is that possible? You're thirty-one."

"I started sleeping with women when I was a teenager." He pauses as his glides his hand over my arm. "I've dated a few women but it never went anywhere. I like being alone. I like keeping my business life separate from my work."

"That's why you had a phone just filled with women you fuck?"

"I could leave it alone when I wasn't in the mood. I could forget about all of them. I wanted to leave that all behind me. When I took your number that night, I had that phone in my pocket. It wasn't because I was going to call someone else to fuck. It was because I was ready to toss it."

"You put my number in there with all of them." The gravity of the statement stings as I hear myself say it.

"I put it in my phone." He stresses the last two words. "Right after you left, I put it in the phone I have with me all the time. It was a big step for me. I wasn't ready to call you from it because I didn't know how to explain it. I've always kept my fucking separate from the rest of my life."

"That's why you had that hotel suite?"

"I arranged that shortly after I arrived here because I felt the same old urges to…"

"To fuck random women?" I fill in the uncomfortable blank.

He buries his face in my neck. "I'm not proud of who I was. I wanted to change. I tried and I didn't fuck anyone until I met Cassie."

"You took her to the room?" I need to know. I want to tell myself it doesn't matter if he did, but that's a lie. He told me he only had sex with her twice. He told me it never happened in that hotel suite.

"No, never." The words whisper across my skin. "You were the only one."

I pull back. I can't absorb that when he's so close to me. I can't think straight when I can feel his breath hot on my body.

"Jessica, don't run." He grips my arm. "Don't do this."

"I'm not." I try to reassure myself as much as him.

"You are." His tone is level and calm. "You want to race out of here because you're afraid I'm lying to you."

"You are lying." There I said it. It's what I feel.

"You were the only woman who ever set foot in that hotel suite other than my sister. The only one."

"I don't believe you." I can't lie. I won't lie to him.

He pulls me back into his body. "I'll prove to you that I'm not the man you think I am."

Chapter 18

"I was wondering if it was possible for me to get tomorrow night off?" This is the first time I've asked for a night off from work since I've started. It's a special occasion though. Rebecca just got a promotion and a group of people she works with are celebrating. I want to be there for her.

The kitchen manager smiles at me as she looks at the schedule on the wall. "Sure, I don't see any reason why not."

I almost reach over to pull her into a tight embrace. "This means so much to me."

"What does?" Drew's voice echoes in the air behind me.

"I'm taking tomorrow off." I'm going to do this in front of the kitchen manager so he can't twist things around and fuck it up for me.

"That's not going to work for me." His voice is harsh and unyielding. "We'll be too busy."

"I'll come in early and do all my prep." My words are meant for the kitchen manager although my eyes never leave his.

"We're good, Jess." She pats me on the back. "Take the entire day. You've been working really hard."

Drew stands in stunned silence as we both watch her walk away.

"I need to get back to work." I pivot on my heel to turn back towards the stack of cucumbers I've been assigned to julienne.

"Where are you going tomorrow night?" His breath is on my neck.

I move to the side. "It's none of your business, Drew."

"Are you going out with the lawyer?" There's no denying his distaste for Nathan. "Is that why you need a night off?"

I turn sharply and tap my finger against his chest. "Back off, Drew. My life is none of your business."

"You're actually going out with him again?" He's so smug.

"I'm going to a party with my roommate. I'm not going out with him."

"When you kissed me that night, you wanted me, not him."
It's meant to provoke me and it does.

"Shut up."

"You would have slept with me when we went out for
dinner that night, but then he showed up at your place before I got
there." The mention of that night hangs in the air, thick and heavy,
between us.

"Maybe things would have been different if he wasn't
there." It's a small offering. It's the truth. I was so fucked up then
that I can't be sure what I would have done if Nathan hadn't
appeared in my doorway.

"He's going to dump you." His eyes rake me over. "I'll be
waiting."

"Don't hold your breath."

***

"You should have invited the cute chef to come with you."
Rebecca smiles at me across the table.

I pull my hand through my hair, wishing I had tied it up for
the night. "That makes perfect sense." I don't even try and hide the
sarcasm in my voice.

"Drew is so angry because he's so horny," she tempers her
tone as she gazes at her coworkers who are seated around us.

"Do you still work for Cassandra now that you're
promoted?" I noticed almost immediately that she wasn't in
attendance. I was grateful given the fact that I still carried so much
guilt about what happened between her, Nathan and me.

"We're colleagues now." She pulls air quotes around the
words. "I get to travel, and wine and dine clients and I get an
expense account."

I smile knowing that all her Manhattan dreams are finally
coming true. "Things are looking up for you."

"I guess." If I was looking for excitement, there was none
to be found in her dismal mood.

"What's going on?" I push the bland food around on my
plate. If there was one thing you could count on with this group of
people, it seemed to be their lack of culinary taste. I was going to

need to make myself a sandwich after this sorry excuse for grilled tuna.

"Do you think I'm too young to get married?"

That came out of left field. "Married?" I try not to choke on the bite of risotto I just took.

"I think I want to have a family soon." She pouts her lips. "I'd make a good mom, don't you think?"

"Are you pregnant?" I spit the question out with way too much shock and surprise attached to it.

"Pregnant?" For the first time this evening she's finally got a wide grin on her beautiful face. "You have to get screwed for that to happen and there's no action going on in there." She points towards her lap. "It's a virtual dead zone."

"You'll meet someone," I offer. I know she will. She's got everything going for her.

"Right now, Jess." She scoops her finger towards me and I lean in closer. "All I need is a really good fuck."

Chapter 19

"You're such a good fuck, Jessica," he purrs into my ear.

"What?" I almost knock him completely off my bed. "How did you get into my room?"

"That guy you live with let me in. Bryce, right?" His hands deftly pull the sheets off of my body. "Why the hell do you sleep in the nude? What if he walked in on you?"

I leisurely rest my hands over my head, putting my entire body on display for him. "I like the way it feels."

"I like the way you feel." His eyes rake slowly over my body. I can barely make out his face in the dim light of my bedroom but I sense his gaze. I know he's drinking in everything he sees.

"Why are you here?" My eyelids are so heavy. I had too many glasses of house red wine at the restaurant with Rebecca and her coworkers. When they took off for a club I got into a cab and came home. I must have fallen asleep almost instantly.

"I'm here to fuck you." His clothes are off now. He's supporting his entire weight with one hand while the other softly caresses my thigh.

"I want that." If I can keep my eyes open, I want that.

"Was the party fun?" His lips are on my neck now. It feels so soothing, so natural to have him touch me. He knows exactly how I like to be touched.

"The party?" The words escape my tongue in a breathless whisper. I moan slowly when his hand snakes up my leg and gently pushes them apart.

"Your roommate? You went to a party for her." His mouth moves lower.

"Did I tell you that?" I haven't talked to him in two days. I was working. I needed space after he said he didn't take anyone else to the hotel suite. I needed time to absorb that, to decide if it was real or fiction.

"You're so wet." His index finger circles around my clit and I groan spontaneously.

"Put on a condom." I don't mince words. I don't want to.

"You can't stand another minute without me can you?" He moves briskly and I hear the tear of the foil packet.

"I want to be fucked." The words reflect my body's need. I need to be taken. I need to be consumed. I need to not doubt him so much.

"Goddammit it," he hisses as he pushes himself completely into me. "You're so ready for me."

"Hard." I wrap my legs around his waist. "Fuck me, hard."

His lips push into mine as he slams his cock into me. I moan into the kiss and I feel his breath hitch.

"You're so greedy, Jessica." The words whisper across my mouth. "You'll never get enough of my cock inside of you."

He's right. I won't. I can't. It's so good. It's always so good.

"Harder," I clench my sex around him, pulling him deeper.

"Christ." He bucks back and grabs my ass check in his palm, tilting my pelvis to take more of him.

"You're cock is so big." I bite his shoulder. "So fucking big."

A deep groan pulls through his body as he ups the tempo. "Tell me how good it feels to be fucked by me."

"Nothing feels like this," I confess as I push myself into him. "Nothing is this good."

"You want my cock, don't you?" The headboard pounds against the wall as he rams himself into my core.

I flinch at the bite of pain that always comes when he's this deep. "I want it."

"Tell me you crave my cock."

"I crave it." I can barely form the words. It all feels like so much.

"After I fuck you, I'm going to lick you until your sweet, little body can't take anymore."

"No." I shake my head. "Just make my come."

He pulls out and flips my body over in one movement. I claw at the sheets, wanting more. I reach down to touch my clit but his hand pulls it away.

"You don't get to have this." His breath is there, it's on my center. I can feel it skirting across my wetness. "I own this orgasm. Just me."

I bury my head in my pillow as I scream when he licks my folds. He's not gentle. He's needy, and rough and it drives me over the edge. I almost collapse before he's on me again. I come once more when he pushes two fingers inside of me and rubs my tender spot over and over.

"Nathan, no more." I wave my hand behind me. "It's too much."

"You're mine." He drives his cock into me so hard my head slams against the headboard. I cry out from the pain and he pulls my body up and against his, tilting my pelvis so his cock never leaves me.

"God, please." I moan into the air. "This is so good. I can't come again. Please."

"You never want me to stop." His fingers circle my clit as his other hand holds steady around my neck, pulling my body back. "I'll fuck you forever. Only me."

"Only you," I repeat. "Only you."

Chapter 20

"I need a good lawyer." I sit in the chair opposite his desk.

"You need a lawyer?" He's behind me, his hand resting on the curve of my neck. I wore my hair in a ponytail with the hope that he'd do just that. I love the way it feels when his hands touch me there.

"Yes." I try to catch the giggle that's building inside of me.

His hands leave my skin and I feel instantly lost. I'm becoming too attached to him again. Even though I haven't spent a night at his place since I was at the hotel when he walked in with his sister, things are becoming heavy again. My feelings are racing to the surface and I'm scared I'm going to crash and burn just like last time.

"What do you need a lawyer for?" He's kneeling in front of me now, his hands clenching either side of the chair.

"I have a concussion." I pull my bottom lip out in a fat pout.

His eyes are riveted to it. He licks the pad of his thumb before he pulls it over my lip. "I would give almost anything for you to suck me off right now."

"Is that how you handle all your potential clients?" I frown. "No wonder you make so much money."

He lifts a brow and a warm smile covers his handsome face. "How did you get a concussion?"

I lean forward so my hand is resting lightly on his shoulder. "I was being fucked by this man the other night. Not just any man, but *the* man. I mean his cock is like this big." I hold my hands a few inches apart.

"That big?" His brow furrows.

"This big?" I push my hands even farther apart.

"More like, this big." He pulls my hands wide until there's a definite gulf between them.

"He thinks so, but it's more like this." I push them back together just a bit.

"I gave you a concussion when I was fucking you?"

"You sometimes tell me that you're going to fuck my brains out so technically I guess I had a warning." I reach to touch the side of his face softly.

He doesn't say anything. He just stares intently into my eyes.

"When did you know you were so irresistible?" I trace a path across his top lip and then the bottom with my finger, watching how they part ever so slightly with each graze of my touch.

"The first moment you looked at me." He doesn't break a smile at all, even though I do.

"Women found you irresistible before I did." I move my finger along his cheekbone to his eyebrow. They're so thick and black. They make him look so imposing, serious and dangerous.

His long eyelashes flutter softly. "Other women thought I was interesting or intriguing for a time. That's different."

I move my finger across his forehead, marvelling in how strong it is. I rest my hand just on his hairline. "It's not that different."

"No one knows me, Jessica." His breath breezes over my cheek. "No one has ever wanted to know me."

I push my fingers into his hair and he closes his eyes and moans softly. "How is that possible?" It's a genuine question. How could any woman not want to know him?

"I wasn't like this with them." His breathing increases slightly. "I wouldn't let them in."

"You let me in." My hand falls to the back of his neck.

A shudder courses through his strong, massive shoulders. "I meant it when I said it."

"Said what?" I run my fingers lazily over the skin at the side of his chin, relishing in the feel of the mid- afternoon stubble.

"That I love you." It's barely audible. I see it within his eyes before the words leave his lips.

I finally break his gaze and look down at the skirt of my dress. "Please don't say that."

"I love you, Jessica."

"I can't say it yet. Please don't ask me to." I pull my eyes up to meet his.

"I won't. You feel it in here." He lightly rests his hand on my chest. "Soon, you'll be able to say it too."

I want to. "Yes." I can't offer anything more now.

"Until then, Jessica…" his voice trails as he pulls his soft lips over mine.

"Until then?" I ask into his mouth.

"You can suck me off."

Chapter 21

"There was a delivery for you when you were out."
Rebecca motions towards a large bouquet of flowers sitting on the
kitchen counter.

I race over to pull the card from the fragrant arrangement.

Until then, Nathan is written in black ink across the card.

"From Fingers?" she asks casually over her shoulder.

. I nod as I settle down next to her. "What are you doing
tonight?"

"Tonight?" She taps the side of her forehead with the
spoon. "Masturbating, most likely."

I laugh at her willingness to overshare. "I'm sorry I asked."
I hold up my hand.

"You're not working tonight?" She finishes the last bit of
her dessert. "Where's Fingers?"

"Hanging out with a friend." I want to sound as though I'm
casual about it but ever since Nathan told me he was going out for
a beer with a buddy, my mind has been playing tricks on me. I
don't want to get caught back in a hotel room rummaging through
his things when he walks in with yet another member of his family.

"His sister?" The amount of sarcasm dripping from the
comment is palpable.

"That was his sister." I try not to convey too much *'I told
you so'* in my tone.

"He says it was his sister, that's different."

"Actually, last weekend, we did a video chat when he was
away and I met them all." I hadn't mentioned it to her because I
knew that she still didn't trust him and she'd have wanted to lurk in
the background to make sure I wasn't having the proverbial wool
pulled over my eyes yet again.

"All of them? How many are there?" She tilts her head to
the side in mock surprise.

"Just four." I smile. "His sister, her husband and the two
kids."

"The perfect family." She picks up the empty bowl and I
swear for a minute it looks like she's going to lick it clean.

"No family is really perfect, are they?"

"No," she almost spits the word across the table at me. "They aren't."

"So, a movie?" I offer. "I got paid yesterday so it's my treat."

"I'll grab my coat."

***

"I ate way too much popcorn." I loop my arm through Rebecca's as we step out into the busy pedestrian traffic. Manhattan never seems to slow down and as much as I missed the quiet, breezy, still air back home, I was beginning to relish in the fast pace and vibrant nature of this city.

"I want a beer." Rebecca pulls me to the left so abruptly I almost fall off my heels into her.

I follow her lead while I check my phone and see a message from Nathan.

I miss you, Jessica.

Simple, sweet and to the point.

"Did Fingers text you?" Rebecca calls over her shoulder as she scans the storefronts across the street. "Where can a girl get a beer in this neighborhood?"

"There's a pub a few doors down from the restaurant. Everyone says the beer on tap there is great. We can go," I offer, even though I'm ready to climb into my bed and sleep the night away.

"Did he text you or not?" She points to my smartphone. I know she's just being protective. I don't have all the answers I want from him yet but I have enough for the moment.

"He said he misses me." I feel giddy just from repeating the words. It's just a simple text, Jessica. You can't invest too much in him yet. One day at a time.

She stops to stare at a pair of designer shoes in a window. "I should come back tomorrow to get those."

"I think you should." I pull on her arm to egg her along. I just want to have one beer and then get both of us in to a taxi so we can get home. I know she has an early morning tomorrow.

"The new job is great." The half-smile on her face suggests otherwise.

"It's always an adjustment when you start something new." I steer us to the left so we whip around the corner. "Just up the block here." I point.

"I haven't said this yet." She stops in the middle of the sidewalk and people curse as they have to weave their way around us. "I'm happy that you're here. I'm happy that you moved to New York, Jess."

"It was the best decision I ever made." I pull her into an embrace. "You're the one who convinced me to do it."

"Just think." She turns sharply on her heel as we near the entrance to the pub. "If you hadn't come here you never would have met Fingers and his dick."

I giggle as I push the door open and walk through into the crowded space.

***

"Just one more and then we'll call it a night." Rebecca waves one finger in the air over her head. "Please, Jess. This is like our own private celebration of my promotion."

"If you put it like that…" I laugh from the slight buzz I got from my own glass of beer. Rebecca is already on her third, heading towards her fourth. I don't know how she stays awake. I'd be under the table by now.

"We should totally go back to Connecticut." She slams her hand against the table. "You could show Josh what a cosmopolitan woman you've become."

I glance down at my worn jeans and pink sweater. "I'm not there quite yet. Maybe when I get a promotion, I can do that."

"You have to get away from that asshole." She spits the words out with obvious disdain.

"What asshole?" I don't want to get in another argument with her about Nathan. It's the same song and dance every time. She'll tell me that he's just using me as his temporary fuck toy and I'll tell her I think she's wrong.

"Drew."

"Drew?" I'm surprised when that name jumps from her lips.

"You need to quit that place." She grabs hold of my forearm. "He can fuck up your career. You know that he can."

I wish I hadn't confided in her about what he was doing to me. She was fiercely loyal and if she thought anyone was fucking over someone she loved, she'd fight tooth and nail to protect them. She did it with me when I was with Josh, and now with Nathan too. Since I've planted Drew squarely on her bad side, he was in the line of fire, just like the rest of them.

"I should go over there and give him a piece of my mind right now." She stomps her foot as if she's about to storm out of the pub, go to the restaurant and wring Drew's neck.

"At least wait until his shift is over," I joke. I motion for the waitress again but she throws me a hurried glance and I can tell she's got way too much to handle.

Rebecca's hand flies past my face at break neck speed. "His shift is over. The low life is right there."

I peer through the crowd to steal a profile view of Drew sitting at another table. He's talking animatedly to someone else. He's got a tall glass of beer in his palm. "I should go over there and dump that over his head." The mental image of that alone is enough to satisfy me but Rebecca now has a seed planted in her mind that's going to be hard to weed out.

"Do it, Jess. Just fucking do it." She pushes on my arm, almost knocking me from my chair.

"I can't." I shake my head. "He'll get me fired."

"It'll be so worth it."

"I'll get us a couple more drinks." Or her a drink and me another sparkling water.

"Be quick when you dump it over his head and then run. Kick your heels off if you have to." She nudges me in the side. "I'll grab them on my way out." She takes a quick glance at my worn heels. "Or not. You can borrow a pair of mine."

I shake my head in laughter as I launch into the crowd. I push my way past a few people before I realize that Drew's eyes are locked onto my face. He's raised his brow as if to taunt me. We're not standing inside Axel NY. He's not my superior in this moment. How much would it really hurt if I marched up to him and told him to fuck off?

His eyes don't leave mine as I steadily walk closer and closer to his table. I can see his mouth moving. He's talking to whoever he's with but his attention doesn't divert from me. The soft hum of the noise in the room mutes out his voice until I'm just mere inches away. I walk right up behind the dark haired man he's sitting with.

"I owed you the drinks." Drew rakes his eyes over my body, settling on my sheer sweater and the pink bra that's poking past the neckline. "I bet she couldn't get enough."

"She was so hungry for it." The voice of the man sitting in front of me, with his back to me, sounds so familiar.

"I can't believe you got her in your bed before me. When we saw her in the line at the club that night I thought I'd taste her first." Drew cocks a brow as if to challenge me to say something.

"Jessica always wanted me. I won fair and square when I fucked that sweet, little body for the first time."

I close my eyes. I feel the air leave my lungs as I tap Nathan softly on his shoulder.

PULSE
The Complete Series

Part Four

Chapter 1

I lace my fingers through the hair on the back of his head and pull back sharply since he completely ignored the first time I touched him. It's not surprising. He's floating in a world of gloat right now. He won their disgusting bet for getting between my legs first. I briefly imagine pushing on his head and slamming his face into the wooden table. I'm stronger than I look. I know I could break his nose.

"What the hell?" He tries to swat my hand from his hair just as his eyes lock on my face. "Jessica. Shit, no."

"Shit, yes." I release his hair after giving it a firm tug. "I'm not too late for the celebration, am I?"

He moves to push himself from his chair. "I barely know this guy." He nods towards Drew who is taking a leisurely sip of his beer. "I came here to meet an old friend."

"You seriously think I'm an idiot, don't you?" I lower myself into a chair next to Drew. "You are both so fucked up."

"I can explain." His hand darts out to reach for mine. I pull back as if I'm about to be bitten by a poisonous snake. I am. I was. That's exactly what Nathan Moore is. He's a revolting, narcissistic, piece of shit snake.

I turn my entire body so I'm facing Drew directly. Right now, in this exact moment in time, he's the lesser of the two fucked up evils. This one hasn't put his dick in me so maybe something, anything that comes out of his mouth will be less of a lie than what Nathan spits in my direction.

"What's the prize?" I nod towards the glass in his hand. "Beer?"

Drew's eyes float past me and I can only assume they're glued to Nathan.

"Drew. Asshole, look over here." I wave my hand past his face. "What did he win for fucking me first?" I don't know why it matters, but it does. I want to know what they think I'm worth, even though right now I feel worthless.

He pulls his gaze back to me and his eyes are cold and hard. "Ask him."

I feel Nathan's hand on my back now. "Don't touch me," I snap as I twist around in my seat to glare at him. "Keep your filthy, disgusting hands off of me."

"This isn't how it looks." The words sound so simple coming from his lips. This isn't how it looks? It looks like the two of them made a bet on my body weeks ago at the club and Nathan won because he convinced me to go up to that hotel suite and jump into his bed. That's how it looks because that's what happened. There's no disguising the truth. No smoke or mirrors required.

"Shut the fuck up." I pull each word slowly across my lips as I stare straight into his eyes. "Shut your lying mouth."

"The line at the bar was ridiculous." A male voice drifts from across the table as a glass of beer is pushed in front of Nathan. "Who is this lovely thing?"

"Who are you?" I throw the question right back at him as I pull my gaze to his face.

His green eyes take in my chest before they settle on my eyes. "I'm Garrett."

"Were you in on their bet?" I circle my finger carelessly in the air above the table.

"Stop it," Nathan spits out in haste. "Don't, Jessica."

"Don't?" I throw the word back at him while my eyes are still locked on the handsome stranger's face. "Were you in on their bet?" I repeat. "If you were I definitely would have fucked you first." It's meant to hurt Nathan. I'm flailing but I'm not about to show it.

He cocks a brow and licks his bottom lip. "The night is still young. I'm in."

"What did you get?" I turn towards Nathan again. "What did you get for fucking me before he did?" I nod in Drew's direction.

"Cash." Drew's hand waves in front of my face as he points in Nathan's direction. "I paid him weeks ago. I just have one question, Jess."

I close my eyes to try and absorb the fact that they bet money on who would get me in bed first.

"Leave her the hell alone," Nathan seethes. "Get lost."

"Jess." I feel Drew pull on my elbow as he rises from his chair. "The night we made the bet, you remember it, right? That first night you were at the club."

I nod slowly as I jerk my arm away. How could I forget? I remember every single detail of that night. I remember the way Nathan stared at me across the club. I remember the way it felt to kiss him, and I remember exactly the way it felt to come when he touched me.

"He already knew your name when we were dancing." His breath courses hot over my neck and I pull back. I can't have any part of him touching me. I can't.

"When you and I were dancing? That night?" I stare at my hands. That wasn't the first night. He's wrong. Nathan and I had been in the hotel room so many times by then.

"Fuck off, Drew." Nathan slams his fist against the wooden table. "Leave it alone."

"If you would have seen me first that night, I would have won, right?" The question is so ripe with arrogance.

"You made a bet with him that night?" I turn to look at Drew. This doesn't make any sense.

"Would you have left with me if you saw me before he talked to you that night?" He ignores my question and pushes. His bruised ego wants to be reassured that he's more appealing than Nathan.

"Wait." I push myself up and turn to face Drew directly. I sense Nathan rising next to me. "You made a bet with him the night when you asked for my number?"

"It's true what they say about blondes." The smirk on his face is pulling every ounce of anger I possess to the surface. "Try and follow the conversation. Before you came in the club that night we bet on who would ride you first. "

"You made the bet that night?" I need him to clarify that.

"No wonder they only let you peel carrots at the restaurant. You're too stupid to do anything else." He pivots on his heel and turns to the side. "I'm going back to my table." He motions towards a group of three men staring at us.

"Drew." I tap him on his back. "Hey, Drew."

He turns sharply. "What now, Jess?"

"This." I swing my right hand back, pull it into a tight fist, take a heavy breath and almost fall forward as I punch him square in the jaw.

Chapter 2

"Someone call the police." Drew stumbles back to his feet by grabbing hold of the edge of the table. "That bitch broke my jaw."

"It's not broken," I whisper under my breath. I can't say the same for my hand. I'm thankful for the throbbing pain in it. It's chasing away the ache I feel inside. The ache that came when I realized Nathan was nothing but a disgusting bastard.

"You're not calling anyone." Nathan's voice barrels through the loud hum of the room. I feel his hands encircle my waist and pull me to my feet.

"I'm pressing charges." Blood is dripping slowly from the corner of Drew's mouth onto his white t-shirt. "She's going to jail tonight."

"Listen to me, you dumb fuck." Nathan pulls me closer to him with one hand as his other darts out to push on Drew's chest. "You drop this now or you're going to regret it."

"Fuck you," Drew mumbles through a wad of paper napkins that are covering his mouth. There's so much blood. "She needs to be charged with assault."

"You push this and..." Nathan's hand drops from me as he takes a heavy step. "I'm going to have Cassie drag your ass into court for all that past child support you owe."

I reach back to grab hold of a chair. Cassie? Did he just say Cassie's name to Drew?

"Cassie?" Drew's voice cracks as the name leaves his lips. "My Cassie?"

"You're a pathetic piece of shit." Nathan fists his hands in the front of Drew's shirt. "What kind of man doesn't provide for his own children?"

I stare at Drew's face as the color leaves it. He's ashen. His expression stoic as he lowers the napkins from his mouth.

"He's their dad?" I hear the words leave my lips before I register them within my brain. He's the twins' father? He was married to Cassandra?

"You know her too?" Drew's eyes dart to my face. "What kind of fucked up game are you two playing?"

"You're her ex-husband?" My hand glides across my forehead. How can that be? Why didn't Nathan tell me that Drew was Cassandra's ex?

Drew lunges past Nathan towards me. "You set me up, you bitch."

Nathan steps to the side to intercept him, his hands jumping to Drew's shoulders. "I set you up."

I feel my knees buckle as I sit. I can't process all of this. I don't understand why I'm in the middle of this. I twist my neck sharply and search through the crowd for Rebecca. I need her to help me. I want her to help me understand what's going on.

"Give me back my money." Drew pushes against Nathan to no avail. "You set me up."

"That money was for Cassie." Nathan pushes him back. "It was for your kids."

The mention of Allie and Aaron stops Drew in his tracks. "You don't know anything about my kids."

"I know you're a sad excuse for a father," Nathan scowls. "You gambled away everything."

I feel so lost. It's almost as though I've stepped into another universe. I need to leave. I push myself back up from the chair and my eyes settle on the green-eyed stranger who brought Nathan a beer.

"I have to go," I whisper as much to him as to the heavy, emotionally filled air that is suffocating me.

"I'll take you." He stands and reaches out his hand.

"My friend is here." I motion towards the table I shared with Rebecca. A group of older men are sitting there now. I scan the people gathered near us and her face doesn't appear.

"Cassie put you up to this, didn't she?" The distant sound of Drew's raised voice arguing with Nathan rings through me as I step out into the darkness and the heavy night air.

Chapter 3

"Where did you go?" I place the mug of hot coffee I've been nursing for the past ten minutes down on the table. "You bailed on me."

"I saw you with Fingers." Rebecca pours herself some before she turns to me. "You never mentioned that he knew Drew."

She's diverting the conversation. "You just got up and left. You didn't think to come tell me?" I'm pissed and I have every right to be. It was her idea to go get a beer in the first place and because of that my entire life fell apart in the space of five minutes.

"Jess, you were sitting with Nathan." She spits out his name as if it's vile. "You were busy so I called it a night."

"You knew, didn't you?" I ask even though I'm sure of the answer. "You knew Drew was married to Cassandra."

"What?" The coffee that was just in her mouth is now spread out unceremoniously all over the table and the front of my robe.

I cock a brow at the reaction. She may be good at manipulating people and getting her way but I doubt that even she could mock surprise so convincingly. "You didn't know?"

"You're wrong." She reaches for a paper towel to soak up the mess. "There's no way he was married to her."

"They were married." I still can't absorb the fact even though I heard it firsthand last night. I spent hours after Nathan's friend, Garrett, dropped me off trying to decipher exactly what happened.

"I never met the ex." She takes a generous mouthful of coffee. "She's still hung up on him."

"On Drew?" I almost burst out laughing. After learning that he was shirking his child support duties, I can't imagine what Cassandra sees in him.

"How can it be Drew?" She leans both elbows on the table as she shakes her head. "She talks about her ex like he's the best thing that ever happened to her. His name is Andrew. Ah, that makes sense I guess."

I shrug my shoulders. "Nathan knew all along. He knew when he made the bet." The word slips out with my thoughts. I didn't want to confess any of this to my best friend.

"What bet?"

"I can't talk about it." Technically I won't. I don't want to humiliate myself even more.

"Jess." She inches her chair on the floor so she's sitting next to me now. "Spit it out. What bet?"

It would feel amazing to just let this all out. I'm just not in the mood for all the reminders that she warned me that Nathan was just using me for sex. "You're going to tell me that you knew he was a mistake all along."

"Fingers?" A thin smile covers her lips. "That goes without saying. Spill the beans. What the hell is going on?"

"Do you remember that night when we went to the club with Bryce? Right after he moved in?" I don't want to make Nathan the centerpiece of this recounting. "That was the night when I met Drew."

"I remember." She rolls her eyes. "I was drinking Bloody Marys and trying to get a pharmacist to prescribe his dick to me."

I laugh out loud. "That was the night."

"What about it?" She reaches for a peach from a bowl in the middle of the table. "Who bet what on what?"

I just need to say that Nathan and Drew bet money on who would nail me first. I wish I could just say it without feeling like my heart is falling out of my chest at warp speed.

"Apparently, when we were in line, Drew and Nathan wagered a bet on me." There that's it. It's out in the universe now and Rebecca can have at it and me for being so reckless.

"Those bastards." She bolts to her feet so fast the entire table jerks upwards causing the peach to roll off the edge. "He's an asshole."

Sadly, I feel the need to clarify which of the two assholes she's referring to. Such is the life of Jessica Roth in the big city. "Which asshole?"

"Fingers." She once again reaches to mop up the stray coffee that spilled over the rim of her mug when she upset the table.

I take the paper towel from her hand as I wipe the area directly in front of me. "What about Drew?"

"Yeah, him too." She storms off leaving me with even more questions than I had before she sat down.

Chapter 4

"Don't even bother." I point directly at Nathan's receptionist as I scoot past her on my way to his open office door.

"Ms. Ross, he's not…" her voice trails behind me just as I reach the doorway.

"Jessica?" The surprise in his tone is unmistakable. "What are you doing here?"

Normally I'd take offense at his reaction to my showing up unannounced at his office, but seeing how I almost decked him alongside Drew at the bar two nights ago, I can't blame him for the question.

"Come in." He motions towards one of the chairs in front of his desk as he closes the door. "I need to be in a meeting in a few minutes."

"We do this now, or we don't do it." I don't move my gaze from the bank of windows behind his desk. I haven't slept more than an hour since I saw him with Drew at the bar. If I don't get answers now I'm going to cease to be responsible for my actions. Call it a plea of temporary insanity or better yet, a plea of sanity. Who in their right mind wouldn't want to torture these two bastards after what they did?

I don't make eye contact with him as he picks up his desk phone and punches three keys. "Cancel the rest of my day." I feel his gaze burning into me as he pauses before continuing, "I don't give a shit, just do it." He slams the phone down before sitting in front of me on the edge of his desk.

"Why?" It's really the one and only question I have.

"Why what?" His tone is even and controlled. He's not going to make this easy for me.

I pull my eyes up the lapel of his navy suit jacket before settling on his icy blue eyes. "Why do this to me? Why?"

"Do what?" he chirps back.

I run my hands over my face trying to erase the distress from my expression. "Seriously?"

"What you heard at the bar was out of context." Naturally, he'd say that to me. It's what any good lawyer says to someone when they're trying to win a case. The only problem is that this case is my life and he's already fucked it up so badly that I can't tell up from down anymore.

"I heard you say that you fucked my sweet little body," I sneer as the words leave my lips. I've replayed those five words in my mind repeatedly every second since I first heard him say them. "You talked to him about fucking me." I point my finger into my own chest as if to distinguish my body from all of the hundreds of others he's fucked over the years.

"Jessica." He takes a heavy swallow. "None of this was about you."

It couldn't sting more if he would have slapped me directly across my face. "It was all about me."

He drops to one knee now, trapping my body in the chair. There's nothing floating in the air between us this time but bitter anger and resentment. Anything his body may be trying to convey to me is being swallowed by my loathing for him. "It was about Cassie."

"Cassie?" I parrot her name back. "You fucked me because of Cassie?"

He shakes his head and I watch his eyes skirt over my body. "I fucked you because I can't get enough of you. I want you more than anyone. I've told you all this."

"Before I knew that you bet money on my ass." I try to stand but his frame is unyielding. He doesn't budge. His expression remains serious and passive.

"Do you want to hear what happened or not?" The question is a challenge. There's an undercurrent of impatience woven into it.

I lean back in the chair to try and find some air. "Tell me then."

"You'll listen?" He cocks both brows expectantly. "Jessica, you're going to listen to me?"

"Whatever. Talk." I push back on his shoulder wanting him to retreat. I can't breathe when he's close to me and I can't sort through my tangled thoughts when I don't have space to think.

"It's complicated." He pivots back on his heel. "It's so fucking complicated."

"Don't bother then." I shove his chest to try to skirt my way around him. "Coming here was a mistake."

"I met Cassie at the same club I met you." His gaze is direct. "She was a wreck."

"A wreck?" I exhale. I can already sense where this is going. He's going to use Cassie's emotional wellbeing as an excuse for him being a complete and total douchebag.

"She was so wasted." He rolls his eyes. "She was falling over and some guy was ready to drag her out of the club to his place."

"So you recused her?" The words are fraught with sarcasm. I don't give a shit if they have scepticism written all over them. All I want is the truth, plain, simple and no holds barred.

He leans forward again, his breath skirting across my cheek. "I helped her avoid a situation she'd regret." His tone is cold, clipped and harsh.

"Then what?" At the rate this is going I'm never going to get to the bottom of his bet with Drew.

"Jessica." His finger jumps to my jaw and I recoil at the touch. "You came here for answers, so you need to listen."

I regret coming here. It was reckless of me to get in a taxi and race over here hoping he would actually tell me anything that even bordered on the truth. I should have followed my gut instinct and gone to see Cassandra.

"I'm listening," I bite back. "You met Cassandra at the same club you met me, you saved her from a big bad wolf who wanted to stick his dick in her and you fucked her instead."

"Jesus, Jessica." He leans back to pull himself to his feet. "Shut the hell up and listen to me."

Chapter 5

"I didn't come here for this." I jump to my feet and bolt towards his office door in one swift movement.

His hands are around my waist before I have time to react. "You came here to get answers and unless you sit quietly and listen, we're never going to get anywhere."

"Never tell me to shut up." I push my index finger against his hard chest. "Never say that to me."

He scoops my hand within his and brings it deftly to his lips. "I'm sorry, Jessica. Please. This is killing me. You're ripping me apart. Can't you see that?"

I tear my hand from his grasp as his words assault me. "I'm ripping you apart?" My voice is barely more than a whisper even though my intention is a scream. I'm so tired emotionally. I'm so overwrought with everything that's happened. Why can't I just turn around and walk out of here? Why can't I just see that he's not good for me?

"Please, just listen. Jessica, you have to listen to me." The tone is pleading and edgy.

I swallow the bitter sting of my anger and lower myself back into the chair. "Five minutes, Nathan. Five minutes." It's all my body will allow me. Hell, I'm not certain I can even make it that long without falling apart.

"I met Cassie at the club like I said. She was so drunk, Jessica. I took her home that night and that's when I realized she had kids." He sits on the corner of his desk. "The babysitter who was there whined about how Cassie never paid her so I covered it. I slept on her couch because I was scared the kids would need something and she was passed right out."

"Allie and Aaron," I whisper their names.

"I fell in love with them." A small smile skirts the edge of his mouth. "Christ, you've seen them."

I nod at the reminder of how sweet they are. "They're beautiful."

"I made them breakfast and played with them." He closes his eyes and looks down at the floor. "There wasn't much to eat at their apartment so I took them to buy groceries before Cassie woke up."

I look away and scratch my neck, trying in vain to ward off all of the conflicting emotions that are racing through me.

"She couldn't cover her bills." He exhales audibly. "I just started paying for things. Almost every date we had was at her place so I could see the kids. I love kids."

It's a confession that catches me off guard. I know he loves his niece and nephew in Boston but this is the first I've heard of his love for children in general. I've never viewed him as the fatherly type. I'm no judge though. To me he's only ever been the type of man who loves to fuck. He's not exactly multi-faceted in my eyes.

"Then she told me that she would go to the club to spy on her ex because he wasn't paying child support." His fist clenches at the mere mention of Drew's role in Cassandra's life. "I offered her legal advice. I set her up with a family law attorney so she could sue for back support, but she backed out."

"He pays nothing?" It's surprising given the fact that I know that he must be making a decent salary at the restaurant.

"She told me that he'd throw her a few hundred dollars here and there but he's so far behind on what he owes." He clears his throat. "Before they divorced he quit his job on Wall Street and decided he wanted to be a chef."

"Why?" I ask not because I expect Nathan to have an answer but because I don't see the logic in anything Drew does. "Why would he give up a good job?" I bite my tongue the moment the question leaves me. I did the same thing. I'd thrown away a great job in Connecticut to come to New York to try and make it in the culinary world.

"He's so fucked. He gambled away virtually everything Cassie owns. She had to go to her parents for help after she and Drew split."

He knows so much about their relationship. He's so immersed in Cassie's divorce and her relationship with Drew. "How could you let me work with him and not tell me he was Cassandra's ex?"

"I didn't think it mattered, Jessica." The words sound genuine, even if I'm not absorbing them that way. "I didn't want it to matter."

"It all matters." I glance at the clock on the wall beside his desk. "Your five minutes are up."

"Don't go." He's back on his knee in front of me. "I'm not done explaining all of this."

"You should have told me who he was when you saw me with him at the club." I can't meet his gaze. I'm so empty right now and he'll see that and press to make things better. "You should have told me everything."

"None of it mattered."

"It didn't matter to you." I tap my hand on his chest. "It all matters to me. Every single detail."

"Let me explain about the bet." The reminder feels like a razor slicing through my skin.

"Why bother?" I push on him so I can rise to my feet. "We're done."

Chapter 6

"Hey, Jess." Cassandra pulls me into a weak embrace. "I was surprised to hear from you."

I settle back onto the park bench as she sits next to me. "I'm glad you brought the kids."

She nods towards the playground equipment. "They love it here. They miss you, you know. They talk about you a lot."

"How are you?" It's the expected question and one that will give me some time to gather my emotions before I dive into the subject of her ex.

"Great." The wide smile that covers her face says more than the word. "I've been struggling, but things are looking up."

"With the new guy?" Another momentary reprieve before I bring up Drew. How exactly am I going to do that? I wish I had given this more thought before I texted her after rushing out of Nathan's office.

She looks down at the ground before she answers. "With Nate. I saw him last night."

The words bite as they hurl their way through me. It's just another unwelcome reminder of her connection with him. My entire relationship with Nathan has been a lie just so he could help her. "Great." It's weak. It's lame and it's the only syllable I can utter right now.

"He's in love with someone." She waves to the twins as they race through the sand towards a set of swings.

"Oh," slips past my lips. "Do you still care about him?" That's not my business but my brain doesn't have any guardrails at the moment. I'm going to drive my entire life over a cliff just because I can't temper what I feel for Nathan Moore.

"As a friend." She pulls her long, brown hair into her fist to keep it from flying into her face in the wind. "We were never a good fit."

"You seemed to care a lot about him when we were at his apartment," I counter. Why am I doing this? Why push her to share things that don't matter at this point? He wagered money on whether he'd sleep with me before Drew. The fact that he made the bet after we'd already fucked isn't lost on me. It's just semantics. A man who claims to care about a woman doesn't do that. Plain and simple.

"He helped me when no one else would." She takes a deep breath. "I guess I needed a knight in shining armor and he wanted to be one."

I'd never use that phrase to describe him and my brain was having trouble wrapping itself around the concept. "What happened last night?" It's not my business. I know it's not but I can't help myself.

"He gave me a lecture about my ex." She takes a heavy swallow before she turns to look at me directly. "He told me it was time for me to stand up for myself. He wants me to go after my ex for support."

I feel my stomach drop at the mention of Drew. "Your ex doesn't pay support?" Another useless question to try and bide myself enough time to learn more about Drew.

"He's got issues." She laces her fingers in mine on my lap. "I still love him, Jess. I don't know how to stop."

I glance at her trembling hand and think about how mismatched Drew and she are. "He should be helping you with the kids." I know it's not my place to offer any opinion on her relationship with Drew. If I was actually going to be honest, I'd tell her to kick him square in the groin the next time she sees him, not only for being a deadbeat dad but for being an asshole too.

"Nate helped me see that last night." A thinly veiled sigh escapes her lips. "He told me that unless I make him responsible for the kids, he's going to keep doing what he's doing."

What he's doing is he's out trolling clubs looking for women he can bet on. I want to tell her but now isn't the time. Is there ever an appropriate time to tell your ex-boss that her ex-husband is a low life piece of shit?

"You're going to try and get your ex to see that?" Good luck with that Cassandra, I want to add. Good luck getting Drew to see anything.

"Nate gave me the name of a friend of his who can help me get back some child support." She pauses before she continues, "I just need to tell Andrew that's what I'm doing." She winces as she says his name and I realize it's the first time I've heard her use it.

"You've never said his name before." Way to point out the extra obvious, Jessica.

"It hurts too much," she whispers softly. "I still miss him."

Chapter 7

"I feel like I should be writing this down," Bryce jokes as he takes a bite of his cheeseburger. "You're like living in a reality show right now, Jess."

"Tell me about it." I reach across the table to steal a fry. The salad I ordered may be welcomed by my hips, but my stomach is craving something greasy and bad for me. Why does that conjure up an image of Nathan? I smile inwardly, grateful for the chance to spill everything out to someone I know I can trust.

He pushes his plate to the middle of the table to grant me unlimited access to his dinner. "Have you told Rebecca all of this?"

"Are you kidding?" I almost choke on the food in my mouth. "She works with Cassandra every day. She'd gossip about all of this to her. She has no idea Nathan used to date Cassandra."

"I don't get it though." He takes a long drink of his soda. "Why did he make a bet with Drew knowing he'd banged you already?"

"Who cares?" I throw the response out so flippantly. The truth is that I care. I want to understand Nathan's motivations but there's only one person who can explain that to me and it's him. I've avoided him for more than a week now and I'm finally able to get through an entire day without thinking about him every second.

"You do." Bryce nods in my direction. "You're all torn up inside over this. I can see it."

"You're too sensitive," I joke. "I'm fine." That's a bold faced lie. I'm not fine. I'm finally skirting the edges of okay. Fine is way off in the distance but I'll get there. I have to.

He pulls the wilted lettuce from under the bun before he takes another bite. "I wanted to ask you..." his voice trails as he chews. "I wanted to ask you about work. How's Drew been around you?"

"I talked to my supervisor," I wince as I say the words. Ratting out Drew wasn't something I wanted to do but working with him isn't an option for me anymore. Once I knew about the bet, I realized that allowing him to continue to harass me at work wasn't going to fly. Either he had to leave or I did.

"What did they say? Did he get in shit for it?" He raises a brow as if he's expecting me to confess that they lined up a firing squad to take aim at his crotch.

"He'd already asked to be moved to another restaurant on the Upper East Side." I can hear the relief in my voice so I know it's equally apparent to Bryce too. "I haven't seen him since the bar."

"I still can't believe you clocked him." He lets out a deep belly laugh. "You're tougher than you look."

I take a small bite of another fry. "You have no idea."

***

"Boxing gloves?" I try to stifle a laugh as I throw open the door to the apartment. I half expected it to be Trudy, Bryce's girlfriend. She'd texted me earlier saying she was making a surprise visit and to not warn Bryce. She wanted to crawl into bed with him when she arrived and I was secretly envious of their bond at this moment.

"You pack a mean punch." A deep voice floats into the air as the gloves move to the side to reveal Garrett.

"You're Nathan's friend," I spit the words out without realizing how vile my tone is. I may as well have been talking about finding a rat in my apartment. There was no disguising my disgust.

He reaches to hand me the gloves. "You're not going to hold that against me, are you?"

I look down and realize in that moment that I'm only wearing a robe. I'd been almost ready to hop into bed when the knocking at the door pulled me down the hall. "I haven't decided yet."

"You're wondering what I'm doing here." The statement is swollen with suggestion. Please don't let this be another man who thinks it's fun to get me into bed for sport.

I raise my arm to block his entrance into the apartment. It does little good considering he towers above me. "You'll tell me," I push back. I feel a blush pull across my cheeks when I throw my memory back to the bar and my first meeting with him. I didn't actually suggest we fuck each other, did I?

"I want to talk about Nate." He looks over my shoulder into the apartment. "Can I come in?"

I hesitate briefly. If I don't let him in, I'll never hear what he has to say. Is that such a bad thing? He's likely just another member of the joint committee on how great Nathan Moore is. He's going to sing his invisible virtues just like Cassandra did.

"I won't take long." He taps his foot as if that's going to spur me along.

"Did he send you?" I push the boxing gloves into his chest. "If he did, you can leave now."

He looks down at me and his expression softens. "No. I haven't seen or spoken to Nate since you took that guy down at the bar."

I doubt he's telling the truth. He's Nathan's old friend after all. That is what he called him, right? "Nathan and I are finished."

"You'll want to hear this." He tips his head towards the living room. "Give me a few minutes, Jessica. That's all I ask."

Chapter 8

"You're a lawyer too, aren't you?" I teeter on the edge of the couch, holding tightly to my robe.

"What?" The wide grin that accompanies the question speaks volumes. "You have something against lawyers?"

"I have something against liars," I counter. "Nathan is a liar."

He pulls his hand through his messy brown hair. "Nathan's crazy about you."

I almost laugh out loud. Nathan sent him here. I know it. "Nathan's crazy about sex." The statement escapes me before I have a chance to temper it.

He lifts a brow as if to question whether that's a bad thing or not. "I don't know what went on with that other guy but he sat down to talk to Nate when I went to get a beer."

I know it shouldn't matter to me whether Nathan went there to meet Drew or not, but it does. "So, you were the old buddy that Nathan was meeting?" There's really no purpose in asking him that. He's Nathan's friend. He's going to lie to me for him. I'd probably do the very same thing for Rebecca.

"We had to talk about a case that I'm working on with him. A friend of his…" he stops himself before he offers more. The flash behind his eyes suggests he's just realized that he's confirmed my suspicion that he's a lawyer.

I wait for him to continue but he sits in silence, his eyes glued to me. "Drew just showed up?" I ask. If I can grasp even the smallest bit of understanding about what happened the other night, it will help me push this entire episode into my past, where it needs to stay firmly entrenched.

"He sat down with a beer for Nate while I was at the bar. He wasn't there more than a few minutes before you walked up to them."

I'm at a loss for how I ended up in the very same bar with Drew and Nathan just as Drew felt the need to buy Nathan a beer for fucking me first. "Life isn't that much of a coincidence." I stand with the hope that he'll take the not-so-subtle hint and get out of my apartment.

"I don't know anything about that." He stops right in front of me. "I do know that Nate is in love with you."

***

"Put on some clothes." I push past him the moment he swings open the door to his apartment.

"You could take off some." He sweeps his eyes slowly over my body. I'd thrown on a pair of jeans and a t-shirt before I'd hopped in a taxi to come to his place after Garrett left.

"Nathan." I sigh heavily. "Please put on some clothes." It's as much a demand as a plea. I can't look at him when he's standing in front of me only wearing boxer briefs and a smile on his face. He's too handsome, and muscular and everything. Why do I still want to feel him inside of me when he's such a fucked up excuse for a human being?

"I'm hot."

"You're what?" He's right but why the announcement?

"It's hot in here, Jessica." His hand glides through the air. "I'm too hot for clothes."

In more ways than one, I want to say. "Okay, well…" I have nothing. Now I have to interrogate him when he looks like he stepped off the pages of an underwear ad. Why hadn't I called first to see if he could meet me somewhere?

"What do you need?" He brushes past me and walks towards the small bar. "Do you want something to drink?"

I watch as he takes a long, leisurely sip from a bottle of water. I can't look at him anymore. I wish I had never laid eyes on him. I'll never meet another man as beautiful as he is. "You said no lies." He did say that. He's always said that to me.

"I've never lied to you, Jessica." He cocks a brow but stays firmly in place. I'm a little shocked, and admittedly, a bit disappointed that he hasn't tried to embrace me. I miss his hands on my body. I wish things hadn't become so complicated.

"You lied about Drew." I can't look at him as I say the words. "You lied about knowing him."

"I don't know him," he says softly. "I only know him as Cassandra's excuse for an ex-husband."

"You were in love with her," I snarl. "Everything you do is for her." It's petty and childish and I don't mean it. I'm just so tired of trying to wrap my brain around the fact that he made a bet on my body with her ex.

He raises both brows as a sly grin slide over his mouth. "Jealousy suits you, Jessica."

"Jealousy?" I scoff. "I'm not jealous of her." Did that sound even remotely genuine to him? Of course I'm jealous of her. He's kept the depth of his connection with her hidden from me the entire time we've been fucking each other.

"You're protesting too much." He tips the bottle of water in my direction before he takes another sip.

I shake my head slightly as I sit down in a chair. "You're being a fucking lawyer again, Nathan."

"I'm being reasonable, Jessica." It's a comeback that tears into me. The suggestion that I'm not being reasonable stings.

"Speaking of lawyers, your friend came to my place tonight," I say the words as nonchalantly as I can manage. I want to gauge his honest reaction.

"What friend?" He doesn't even bat his long, perfectly shaped eyelashes.

"Garrett." My eyes are glued to his face as the name leaves my lips. I know he's not going to be surprised in the least considering he probably sent him over there with an agenda and a pair of boxing gloves as a nice touch.

"What?" He slams the now empty bottle of water onto the bar and it teeters slightly before it falls over. "Garrett was at your place? Why?"

He's either been taking acting lessons or he really has no clue Garrett was on a mission to convince me that Nathan loves me. "You didn't know he was coming over?"

"What the hell is going on between you two?" He's rounding the bar now and it's only going to be three, two, one second until I see his entire body on display in his underwear again. There it is. Dammit.

"He brought me a present." I know my eyes are dancing with the words. I can feel the tension in the air. Nathan can't tolerate the idea of my being alone in a room with a man. I'm taking some perverse pleasure in watching him squirm over this. It's nothing compared to how he's made me feel over his bet with Drew, but it's a start.

"What the fuck?" He pulls his hand across his forehead to remove a few stray beads of sweat. Great, now he's not only semi-nude, he's glistening.

I pull on the collar of my t-shirt. It does feel extra hot in here. "He came over tonight." Way to drag it out, Jessica. Just tell him that Garrett was a messenger of love who visited you to convince you that Nathan has real feelings for you.

"Jessica." He's across the room and sitting next to me before I can process it. "Tell me there's nothing there."

"Nothing between me and your friend?" The words are barely audible. I can hardly think, let alone string a question together. He's too close. I can smell his cologne and almost touch his bare leg.

"Christ." He grabs both my shoulders in his hands. "This needs to stop tonight. Tell me how to fix this. Now."

Chapter 9

How bad would it really be if I stripped right now and sat on his lap? What would that say to him about me? That I'm weak? That I can't stand up for myself? That I'm like one of those female characters in a romance novel that has no backbone? Or that I crave his body so much that I don't give a fuck what he does? That's the ticket.

"Jessica." His voice pulls me from my thoughts of riding his glorious cock into the sunset. "Are you okay?"

"I'm just super..."Jessica, stop. Do not tell this man that you're super horny and you want him. Don't, do that. Don't. "I'm just super." What?

He pulls back slightly and raises his eyebrows as the corner of his lip rises in tandem. "You're just super?"

I shake my head and inch away from him on the couch. "Tell me about the bet."

"The bet?" he parrots back. "The bet between Drew and me?"

"How many bets are you a part of?" It's a half-joke if I'm being honest. If I'm being brutally honest, it's meant to bite into him but I know that he'll skirt over it the way he always does when I subtly try to stab him with a verbal knife. I'm beginning to think I need to switch to a more direct verbal hatchet if I want to get my point across.

"You went to the club that night with your roommates." He's so direct and matter-of-fact in his tone. "I saw you in the line."

"You didn't say anything." I shift slightly in the seat, feeling suddenly apprehensive about the conversation. It was my intention, when I hopped into the taxi earlier, to find out why he'd sent Garrett over to talk to me, now I'm on the brink of learning all about their disgusting bet.

He glances towards me and his eyes briefly scan my face before they drop. "You railed on me about kissing you in front of Bryce. You told me not to interfere when you were with other guys."

I nod. I remember that conversation. He'd promised me he'd keep out of my way if I was interested in someone else. The whole concept seems so foreign to me now. How can I possibly want another man? How am I ever going to get myself back to a place where that feels okay again?

"I was coming up behind you and heard Drew talking to some guys." His fist clenches on his lap and he pulls it across his leg. "They were talking about you."

"About me?"

"He said the curvy blonde was ready for him." His jaw tightens. "He was pointing at your ass, waving a wad of cash in his hand and asking who wanted to bet him that he could nail you first."

My stomach recoils at the sound of the words. I'm appalled by the image of Drew staring me down in line and wagering a bet on my body. "You already knew who he was?"

He nods slowly. "Cassie pointed him out to me months before that. I'd go to the clubs sometimes and I'd almost always see him there. I knew he was a gambling addict. He was blowing money left and right on anything he could place a bet on."

I'm not sure if I'm more bothered by the fact that he knew who Drew was for months before that night or by the mental image of Nathan interacting with women at clubs before he knew me. I sit in silence hoping he'll take the hint and continue his confession.

"I asked him if I could get in on the bet." He reaches to cradle my hand in his but I pull back. I can't manage any skin-to-skin contact with him right now. I can't.

"We'd already fucked, Nathan," I say the words slowly, enunciating each syllable.

"It wasn't about that, Jessica." His breath hisses out. "It was about helping Cassie."

I close my eyes to temper everything I'm feeling. "Why would you do something like that to me? It's so degrading and so disgusting."

"I'm not proud of it." The words are genuine but they offer nothing to me. "I barely knew you then."

He's right. He barely knew me. We'd only fucked up to that point and if I was being truthful, that's all we'd ever really been. "You barely know me now," I whisper. "You don't know me."

"Jessica. Listen to me." He turns to look directly at me. "I was trying to help Cassie and her kids. I never meant for it to hurt you."

"You made a bet on my body." I slide my hand over my breasts and down my stomach. "You made a bet about my body with him."

"Jessica, please," he breathes, his hand pulling on mine. "I got caught up in helping her and didn't realize how it would hurt you."

"I worked with him." I sigh. "You knew I had to work with him. I went on a date with him and then he harassed me every single day."

"He was so pissed that he lost the bet that he kept after you for weeks. I told him to fuck off over and over again." The words are meant to comfort me but they only push me closer to the edge of the emotional abyss I'm already teetering on.

"You put me in a horrible position to help her." It sounds childish as the words hit the air. It sounds as though I'm being petty and juvenile. "You allowed me to be a pawn in your stupid little game with him to help her."

"No." The word is breathless. "Jessica, no."

"Nathan." I shut my eyes briefly before opening them to stare at him. "You made a bet with Drew about fucking me when we'd already fucked each other so you could help his ex-wife." I hadn't signed up for any of that when I first went to the club.

"It's not that simple." His tone is raspy and low. "She was getting eaten alive by creditors and he was blowing his money. This was finally my chance to get something from him. I was just taking from him to give to her."

"By using me," I say decisively. "Why can't you see how completely fucked up this is?"

"You don't think I know that?" He jumps to his feet. "You don't think I realize how badly I've fucked up the only thing that's ever mattered to me?"

"Why didn't you just tell me?" I ask while trying to temper all the mounting rage that I'm feeling. "Why the fuck didn't you just tell me what was going on?"

"How?" He's on his knees in front of me now. "What was I supposed to say? You don't think I realized that I was going to lose you the minute I brought it up?"

"The night I danced with Drew..." I stop to pull in a heavy, much needed breath. "That was the night you finally told me your name."

"Making that bet was a mistake the minute it happened." He's pulling on my hands. "When I saw him dancing with you something inside of me switched on. I couldn't stand it. I fucking hated him more than I ever had before."

"That was when you should have told me." I can feel tears racing to the surface. I don't cry. I'm not like that. Please don't let me cry in front of him.

"Jessica." He lifts his chin to look directly at me. "Don't let this come between us."

I thrust my back into the couch at the request. "Don't let this come between us?" I push the question back to him. "This? You mean the fact that you let me trust in you when you were fucking with me the entire time? That? Is that what you mean?"

"No." His head shakes rapidly from side-to-side. "Listen to me, Jessica. Just listen."

"I've been listening to you for weeks." I know he can hear the exasperation in my voice. It's unmistakable. I'm so tired of his bullshit. First, the fact that he was dating Cassandra, then the fuck phone and now this goddamn bet he made with Drew.

"I made that bet knowing that it wasn't even real." He rests his hands on either side of me on the couch. "I'd already been with you. I told him later that night that I fucked you and he paid up. He just couldn't drop it. He kept circling you like a fucking vulture."

"How much?" It's a question that has been pulling at me for days now. Part of me wants to know and the other part knows that once I hear the amount I'll be scarred for life.

"The money doesn't matter." His tone is flippant and dismissive. Of course it doesn't matter to him. He's not the one who had a price tag placed on his ass like I did.

"It matters to me." I squirm on the couch cushion, trying to break free of the wall he's built around me with his body.

"Jessica, please." His voice is so soft and ripe with emotion. "Don't ask me that."

"You said you'd never lie to me." I know it's underhanded but it's going to get me exactly what I want from him. "Tell me how much."

"Jessica." He's tapping my hip with his hands. "Please, don't ask that."

"Now, Nathan." I tilt his chin up with my index finger. "Look me right in the eye and tell me."

Chapter 10

"Five thousand dollars?" She spits the words out right along with most of the saliva that's been in her mouth.

"Rebecca." There's no reason to try and veil the disgust in my voice. "You spit all over me."

"You're saying that Fingers and Cassandra's hornball hubby bet five thousand dollars on fucking you?" She taps her finger on my bed to accentuate each word.

"I'm saying that exactly, yes." I needed to tell someone after I raced out of Nathan's apartment and Rebecca was the lucky recipient of that news since Bryce was nowhere to be found when I got home.

"That's so weird." It's not the response I expected but if you looked at the situation as a whole, it was actually more than weird. It was bizarre.

"It's weirder than weird," I offer, realizing immediately that comments like that weren't about to help me beat the stereotype of the blonde, big breasted bimbo that I've been fighting against for years.

"Fingers made bank when he fucked you." She laughs until she realizes I'm not joining in on her merriment. "What's got you so worked up?"

"Rebecca." Her name leaves my lips in a rush. "You're not serious? You wouldn't be pissed if a guy you were dating made a bet on you?"

"First things first, Jess." She stretches her body out so she's lying right next to me. "You two were fucking back then, not dating."

"True," I acquiesce. She's right about that. We had only fucked a few times at that point.

"Second, Drew is a scumbag." She shakes her head as if to ward off any Drew germs that may have infected her just from saying his name. "I'm the one who has heard story after story from Cassandra about him. The guy is a waste of skin."

"He still shouldn't have bet on me." I'm getting tired of trying to convince everyone that Drew and Nathan were wrong. "Neither of them should have done it."

"No arguments from me." She pulls her legs under my blanket. "Just think about one thing."

"What?" I ask as I settle in next to her. "Please don't say anything about Nathan's cock."

She giggles into my hair. "I don't have to. You dream about Fingers and his magical dick every night."

I laugh out loud and realize this is the first time in weeks I'm actually enjoying myself. "What should I think about?"

"Think about how much he's changed since that night when you first met him." She pokes me playfully in the side with her index finger. "He wouldn't have made that bet last week or two weeks ago, Jess. He didn't really know you back when he did. Don't throw him away for one mistake."

Chapter 11

"You hurt me." My lips skirt over his neck. "You tore me to shreds."

His breath courses hot over my forehead. "I'm lost right now. You get that, right? You know that I can't think or eat or breathe because you fucking hate me, Jessica."

"I hate what you did," I qualify his statement. "I hate that you used my body to get something for her." I do hate that. I detest that he used his knowledge of Drew's addiction and his desire for me to manipulate money from him.

"I hate myself for that." His hands reach past me to rest on either side of the door to his office. "I hate that I hurt you. It makes me sick when I think about it."

"I'll never forgive you for this." I mean every word. I can't forgive him. I've thought all morning about what Rebecca said to me about throwing Nathan away for the one mistake. It's more than that though. It's the endless lovers he's had, it's the half-truths about Drew and most of all, it's the fact that he sat in that bar and boasted about my body.

"I won't give up until you forgive me, Jessica." His lips graze across my cheek. "I'm never giving up until I'm back inside of you."

"You're going to forget about me." It's not meant as a challenge, it's only an observation based on everything I already know about him. "Your cock is going to need someone and you'll find her and she'll be your new obsession."

He takes a heavy step back as if I've physically assaulted him. I see a veil of pain wash over him, bouncing through his eyes. "No." His tone is raspy, direct and measured.

"Stop it." My words are ripe with impatience. "Just stop pretending I meant anything to you."

He's on me in an instant, his heavy body pressing into mine. "I love you, Jessica."

I cringe when he says the words. I don't want to hear them. I believed them for a brief moment weeks ago. I felt something when he said them in this same office right before I found out about the bet. Back then, I thought there was a chance that this could turn into something substantial. Now, all I feel is regret and distance.

"I love you," he repeats the words, saying them louder this time. "I'm not forgetting about you. I'm going to fix this."

"You can't," I spit back at him. "This is so far past fucked up that it's not fixable." I don't mean that. If I meant it, I wouldn't have come to see him this morning. I wouldn't have thought about throwing all caution to the wind and kissing him. I wouldn't have felt my heart breaking within my chest. If I meant it, it wouldn't hurt this much.

"I can fix this." His tone is determined and strong. "Tell me how. Jessica, tell me."

"You said..." I feel every defense I've built up since I met him crumbling to my feet in a pool of heated dust. "You said that you fucked my body to him. I heard it. I heard you talking about me like that."

"Christ, no." He pulls my head into his chest, cradling his arms around me. "I didn't mean it like that. You're not just a fuck. You've never been just a fuck. Please tell me you get that, Jessica. Tell me."

"I can't stop hearing those words in my head." I pull my hands to my temples. "Hearing you tell him that. Hearing you say it to Drew."

"I just wanted that to be over." His voice pleads as his hands claw at my arms. "I just wanted to get all of that over with and behind me."

"You can't talk about me like that." The words pale in comparison to their meaning. I can't shake the sound of his voice boasting about bedding me.

"Jessica, please." His body is steely against me. His resolve is unwavering. "Tell me what to do. I can't lose you. I can't go back to before you."

"Take back what you said to him." I'm asking him to do the impossible. I'm asking for something he can never give to me.

He pulls me even closer. "I'll make you forget you heard that. I'm going to drown it out. I'll show you."

Chapter 12

"I worked for Cassandra for about two weeks." I'm so tired of all the secrets. I feel like I'm the missing piece in the jigsaw puzzle that makes up all of these people's lives. It's time for me to grow up and take responsibility for my part in the mess that's become my not-so-glamorous life in New York City. He's been texting me for days now asking about Cassandra. He wants answers, so do I. That's why I'm here.

"What? When?" Drew throws both questions at me with lightning speed. "You worked for my Cassie?"

"I started the day after you and I met at the club." The timing seems insane now that I'm thinking about it. "She was the boss of a close friend and I had an interview. She hired me on the spot."

"You cooked for Allie and Aaron?" Hearing the twins' names coming from him gives them more meaning in some way. Maybe coming to see him at work wasn't such a bad idea after all.

"They're great, Drew." I smile when I think about their angelic faces. "They're so beautiful. You should be really proud of them."

"I am." He nods his head slowly. "I'm trying to be a better dad."

"I didn't know you even knew them." It's not an excuse, it's the truth. "How is it possible that I could meet you and then the next day be hired by your wife?" I cringe once I realize that I should have prefaced that with an ex. Cassandra and him are divorced. I need to honor that and not remind him of the family he isn't a part of anymore.

"You were good to them, weren't you?"

"All three of them are amazing." I confirm though a smile. "I loved working there."

"I need to say something, Jess." He looks over his shoulder at the kitchen manager. "I only have a few more minutes on my break. I can't get another warning here or I'm out."

"What is it?" I ask suspecting that he's going to bring up the harassing way he treated me back at Axel NY. Since he'd left I'd been promoted to dessert prep and going to work every day was now a joy instead of a nightmare.

"It's about the lawyer," he grumbles. "About that night when you saw us together."

"At the bar?"

He nods before he pulls in an audible breath. "I saw him at the bar when I first got there with some buddies after work."

I'm not sure I want to know what he's about to share. I'm definitely not sure any of it is going to be the truth. "You decided to bring up the bet with him?"

"Not until I saw you." He casually adjusts the buttons on his chef jacket. "I took him a beer and sat where I knew you'd see me."

"Why?"

"I'd been pushing you for weeks, Jess. I thought you'd come over and blast me." He taps his finger on the edge of the table. "I wanted you to come over and blast me."

"You wanted me to get mad at you?" I'm beyond confused. He's not making any sense at all. "You wanted me to punch you?"

He runs his hand along his jaw and chuckles. "That I didn't expect but I deserved it."

I nod and pull a slight grin over my lips. "You did."

"Guys like him have it all. I didn't think anyone would take me up on that bet. When he did and he won, I was gutted." He peers behind me. "I don't have much longer."

"Just tell me, Drew." I try to keep an even tone. "What about that night?"

"He was telling me to go to hell when you walked over and I brought up the bet." He pulls his hand across his brow. "I was telling him that I knew I could fuck you if I really tried. I was pushing him."

Hearing him tell me that they were discussing my body isn't offering me anything but more fodder for another rage filled outburst. "It doesn't matter." It really doesn't matter. That's the truth. Knowing that Nathan discussed my body with Drew only adds to my confusion and regret.

"I told him to spell it out. I told him to just say it so we could be clear about what happened with you." I can hear something in his voice that hasn't been there before. It may be regret or it may just be more bullshit.

"I don't really care why he said it," I lie. "You're both still disgusting for making the bet in the first place."

"You're right," he agrees a little too swiftly. "My kids would disown me if they knew I was that pathetic. I need to man up for them. I'm learning to cope with the addiction. I'm going to be a better parent."

"I'm glad." At the very least, maybe the one light at the end of this fucked up tunnel was that Drew was finally going to get his act together.

Chapter 13

"Goddammit, Jessica." His body hovers above me. "You've got to let me fuck you."

"I came here to talk to you." I push my hips back into his couch. I can't let him feel how wet I am.

"You want my cock in your body. Don't try and deny that." His voice is a low growl.

I can't deny that. How am I supposed to? I arrived not more than five minutes ago with the full intention of setting ground rules. Now the only barrier between my body and his was the thin silk of my panties and his trousers. "I don't…well….let's just say that I…." good for you, Jessica. Blabber on like that any longer and you won't need to tell him no, he'll push you out of his apartment door himself.

He skirts his lips across my forehead with a heated touch. "I'm so fucking hard right now. Why the hell did you come here wearing that?"

I look down and realize my breasts are very close to popping out of the top of my dress. "I'm on my way to dinner with my roommates."

"Like hell you are." His hand is on my waist now, slowing inching towards my uncooperative breasts. "Your tits are so beautiful."

"Don't say things like that." I want to sound firm and controlled. I'm pretty sure every one of those words I just said sounded like a moan.

He rubs his groin over me and I can feel how hard he is. "I want to be inside of you."

"You want things you can't have," I whimper.

"I'm going to lick you until you come all over my face." His voice is nothing more than a breathless whisper. His groans are drowning themselves in my hair as he pushes himself into me.

"You want to fuck my sweet little body." I push the words out in a slow measured tone. I'm still reeling from hearing them come out of his mouth when he was talking to Drew.

"Jessica." He pulls himself back up to his knees. "Listen to me, now. Listen, Jessica."

I close my eyes briefly to ward off how hot he looks. His shirt is partially unbuttoned, his hair is a mess and his eyes are full of un-tempered want. "What?"

"Open your eyes now."

I do. "Happy now?"

His expression is torn. His brow is furrowed, his mouth a firm line. "I fucked up when I told Drew that I fucked your sweet little body, but..." the words trail away as his hand runs up my leg. "I can't contain what I feel. Fucking you is my sweet heaven. Nothing has ever felt like that to me. I fucked up when I said it, but I meant it. You want me. You've always wanted me."

"You don't know what I want." I need to get out of here. I have to get away from him before I give in again.

"You can run away but I'll always find you."

My body tenses as his hand inches up my thigh. A slow moan escapes my lips. "Stop," I say it, trying to make it sound genuine.

"You want me to stop?" His hand doesn't follow his mouth's suggestion. His finger skirts against the soft silk of my black panties. "I need to touch you. I've been aching inside for weeks."

"Stop." My hand bolts to cover his. "Stop now."

His eyes search mine before they rest on my lips. "You want me to stop? Jessica, say it again."

"Don't touch me." I push against him wanting to get myself up into at least a semi put together state. "Stop touching me."

He pulls himself to his feet and stares down at me sprawled on my back. He'd embraced me the moment I arrived and pushed me down without any resistance. He knew then that I'd give in to him. He knows instinctively that my body craves his too. He senses that I have no resolve when it comes to him.

"I want you." The words are meant to be simple. They should convey a direct need, a desire and a want. Coming out of Nathan's mouth they carry so much weight. They mean more than I can handle.

"You said you'd never lie to me." I push myself up until I'm sitting. "You lied about Drew."

He paces in front of me. "That's bullshit, Jessica. I didn't lie to you about him. I told you to stay away from him because he's fucked up."

"You should have told me." My voice is loud, almost too loud for this space. Everything is racing full speed ahead to the surface now. "You fucking should have told me you bet on my body, you asshole."

"Don't call me that," he spits the words at me. "Don't call me names, Jessica. You'll regret it."

"How?" I want to stand but I know all my energy is pulled into my emotions at the moment. "How will I regret it? You'll stop harassing me? That's not a bad thing, Nathan."

Before I can react he's sitting next to me. "I can't stop. Fuck, Jessica. You think this is something I can turn off?"

"Why are you doing this?"

"Doing what? Wanting you?" His face is rigid as he asks the questions. "Everything in my life is about you now. Everything. I fucked up. I get that. You can't throw me away because I'm not perfect. Everyone makes mistakes, Jessica. Everyone."

"You let me work with him." I push the subject. "I don't understand that."

"Understand what?" He's pulling on my hands, trying to capture them within his. "You want to be a chef. I want that for you."

I inch back on the couch trying to gain some distance. "You should have told me he was such an asshole."

"Christ, Jessica." He pulls himself closer to me again. "You think I knew how completely fucked he was? I would have killed him if I knew he was harassing you. I would have literally wrapped my hands around his neck and choked the life out of that asshole."

"You knew he was chasing after me." I'm not going to let him drop this and pretend it's not important. "You saw him with me at the bar. You came to my apartment when I was going on a date with him. Wait." I stop myself when I realize that he always showed up whenever Drew was there.

"You were following me." I bolt to my feet. "Jesus, Nathan. You've been following me all along."

"Jessica." He hangs his head in his hands. "No. Jessica, no."

"Why were you always right there?" My hands are trembling so hard I have to fist them together just to control the shaking that is now coursing through my entire body.

"I'm not always right there." His tone is different. There's something vulnerable there. A small crack. "It wasn't me."

"Nathan, please." I'm almost sobbing now." Please, Nathan, please."

"Jessica. You're going to fucking hate me more than you already do." He's on his feet. "You're going to fucking hate me."

"Oh, God." I close my eyes waiting for the assault of his words. "Just say it."

Chapter 14

"Did you meet him when he tried to fuck you?" I expect her to choke on that bite of soft pretzel she just took. Lucky for her I have medical training. I'll save her depending on how truthful she's going to be.

"Who?" She chews as she throws me a quick glance. "The pretzel guy? He didn't try and fuck me. He winks at everyone who gives him a tip."

"Nathan." I don't want this conversation to go on any longer than it needs to. I've already packed most of my things this morning even though I had no idea where I'll live. On my measly salary, the options in Manhattan are limited to a cardboard box or a closet.

"What?" A one word response isn't going to cut it.

"He told me last night." I look off into the distance. This is the same bench where Nathan and I sat weeks ago when he told me he couldn't stand the idea of missing me. I thought back then that everything between us would be simple and fun. Now, everything had turned horrible and painful in an instant.

"What?" Again? Really? We're not going to get anywhere if she can't expand her vocabulary.

"He asked you to report on me." I practiced saying that over and over again all morning. "That's why he always knew where I was."

"He's lying." Finally, more than one word pops out of her. The panicked look on her face is all the confirmation I need.

"He's not." I can't look in her in the face. "He showed me some of the texts you sent him when we were at the movies. You told him I was going to take you to that bar so he went there with his friend."

"Shit." The pretzel falls from her hands onto the grass. "Jess, I'm sorry."

"You took me to that hotel room for a reason, didn't you?" I ask in an even tone. It's nagged me since that day. I've always wondered why she was so righteous as she pulled me into that elevator and up to the eighteenth floor so she could watch me fall to pieces once I realized he still had the room.

"I don't trust him." The words aren't meant to be tempered. She's simply telling it like it is. "He used to date Cassandra."

I laugh at the announcement. "I know." I've been trying to shelter her from that tidbit of information for weeks and now she's telling me that she knew all along? What happened to the honesty in our friendship?

"That's where I met him." She turns to face me directly now. "I saw him in her office one day. I introduced myself."

"Why didn't you bother to tell me that when I first went up to his hotel suite?" The question is rhetorical at this point. It wouldn't have changed a thing. I wanted him then. I want him now. As much as I know I shouldn't, I can't help what I feel.

"She told me that morning that they were on a break." She reaches past me to grab hold of the back of the bench. "When I saw him at the club, I knew it was over for him. I knew he was going to end it completely with her."

"So there was nothing to hold you back from telling me?" I push the issue. She could have simply told me that night that Nathan had dated her boss.

"I wanted him but he never wanted me." Her voice cracks with the confession. "I came on to him once and he very politely told me he wasn't interested."

I feel a slight pang of jealousy at the admission. Of course she would have tried to get him in her bed. Any woman would have given the way he looked. How could I blame her for that? I was all over him the first moment I saw him at the bar.

"I started it when I texted him that we would be going for lunch and meeting Bryce." She taps her finger behind my back. "I couldn't believe he was there with that chick. I thought he'd be alone."

"You told him we would be there? Why?" I stare down at my skirt, tracing my finger along the bright pattern.

"I still thought I'd have a chance with him." She shrugs. "I thought he'd see you with Bryce and think you were taken and I'd have my opening."

"That's why you went to pay the check?" I feel as though everything is falling into place. "You left us alone."

"He only ever wanted you." I feel her hand on my hair, pulling it back.

"You still want him." It's not a question. I don't need to ask that. It's more an observation. She obviously has been trying to get me to doubt Nathan. That's why she told him about my date with Drew and let him know when we went to the other club that one night.

She shakes her head slightly. "Not anymore. He's so hung up on you, Jess."

"So why help him?" I'm half-expecting her to tell me that he's paying her. Men like Nathan Moore can pay for whatever they want. Money means nothing to him.

"I love you." She runs her hand along my shoulder. "You're my best friend. I knew Drew was bad news. I just gave Nate a heads-up whenever I knew Drew was around you. "

"There was that night at the bar when I went for drinks with Drew after my interview at the restaurant." It's open-ended on purpose. I want her to fill in the blanks so it can finally make sense to me.

"I knew Fingers was there…" she stops herself. "Or at least coming there. I told him where you were going when you texted to tell me the interview went well. I wanted him to see you with Drew so he'd finally tell him to fuck off for good."

"You're serious?" I ask, not expecting anything in return. I can't help but doubt her motivations.

"I've never seen you as happy as you are when you're talking about him, Jess." She pulls her gaze down to her own lap. "I just want you to be happy."

That's easier said than done. There's one only person that truly makes me happy and he's the one man I keep trying desperately to avoid.

Chapter 15

"Christ, Jessica. Please." His voice rumbles through the room, bouncing off the walls. "Don't make me give this up."

"It means nothing." I clench my sex around his cock. "It's just a fuck."

"It's not." He pumps slowly, his hands gripping mine, pushing them into the bed. "You know it's not."

"Fuck me, harder." I'm almost begging. "Please make me come."

"I'm going to lick you again." He starts to pull back and I feel the tip of his cock slide over my folds.
"No," I scream the word into his mouth. "No more." I'd already come twice beneath his tongue and now all I wanted to do is feel him inside of me. I'd shown up on his doorstep and jumped into his arms without a word. Now, thirty minutes later, I'm sprawled out naked in his bed, my clothes littering a path down the hallway.

"Fuck," he grunts as he pushes himself balls deep into my body. "I love fucking this sweet, little body."

I slap him hard across the face and he stalls for just a second. "Goddamn it." The words escape his lips with a smile.

"Don't say that about me again," I moan. "Don't."

"Christ, I'm so close." He's pumping harder now, thrusting himself into me. It's deeper and deeper with every stroke.

"Slow down," I beg. "I want it to last."

He slides his hand under my ass and effortlessly pulls us over in one swift movement so I'm now on top of him. "Fuck me, Jessica."

I lean back and glide my body so his cock slides to its full depth over and over again. The sensation is painfully slow and agonizingly delicious. "Like that?"

"Tell me you love this," he whispers.

"No." I pull him from my body and grip his cock with my fist. I pull it across my clit before I push myself back onto it. "I won't tell you that."

"Tell me how it feels when I'm fucking you."

"You talk too much," I whimper as I feel myself reaching the edge again. "Shut up."

"How can you ever fuck another man?" He circles his hips off the bed and the sensation pulls at my core. He knows exactly how to make me come. He knows exactly what my body craves. He's the only man who has ever done that. "You'll never feel like this with anyone else."

"I came here just for this." I close my eyes, warding off all of the emotions I'm feeling. We're so connected like this. When he's inside of me, nothing else in the universe matters.

"You came here because you need me." He grabs my hips and pulls me down onto his cock.

I can't help but moan loudly. My body betrays me when he's touching me. I can't hide the desire. It's palpable. He senses it because it screams his name the same way I do when I'm on the verge of coming hard. "I want to come." It's bold, direct and honest.

"I'll make you come. Lean forward. I'm going to fuck you hard, Jessica."

I plunge forward at the promise and slide my lips over his. I taste my sweetness on his tongue. "Do it," I challenge.

He pulls on my ass as he sits up with me on his lap, his cock still buried within me. "Feel it." He bites my lip as he pushes up with his hips, slowly sliding his cock deeper and then pulling back until the head almost slides between my folds. The sensation is overwhelming. I can feel the edge of my orgasm right there.

"Nathan." His name slides from my tongue into his mouth. "Nathan."

"Take it sweet, Jessica." He rests his lips against mine as I come hard. "Take it."

Chapter 16

"That was a mistake." I get on my hands and knees to look for my stiletto. "Why did I come here?"

"Stay right there and I'll nail you again in about a minute."

I look up to the sight of him fully nude, his heavy, thick cock resting in his palm. "Are you actually jerking off right now?"

"No." He shakes his head as he steps farther apart, making his frame that much more imposing. "I'm getting ready to fuck you again."

"We can't do that again." There's absolutely no conviction in my tone. My eyes don't stray from his massive cock which has now sprung right back to life.

"Jessica." A heavy sigh escapes through his moist lips. "Look what you do to me."

I lick my bottom lip as I cast my gaze from his face right back to his dick. "Nathan, we can't do it again."

"Jesus, I'm so hard." He pulls his large hand over the head of his cock as I stare open-mouthed at it. "I can't get enough of you. I never will."

I pull myself back to my knees. One more time can't hurt, can it? It won't matter if I take that big, beautiful cock between my lips now and slide my tongue over the wide head and…

"Oh fuck, me." The words tumble from him as I slide my mouth over him in one single movement.

I nod, before reaching up to cup his balls in one hand while I circle the thick root with the other. I feel my eyes roll back in my head at the sensation of his cock in my mouth again.

"Jessica. Christ, please." His hands jump to my hair. I wince as he pulls hard on the strands, fisting them as I slide my mouth steadily up and down. "Suck it. You suck me so good."

I rally back on my heels as I hear the words. "Yes," I whisper around the girth.

"You want this," he challenges. "You've always wanted this."

He's right. I can't argue with him. I want to feel him in my mouth and on my tongue. I want him to take pleasure from my body. I want him to feel everything I'm giving to him now.

"I'm going to shoot my load down your throat. I'm going to fill you with it." He's pumping harder now, his cock touching the back of my throat with every thrust. I have to adjust my knees to give myself more traction. It's so much. It's too much. It's way too fucking good.

"Jessica. That's it." His hands pull hard on my head, guiding it, adjusting it to take all of him in. "Suck it like that."

I moan around the root as I feel his balls constrict in my hand. I brace myself. He's going to come. He's going to come for me now.

"Fuck, yes. Fuck." The words are loud, clipped and breathless as he pumps everything he has into my body.

Chapter 17

"I can't come back here." I don't mean it. It's what I should say though, right? He's too controlling, too demanding, too manipulating and too appealing when he's standing naked in front of me.

"Did you find your shoe?" He reaches his hand out to grasp mine. "I think it fell under the bed."

I place my hand in his as he pulls me and my wayward shoe up. "It's here."

He grabs it quickly and tosses it back under the bed. "You need to get back on your hands and knees and look for it."

I cock a brow and look down at his once again erect cock. "How? Just how, Nathan?"

"How what?" He pulls a smile across his delicious lips.

"How can you be hard again already?" I kneel back down to retrieve my shoe yet again. "How many times in a row can you actually fuck a woman?"

"Any other woman, once." He takes my shoe from me and kneels down. "You, endlessly."

"Don't be charming." I rest my hand on the back of his head as he slides my foot into the shoe. "I can't be mad at you when you're charming."

"Are you wet again?" His hands are on my thighs, pushing the hem of my shift dress up. "I want to taste you again before you leave."

"Nathan, no." I push helplessly at his hands. "We can't."

"Do you mean, no, Nathan stop and don't lick my beautiful body until I come?" He grazes his tongue over my thigh. "Or do you mean, Nathan, don't stop until I come over and over again from you licking me?"

I close my eyes as my hands lace through his hair. "Nathan," I whisper. "Please."

He moans loudly as his tongue traces hot over my panties before he pushes them aside and plunges his face into my wetness.

***

"You're actually leaving this time?" The amusement skirting the edge of the question isn't lost on me.

"I need to go." I take a few steps back to try and create a barrier between us. "Don't you have clothes you can put on?" I search the ground for the jeans and t-shirt he was wearing when I arrived.

"I'll get dressed and I can go with you." He races towards his closet to pull out a pair of navy pants and a light blue dress shirt. "Formal, semi-formal? Where are we going?"

"I'm going to look at places to live." I pull my hair back into a hastily thrown together ponytail. "You're staying here."

He drops the clothes in his hands to the floor and bolts towards me. "Wait. You're doing what?"

"I can't live with Rebecca anymore." I breathe in heavily as I continue, "I feel weird about it and she gives you status updates when I'm brushing my teeth and eating a sandwich."

"Only when you leave the crust behind," he jokes. "We're not doing that anymore. You don't have to move out of there."

"I don't trust her," I say it with regret. I don't. Our relationship is on shaky ground right now and it's important to me that we salvage it. I can't do that if I'm living with her.

"I think you should reconsider." His hand rests on my elbow. "She's a good friend."

"A good friend wouldn't have convinced me to sneak into your hotel room that night."

"What do you mean?" His brow furrows. "She told you to go into my suite that night?"

I can't place all the blame on her. "Not exactly," I qualify it. "She said something about you fucking every woman in the place and that made me want to go see if you still had the room."

"Jessica." He pulls my head into his chest and cradles my body next to his. "You've got to get it through your head that I'm crazy about you."

I nod against his skin, relishing in the smell of him and the feel of his strong, steely chest against me. As much as I doubt his sincerity, there's just something so raw and real about his words when he's telling me how much he cares for me.

"I've fucked up your friendship." He pulls me back so he can look directly into my eyes. "Let me fix it. I can fix it."

I reach to cradle his cheek in my hand. "I need to move out. I want to." I can't continue anything with Nathan if I live with Rebecca. I don't know how I can deal with the two of them in the same room together.

"Move in here." He takes a step back and almost jumps up and down. "You can come live with me."

"That's a horrible idea," I smirk. "Really, really horrible."

"Why?"

"Are you seriously asking me why it's a bad idea for me to live here?" How is he a lawyer when he can't understand something this simple? Does he not understand that I don't trust him at all?

"I love you. You should live with me." The words are thoughtful and direct but they bite right into me like a rabid dog.

"I don't trust you," I say boldly. "I don't trust anything you say to me."

"What?" His hands jump to his chest as if I've thrown a dagger into his heart. "You don't trust me?"

I want to reach out and shake him. Maybe he's missing the common sense gene. That would explain a lot about him. "No, I don't." Why beat around the bush? I don't trust him. I see no reason to skirt around the issue.

"You came over here today," he says hoarsely. "We made love."

I have to take a step back when I hear the words. He's never, once, ever said that we make love. "We made love?" I parrot back to him.

"Do you fucking have short term memory loss, Jessica?" He points to the bed. "We've spent the past three hours naked together."

"We fucked." The word sounds harsh. "We just fucked, that's all."

He stalls and his eyes scan my face. "It meant nothing but a fuck to you?" His eyes squint and move past my face to the wall behind me. He's grabbing tightly to his chest as if he's holding back something.

"That's all it was." I shrug my shoulder. "I was horny. I wanted you to fuck me. Nothing else has changed."

Chapter 18

"Maybe you should just reconsider, Jess." Bryce is sitting on the edge of my bed, his heels resting on one of the many cardboard boxes that are now cluttering my space. "You've been looking for more than a week now. There's nothing out there."

"There are places," I correct him as I rest my head on my pillow. "They're all just out of my price range."

"I'd move with you but I'm going to pop the question to Trudy soon and then we'll get a place of our own." His entire face glows with the announcement. Every single time I see him with his girlfriend, I feel a slight pang of envy race through me. They're so happy and content and their history isn't clouded with lies, mysteries and secrets. That's what I want.

"There is one place I can afford to live," I whisper. I haven't even really wrapped my head around the concept yet, but now is as good a time as any to talk to Bryce about it.

"With Nathan?" The scowl on his face speaks more than the tone of his voice.

"No," I scoff. I had considered that option for a hot two seconds before I walked out of his apartment last week. Since then, I've ignored most of his text messages and calls. He wants me to reinvest myself in him again and that stock has crashed enough times that I know I'll just end up burned to an emotional crisp. Men, like Nathan Moore, don't change. It's simple.

"Where then?"

"I'm thinking I should just go back home." It's a coward's plan. When I lived in Connecticut everything was easy. Josh was so uncomplicated and right now I miss that. I don't necessarily miss him but the simplicity that life there offers me is beckoning me like a lighthouse in the dark sea.

"That's not an option." Bryce is on his feet, his hands firmly planted on his hips. "You're going to run away?"

"It's not running." Who exactly am I trying to convince? "It's more about trying something on for size and then realizing it doesn't fit so you return it."

"You're complicated." He laughs. "You can't go back there. You left there for a reason. Don't forget it."

"It's easier there," I confess. "I can just live without all the drama. I can go back to being an EMT."

"When I came to New York I was scared shitless." His expression is even and serious. "You and Rebecca helped me see it's where I belong."

"I don't belong here."

"You're not running away from the city, Jess." He doesn't mince words. "You're running away from him."

***

"Are you opposed to me just using you for sex?" I clench my fist in his hair as he circles my clit with his tongue.

"No," he whispers into my folds. "Use me however the fuck you want, Jessica."

"If I come over here just to get fucked once a week, that's okay?" I lean back on his bed and let the pleasure rip through me.

He shakes his head slightly and the sensation pushes me closer to the edge. "You need to come over every fucking day."

I chuckle at the idea. "This is so good," I moan through parted lips. "Please, lick it like that."

He shifts his large body and cups my ass in his palm so he can lick me harder. "So good."

"I'm going to come." I don't need to say it. I know he can feel it. I know he senses it just by the way my body tenses when he's touching me.

"Slow down," he pants as he licks my folds softly. "I don't want you to come yet."

"Nathan." I pull on his hair causing him to wince. "Please, lick me harder."

"I'd give anything to do this every day. Let me wake up to this, Jessica. This is my heaven." He pulls my clit between his lips and sucks hard.

I race to the edge with an uninhibited scream. "Oh, God. Nathan." I can't control the words. I can't control the way it feels.

He crawls up my body so he's hovering above me. "I was tested." The words are foreign and misplaced in the moment. "Let me fuck you like this."

I look down at his engorged cock. "No." I can't. I won't.

"I haven't fucked anyone else in months, Jessica. Jesus, please. Give me this," he's pleading. His voice is coarse and rough from want. "You have to take the fucking pill. Tell me you do."

I nod as I stare at his cock. I want to feel it like that too. "Do you have proof?" Did I really just ask that right now?

"Proof that my dick is clean?" He's leaning back on his heels now. One hand is slowly stroking his cock, the other circling my clit.

"Yes," I moan as he pushes his index finger into me. "Oh, yes."

"You don't believe that I'm clean?" He groans as he slides another finger next to the first. "You're so fucking tight I can't stand it."

"You say things..." I can't talk. I'm close to coming again already. "You say things..."

"You're so smooth and slick." His eyes are blazing with desire as he kneads his fingers within me. "I want so much to shoot my load in this beautiful body so you can feel my cum inside of you."

"Nathan." The shamelessness of his words spurs me closer. "Don't say that."

"I've never filled any woman with my cum before." His breath is on my lips now. "I want to with you. Let me, Jessica."

I push my hips from the bed to grab more of him. I want him to take me to the edge again. I need to come. "Christ, Nathan."

"This is all mine." He clenches his hand around and in my sex. "Mine." The animalistic growl that flows through the word sends me into the center of an intense orgasm. I cling to his body as I scream out his name.

Chapter 19

"Here." A piece of paper flutters past my face as he sits down across from me in the mid-town bistro.

"What's this?" I scan it quickly with my eyes.

"My ticket to ride you without a saddle." He cocks a brow as he reaches across the table to steal a bite of my fruit salad. "Nice of you to wait to order until I got here, Jessica."

"You're late." I hold the paper steady so I can read every line. "Is this your test results?"

"I was in court." He pulls the entire bowl across the table and steals the spoon from my hand. "I'm so hungry."

"These are your test results?" I ask again. I can't believe he actually got a copy of them to give to me.

"I want in that." He waves the spoon towards my body. "I want in it without any barriers. That's the golden ticket right there."

"You were serious?" I thought he was half-joking the other night when he talked about fucking me without a condom. "You want to have sex without a condom?"

"Where's the waiter? I need a drink." He surveys the entire span of the room in mere seconds.

"Bourbon doesn't go with fruit salad."

"Bourbon goes with everything, Jessica."

I glance at the paper again. "This makes me nervous."

He scratches the tip of his nose and raises a brow. "My cock makes you nervous? You haven't been shy around it up to this point."

"What if I don't want to?" I push back. "What if I say we can't?"

He stops eating and places the spoon down on the table. "Then we don't." There's no emotion in the statement.

"Just like that? We just don't."

"Jessica." His hand snakes towards mine. "Listen to me. Jessica, listen."

I smile at his insistence that I listen. He always does that when he's got something important to say. "I'm listening, Nathan."

"I would never..." He pulls in a heavy breath and squeezes my hand tightly. "I would never do anything with you that you don't want. Ever."

"You say that but... but I don't know." I don't know. I want to believe him. I wish I could believe him. "I feel like you push me sometimes. You want things I'm not ready for."

"Listen to me." He stands and throws his linen napkin on the table before he kneels down next to me. "Please, Jessica, just hear this one thing."

I stare down at his calm, beautiful blue eyes. His face is unshaven and his hair a mess from the wind. He's so gorgeous. He's more striking than the night I met him. "What?"

"I fucked this up more than once." He bites his bottom lip. "I am going to work every single fucking day of my life to make you want me as much as I want you. I will wait forever for you. Forever, Jessica. Don't doubt that."

I don't respond. I just stare at his face. My heart is telling me that he means it. My head wants to embrace it.

"I love you, Jessica. I fucking love you." He swallows hard just as I see the pool of tears in his left eye. "My life is nothing without you. Nothing. The day you get that will be the happiest day of my life."

I can't handle the emotion in the room. I can feel the weight of it suffocating me. "No. The happiest day of your life will be when you get to come in me without a rubber."

He licks his bottom lip. "That's going to happen sooner than you think."

Chapter 20

"How many women have you fucked in here?" I'm sitting in one of the chairs opposite his desk while he works.

"In here?" He doesn't break his gaze from his laptop screen.

"Christ, you're annoying as fuck sometimes," I tease. "Is that like a lawyer thing?"

"Is what like a lawyer thing?" He reaches for a manila folder on his desk.

"That diverting thing you do." I playfully punch my fist into the folder. "You do it all the time. You ask me the same question I ask you."

"I don't do that." He smirks as he pushes my hand to the side. "That's quite a fist you have there."

"Have you fucked that receptionist?" I nod back towards the area outside his closed office door.

"What?" His head bolts up. I finally have his full attention.

I look directly into his eyes. "Have you banged her in here?"

He furrows his brow as he leans back in his office chair. "You're asking me if I've rammed my dick into my receptionist here in my office?"

"Seriously?" I try not to laugh. "You just did it again."

"I didn't," he says softly. "On both counts."

"She hates me." It sounds as childish leaving my lips as it does when I think about it.

"My receptionist hates you?" He can't hold in his obvious amusement. "That makes you think I banged her?"

"She never says my name correctly." I push my bottom lip out in a fat pout. "She did it again today."

He stands, walks with determined steps around the desk and leans against it. "Jessica." He reaches forward as he drags the pad of his thumb across my bottom lip. "You want to suck me off, don't you?"

I laugh at the no-so-subtle request. "The receptionist, Nathan," I whisper as I run my hand down his pants and trace the outline of his erection.

He slowly pulls the belt out of its loop before the sound of the zipper lowering fills the room. "She has a lisp, Jessica."

***

"I just didn't think I'd have to live here alone without you." I hug Bryce tightly at the doorway to our apartment. "You got engaged so fast."

"I love her a lot, Jess." He reaches to pick up the last of his boxes from the floor. "I'm so excited for this. You're going to come over tomorrow night, right?"

"It's my night off." I remind him and myself. "I'll be there at seven. I'm cooking, so don't touch anything. I'll bring everything I need."

"You just need to talk to her, Jess." He motions towards Rebecca's closed bedroom door. "You two need to have it out with each other. Until you do that, it's always going to be like this."

I nod as I watch him walk through the door and out of my everyday life for good. He's right. Until I talk to Rebecca about what happened with Nathan, things are never going to be right between us. There's no time like the present.

"Did he go?" Her voice startles me enough that I almost lose my balance. I have to wonder if she was listening to the two of us talking about her.

"He's gone," I offer as I finally turn to face her. "You didn't come out to say goodbye."

She shrugs her shoulders. "We weren't close. Not like you and I..."

"I'm still looking for a place." I want her to realize that I was serious when I told her that I'd be moving out too. Every night when I get home after work, I scurry to my room like a timid mouse afraid that the big, bad cat will catch me in its grips.

"You don't have to." She doesn't pull her gaze from the floor. "It would be cool if you stayed. We can look for another roommate."

The offer is touching, albeit completely misplaced. I know that she has to feel the same awkward tension floating through the air every time we happen upon one another. She's gotten surprisingly good at avoiding me at all costs. "I think I need to go."

"I'm sorry about everything, Jess." Her voice cracks slightly. "I was just trying to help."

"You've helped me more than anyone I've ever known." They aren't just words strung together to appease her anxiety. They are real, true and meant with love and affection. "You helped me escape Connecticut and my life with Josh."

"Bryce told me you were thinking of going back." She finally looks at me. "You can't, Jess. It's a hellhole."

I laugh out loud at the description. "It is a hellhole." I nod my head in eager agreement. "I don't belong there. I don't really belong anywhere right now," I whisper. It's not meant to garner any sympathy from her. It's just how I feel.

"My door is always open." She glides her hand through the air. "My home is yours."

I feel a sense of comfort with the words. "That means a lot."

"Anything I've done is because I want to protect you." She glances at me. "We're going to work at this and get back to being best friends."

"We are best friends." I pull her into a weak embrace. "We'll fix it," I say believing that in time we will.

Chapter 21

"There's a rule that you keep breaking." He's standing in the doorway of the bedroom, his pajama bottoms slung low on his hips. I can just see a few stray hairs poking over the waistband. Even like this in the dim light of the room, he's the most desirable man I'll ever lay eyes on.

"Whatever." I look back down at my tablet. "I need to become a prostitute I think."

"What?"

"I think I need to start turning tricks." That's hooker lingo, right? That's what they call it?

"You're the most fascinating person I've ever met." He's on the bed next to me now. "Where do you come up with all this bullshit that comes out of your mouth?"

"It's like this." I place the tablet on his lap and pull the sheet up to cover my breasts. "I look up apartment listings and on the side are all these advertisements for call girls."

"Call girls?" He glances down at the tablet. "You mean these listings asking for female models?"

"Yes." I nod. "That's code for prostitute." I pull air quotes around the last word for extra added emphasis.

"I'll pay you to fuck me." He pulls the waistband of his pajamas down to reveal his cock. "You name the price. How much is your body worth?"

I wince at the words. We haven't spoke of the bet in weeks. It's become a difficult, and not constant, memory at this point. Suddenly, it's boiling inside of me again. I feel breathless at the reminder.

"Nathan." I push the sheet from my body and bounce to my feet. "I can't. No."

"Jessica. Jesus. Shit." He's on his feet too, racing around the bed. "Please, don't. Fuck, please don't run."

"I can't." I'm clawing at my throat. I feel as though I can't breathe. This must be what it's like to have a panic attack. I saw enough of them firsthand when I was an EMT to know the symptoms. "Nathan." I feel my legs collapsing and I reach for the side of the bed. He scoops me into his arms and lowers me to the floor before I have time to react.

"Jessica." His hands are around me and I'm resting against his chest. "Don't think about it."

"I can't help it." I press my hands to my temple to try and ward off the flood of thoughts. I'm assaulted with the image of my fist jarring into Drew's face, the smell of the bar, and the sound of Nathan's voice when he told me the amount of the bet. "I can't do this," I whimper. "Why did I think I could do this?"

"Jessica." He cradles my naked body in his lap as he leans against the bed. "You know I love you. You feel it."

"No." I shake my head violently from side-to-side. "I don't know."

"You feel it," he whispers in my ear. "Close your eyes, Jessica. Listen to me."

My head is telling my body to bolt from the room. It's pushing on me to race from his arms and this place. It's reminding me that his past is a cloud of secrets and women. There were so many women. My heart is winning. I can't move.

"You were wearing a beautiful dress when I first saw you at the club that night." His breath grazes across my neck. "I watched you walk in through the door. I had just paid my tab. I was getting ready to leave."

I nod. I didn't know that. I thought he was firmly entrenched on a stool at the bar waiting for someone he could take up to his room.

"I felt my knees go weak." He kisses my forehead. "Not weak like bullshit words weak, but really weak. I had to sit down. Do you know why?"

I shake my head against his chest as I feel my breathing slow down. "Tell me why."

"You were looking around the room. I was scared you were there to meet a guy. I was going to fight him for you."

I laugh at the idea. I was so scared that night. So unsure of what I was getting myself into.

"If I'd known you were a prize fighter I'd have gotten you to be my stand-in." I can feel his smile against my cheek. "I knew right then, at that club, that I'd never want anyone else in the world again."

"You're such a liar," I say the words into his chest.

"I don't lie to you, Jessica."

"You don't always tell me the truth either."

"That's different. I'm a lawyer. It's my job."

"You just wanted to fuck me that night." I don't know how else to put it. Our entire relationship began with a conversation about fucking each other.

"I wanted to take you into that room and never let you go." He runs his hand along my thigh. "I wanted to hide you away from the rest of the world so no one would see what I see."

"What do you see?" My breath hitches as the question leaves my lips.

"My everything. My life."

"You just say those things to get laid," I joke.

"I get up every day happy because somewhere in the world, I know you're there too." His voice cracks slightly at the admission. "I can't live without you, Jessica."

"You can," I counter. "You can live without me."

He shakes his head and pulls my body tighter into his. "If you leave me, I'm done. My heart goes with you."

"You said you don't do romantic, Nathan." I look up into his face.

"This isn't romance, Jessica." He pulls my hand to his lips and kisses my palm. "This is me, telling you, what I feel."

I stare at his lips as they touch my skin. "You're being serious?"

"Completely." He reaches down to brush his lips against mine. "I'd die for you, Jessica. I would jump in front of a subway train if it was going to hit you. I'd kill someone for hurting you. "He lowers his head and rubs his cheek against mine. "I'm not good with words. I want to be with you. However you'll have me."

"You know I'm scared of all of it." I don't have to define it. He knows. He's always known.

"I sometimes think about what my life would have been like if I knew you when I was a kid." The corners of his lips jump into a wide smile. "I never would have touched another woman. I never would have looked at anyone else. My heart would have been yours forever."

"You're romantic." I feel tears welling in the corner of my eyes. "You know that you are."

"I know that with you I have no barriers." He glides his hand over my thigh and up to my hip. "I know that I want to spend every moment I have left on this earth right here in this spot with you."

"We can't stay here forever."

"Not here, Jessica." He points to the floor. "Here." His hand grazes over my chest before resting on his own. "In my heart. In your heart."

"No pressure for anything more?" I cock a brow. "We take it slow and easy."

"You're going to marry me one day and we're going to have a baby." The words spill out so fast I have to stop to think about them.

"Nathan." I tap him on his nose. "That's not slow and easy."

"You're right." His lips glide across mine. "We'll take it however fast you want it, but you're moving in."

"Nathan." I try to sound angry but I can't. How can I when he's almost literally opening his chest so I can see what's in his heart and soul?

"That's what I wanted to talk to you about. You have so much of your shit here. Clothes, shoes, gum wrappers, magazines." His fingertips brush across my cheek. "We're going to get the rest of your stuff tonight and you're living here. No arguments."

"No arguments," I agree as I pull his arms around me. "What will we do until then?"

"I can think of something." His hand lazily runs between my thighs.

"Nathan." The need is more pressing than it's ever been. If I don't do this now I may never do it.

"Jessica?" He tilts my chin up until I'm looking into his eyes. "What is it?"

"It's just that...I wanted to tell you." Shit, Jessica. It's just three words. You can do this. You feel it. You've felt it since he kissed you at the club. Okay, maybe back then that was lust, but who could blame you? Look at him, just look at his gorgeous face. He loves you. He really truly loves you.

"Jessica?" He repeats my name and I melt a little at the sound of it.

"I love you."

"I know."

"You know?"

"I've always fucking known. You can't keep your goddamn hands off me."

Epilogue

Six months later...

"You're fucking going to marry me, Jessica." He pounds his cock into me from behind as I'm bent over the back of the couch. "You want to feel this every day of your life."

"I don't need a ring for this." I push back, milking his dick with my body. I love the way it feels when he takes me completely, quickly, like this without any barriers at all. "You never should have brought me back here."

"Goddammit." His hand reaches around to grab my breast. "I'm going to shoot my load all over your back."

I pull away harshly and his cock falls from my body. I'm on my knees in an instant and the growl that I receive is reward enough for me. "Turn around." I grab both of his calves, trying to move his strong legs.

"Jessica," his whisper is barely audible. I can't hear anything other than the pounding of my heart as he twists his body to give me exactly what I want.

"Ah, fuck. Yes." He leans back against the couch and twists his hands through my hair. "Just like that, baby."

His words are my fuel and I take his beautiful cock deeper into my mouth. I look up at him. He looks exactly as he did the first night I took him in my mouth. He's still almost fully dressed. His pants are undone, his dress shirt a wrinkled mess and half-unbuttoned. His long eyelashes fluttering closed as I pump the thick root with my hand and suck on the tip. I spread my legs wider, putting my entire naked body on display for him.

"Shit, you're fucking gorgeous." He pumps himself harder into my mouth. "You suck cock so good, Jessica. It's so goddamn good."

I stare up at him, lost in his pleasure. I need his release. I need him to give it to me. Even after all this time, I crave his body endlessly. I can't get enough of the way he tastes, the way he smells, the way he feels when he's giving everything to me.

"I'm going to shoot my load right down that beautiful throat."

It's a promise and a threat. He knows I struggle with how much he gives to me. He knows I need and want it all. "Come for me now," I whisper against his cock. "Shoot it into me."

"Christ. Fuck." The words bite through the stillness in the room as he grabs the back of my head with both hands and pumps his desire into my mouth. It seeps out the sides. I can't handle it all.

I feel him soften slightly on my tongue and I lick my lips as he falls from my mouth. "Nathan," I barely whisper his name. "Nathan."

"That was so intense." His long eyelashes are closed. He looks so peaceful. He's gorgeous. He's more beautiful than the first time we were in this room together.

"I have to go." I stand and reach for my dress. He was the one who wanted to recreate this moment so I'm giving him exactly what he asked for.

"Jessica." His firm hand grabs my elbow. "You're not going anywhere."

"I'm leaving." I sigh a bit too heavily while trying to hide my growing amusement. "I left then so I'm out of here now."

"You're running because you know I'm going to propose to you." He traces the pad of his thumb over my now swollen lips. "Don't."

"That's exactly why I'm running, Nathan." I bite the edge of his thumb. "You think it's romantic to drag me back to your fuck pad to propose marriage to me?"

He can't contain the smile that flows over his mouth. "It's sentimental."

"It's not." I pull my dress back over my head. "You need to come up with a better plan than this."

"Can I at least show you the ring?" He reaches into the pocket of his pants to pull out a small, square box.

"No." I slam it shut. He doesn't realize that I sat up for hours last night staring at it after he'd fallen asleep.

"If you can get the proposal right, you know I'll say yes." I take the box and tuck it back into his pocket.

"Until then…." My voice trails as I glide onto my tiptoes to kiss him.

"Until then, Jessica."

A Final Word from Nathan:

Jessica Roth is innocence personified. Everything about her screams young, beautiful and untainted. I'm addicted to her. She knows it. I can't get enough of her. Fucking her is my sweet heaven on earth.

She told me there were only three before me. She didn't tell me that *he* was one of them. Assholes like him prey on women like her but he was the hunted and she was the hunter. He's looking for her. Now that she's sleeping in my bed every night and sharing my life she can't hide from her past. She has to face it and me, head-on before we can have our happily-ever-after.

I had to answer to her for my sins. Now it's her turn. They say you can't judge a book by its cover. The same is true for women. Jessica may seem pure and simple on the outside, but what lies beneath that pretty little surface may burn me beyond recognition.

She thought she was no match for my past. Wait until her past rears its high powered, vengeful head right in our direction.

You've heard her story, it's time for mine.

IMPULSE by Deborah Bladon

A full-length novel told from Nathan's point of view picks up the story of his unending need for Jessica, after the ending of PULSE.

IMPULSE will be available on Tuesday, August 26th.

Thank You!

Thank you for purchasing my book. I can't even begin to put to words what it means to me. Let me know your thoughts! I want to keep my readers happy.

When I initially published Pulse, I knew that women would enjoy the story, (I mean, who could resist Nathan Moore?), but I never anticipated the response that it would actually receive. This series brought me the kind of success that I only dreamed about being possible. I made the New York Times bestsellers list, a dream that I had since I was a small girl. This wouldn't have been possible without my loyal readers, like you. So thank you, from the bottom of my heart, for making all of my biggest dreams come true.

There are exciting things in the wings, so stay tuned to my website for more information www.deborahbladon.com.

If you want to chat with me personally, please LIKE my page on Facebook. I love connecting with all of my readers because without you, none of this would be possible. www.facebook.com/authordeborahbladon

Thank you, for everything.

About the Author

Deborah Bladon has never read a romance hero she didn't like. Her love for romance novels began when she was old enough to board the bus, library card in hand to check out the newest Harlequin paperbacks. She's a Canadian by heart, and by passport, but you can often spot her in New York City sipping a latte and looking for inspiration for her next story. Manhattan is definitely her second home.

She cherishes her family and believes that each day is a gift for writing, for reading, and for loving.

Printed in Great Britain
by Amazon.co.uk, Ltd.,
Marston Gate.